"SEEMS TO ME YOU OUGHT TO REMEMBER A MAN YOU SHOT AND ROBBED AND LEFT FOR DEAD."

Neither man moved at the sight of the pistols aimed at them. Their faces grew slack at their understanding of who the threat was and what it represented.

But Bob Olive was a cool customer. He turned again to his drink sitting on the bar, exposing his back to Jake. Jake shot him in the leg, along the line of the hamstring in the meaty part, just inches above his knee.

Teacup Smith nearly jumped from under his hat as Bob Olive toppled to the floor spitting a string of "goddamns" and "sons a bitches."

"What about you?" Jake said to Teacup. "You want to turn your back on me too?

"Mister, I don't have any idea what you're talking about, I swear to God."

Jake thumbed back the hammer of the Schofield.

"Then we have a problem," he said.

D0028099

Books by Bill Brooks

DAKOTA LAWMAN: LAST STAND AT SWEET SORROW

LAW FOR HIRE: SAVING MASTERSON
LAW FOR HIRE: DEFENDING CODY
LAW FOR HIRE: PROTECTING HICKOK

ATTENTION: ORGANIZATIONS AND CORPORATIONS
Most HarperTorch paperbacks are available at special quantity discounts for bulk purchases for sales promotions, premiums, or fund-raising. For information, please call or write:

Special Markets Department, HarperCollins Publishers, Inc., 10 East 53rd Street, New York, N.Y. 10022–5299.
Telephone: (212) 207–7528. Fax: (212) 207-7222.

DAKOTA LAWMAN
LAST STAND AT SWEET SORROW

BILL BROOKS

HarperTorch

An Imprint of HarperCollins*Publishers*

This is a work of fiction. Names, characters, places, and incidents are products of the author's imagination or are used fictitiously and are not to be construed as real. Any resemblance to actual events, locales, organizations, or persons, living or dead, is entirely coincidental.

HarperTorch
An Imprint of HarperCollins*Publishers*
10 East 53rd Street
New York, New York 10022-5299

Copyright © 2005 by Bill Brooks
ISBN 0-06-073718-2

All rights reserved. No part of this book may be used or reproduced in any manner whatsoever without written permission, except in the case of brief quotations embodied in critical articles and reviews. For information address HarperTorch, an imprint of HarperCollins Publishers.

First HarperTorch paperback printing: February 2005

HarperCollins®, HarperTorch™, and ❦™ are trademarks of Harper-Collins Publishers Inc.

Printed in the United States of America

Visit HarperTorch on the World Wide Web at www.harpercollins.com

10 9 8 7 6 5 4 3 2 1

If you purchased this book without a cover, you should be aware that this book is stolen property. It was reported as "unsold and destroyed" to the publisher, and neither the author nor the publisher has received any payment for this "stripped book."

For Sinclair Browning,
a dirty shirt cowgirl who writes pretty good

DAKOTA LAWMAN

LAST STAND AT SWEET SORROW

Prologue

I T WASN'T EXACTLY how *he'd* planned his day—getting shot five times.

But as it turned out, it seemed like it was the day for shooting.

First it was the horse who took a bullet.

Running at a gallop—a mistake to be sure—the horse found a burrow, prairie dog hole, and cartwheeled madly, pitching him headlong into the tall grass. He tumbled and rolled to a stunned stop, unsure if he'd broken bones. He stood finally, shaky, momentarily disoriented, found nothing to be broken but perhaps his pride.

The horse stood bravely eyeing him, its left foreleg clearly damaged beyond hope.

He looked at his surroundings, saw nothing but the same ocean of grass he'd been seeing for days. The horse tried to walk to him. He said, "Whoa." He slid the pistol from his pocket, blew dust from its cylinders, held it down along his leg so as not to spook the creature and cause it further anguish. He wasn't sure how much horses sensed danger—not like humans, most certainly. Spoke to it softly while holding forth an empty hand as though it held an apple or a sugar cube until he could get near enough to stroke its muzzle.

"Bad timing," he said. The horse seemed to understand.

He brought the pistol up slow, distracting the horse by talking to it, then fired one shot to the brain, just below the ear. The pistol shot rolled like small thunder out across the open range, then faded. Silence returned like a shy guest that had been spooked off once.

He bent and uncinched the saddle and pulled it free, unwrapped the canteen's strap from around the horn and took a long drink.

It was god-awful hot, just as it had been every day since he came into this country—North Dakota Territory, he suspected, by now. He figured the Canadian border was yet two, three days north.

Wasn't anything to do but figure it out somehow: how he was going to reach his destination. Hadn't seen a town to speak of since Bismarck. Just open range grassland, sky, little else. When he rode through the grass it whispered to him, something sounded like a warning: Go *back, go back, go back*.

Wind blew hot through the tall stems causing the grass to sway to and fro like a restless sea—that's what it was, a sea of grass, variegated green every direction.

It was just past noon. He saw a small stand of cottonwoods off in the distance, figured they guarded water, hefted the saddle, and went off toward them. Sure enough, a bright clean creek snaked through the land shaded by the cottonwoods that stood tall and leaning as though wanting to drink of the water themselves. He nearly fell into it just to relieve the heat that prickled his skin. He drew the water to his face, scooped it over his head and hair, splashed it over his neck, drank it. A small oasis in a world full of hurt. Little things had come to mean quite a lot lately: a piece of jerky, wildflowers, the shape of clouds. Where had the life he'd once lived gone? What happened to the man he used to be? It seemed so long ago, and yet, it had only been a matter of a week, possibly a day or two more. Time seemed as lost to him as everything else.

He sat and took off his boots and soaked his feet in the water. He saw small darts of silver fishes come and nibble at his toes, dart off again.

Then the riders appeared. Two of them. Rough-looking men with pinned-back hats and big pistols riding their hips and rifles slid down into scabbards. Dusty shirts dark with sweat and shaggy beards; men who looked like himself. He figured the gunshot had drawn them. He was right.

"Heard gunfire," the one said.

"Had to shoot my horse," he said.

"Damn foolish thing to do out in such country," the man said.

"Stepped in a gopher hole, broke his leg."

"Tough luck."

"For both of us."

"Seen him back yonder," the man said. He looked at the other man who remained silent, watchful.

"There a town nearby I can buy another horse?" he asked the man doing the talking.

"You got money to buy another horse?"

He could see the direction the conversation was headed, wished he had the pistol a little closer at hand than in his saddle pocket lying there on the bank next to his boots.

"I'm not looking for trouble."

The man looked round at the other one with him.

"He says he's not looking for trouble."

The silent one shrugged, said, "Nobody is."

"He says nobody is," the talker said.

It was an odd way to carry on a conversation: having one man repeat everything the other said.

"Where you headed?" the talker said.

"North."

The man looked off toward the north.

"Nothing north of here but the border."

"How far?"

The talker looked him over head to foot.

"You running from the law?"

"No. I got people up there."

"He's headed for Canaday," the man said to his companion.

The other man looked off north, said, "It's two or three days yet. More if you aim to walk it."

"About a town," he said. "Is there one nearby?"

"Yes, there's one not far from here."

"Which direction?"

"I guess it don't matter which direction," the man said standing in his stirrups then lowering his ass down in the saddle again.

"Why is that?"

"How about you show us the money you aim to buy another horse with."

"I don't see how that's going to matter."

"I think maybe you're on the dodge, maybe you got stole money and are running from the law. It'd be my duty to see you brought to justice if that was so."

"It's not. I'm just a man with a piece of bad luck."

He saw the other man's movement out of the corner of his eye, started to turn, then it felt like he was filled with white light. It wasn't a completely unpleasant feeling after the first shot hit him. Not completely, but strange.

He never counted on getting shot that day, but then he never counted on becoming a fugitive, or anything near it.

1

Bᴵʀᴅʏ Pʀɪᴅᴇ, the prettiest whore in Sweet Sorrow, stood on the porch in front of the Rosebud saloon picking nits out of her lover's hair on a Sunday morning so hot that most folks didn't want to get out of bed to go to church.

Roy Bean grew drowsy from Birdy's tender fingers searching through his hair. It was always such a pleasant experience for him and he allowed how he could fall in love and marry a girl like Birdy if it wasn't for the fact he already had a wife and several youngsters down in Texas awaiting his return.

Birdy had outright asked him to marry her on several occasions, but his answer was always the same.

"I'm in my middle years and you are just a child. I've tried about everything a man can try and have failed miserably in the trying. The only thing I've been even mildly successful at is procreation. Why, was I to marry you, Birdy, I'd fail at that, too. No, better you stay a bride to the multitudes than a bride to a wastrel such as myself. You'll fare better. Someday a lonesome cowboy will come along and win your heart and give you a passel of kids and a home with a bed that's got no strangers, nor bedbugs in it and that will be what you deserve."

But still she begged him to marry her.

"I'm nothing but a footloose scoundrel."

"I'd love you even if you was a bank robber."

"No, you wouldn't."

"I would."

"Don't beg, child, it's unseemly."

"If you don't marry me, I'll throw myself into the river and drown," Birdy said. But Roy Bean knew that Birdy had a penchant for being melodramatic, for he was a man who featured himself as an excellent judge of the human character.

"What river? There ain't a decent river within fifty miles of here," he said.

"I'll just find one and throw myself in it and the tragedy will be on you and you'll spend endless nights unable to sleep and end up an old boozehound and crazy in the head from grief."

"Lord almighty, I don't know why I don't take you back East and get you started in a stage career as an actress—why I guess old Lillie Langtry would pale in comparison to you."

"You reckon?"

They laughed. It was one of the things Roy Bean admired about Birdy Pride—her youthful nature. It made him feel young just to be in her company.

"Say, ain't that Toussaint Trueblood?" Birdy said.

"Where?"

"Coming up the street in that wagon—pulled by that raggedy mule."

Roy Bean opened his eyes even though he didn't want to and looked up the street. Birdy was right, it was the French Indian. Roy did not refer to Toussaint Trueblood as a half-breed like some of the others in Sweet Sorrow did, even though he knew like everyone else that Toussaint was half French and half Mandan Indian. For, Toussaint was a man well educated who could speak several languages that included Italian, Spanish, and Latin as well as French and Mandan, and English like a white man. Roy Bean considered Toussaint Trueblood anything but a half-breed. In fact, he might be the smartest man in all of the Dakotas next to himself and was someone to be careful of misjudging.

Birdy and Roy watched as Toussaint pulled his wagon up front of the Rosebud, hauling back on the reins and applying the brake with his foot.

"Mr. Trueblood," Roy said.

Toussaint rested his gaze on the comely Birdy, practically ignoring Roy Bean's presence.

"What brings you in this morning?" Roy Bean asked.

"Him," Toussaint said, turning his head just enough to indicate something in the bed of the wagon.

Roy Bean stood up and walked to the edge of the porch and looked over the side of the wagon. There was a man lying there under a blanket, his face nearly bloodless.

"Where'd you find the body?"

"Out west of here, near Cooper's Creek."

"Just found him, no horse, nothing?"

Toussaint nodded without taking his gaze off Birdy.

"You taking him over to Tall John's to get fixed for burial?"

"He's not dead yet."

"He ain't? He sure enough looks as though he is."

Birdy stepped closed to the edge of the porch and looked at the man lying in the back of Toussaint's wagon, too.

"Except for the blood, he's a nice looking fellow," she said. "What happened to him, do you suppose?"

Birdy saw the way Toussaint looked at her: like a wolf looking at a lamb, she thought, for Toussaint Trueblood was a mystery to her as far as men went. Most said what they wanted of her, offered her money, and she provided them with what they were willing to pay for. But Toussaint Trueblood never did offer her money or otherwise speak to her about the thing she was most knowledgeable about, or otherwise make suggestions to her lewd or otherwise; he simply looked, and his look caused a little shiver of something to run through her—not fear exactly, but something close.

"I better get him on to the physician, Willis," Toussaint said. "He's got several holes in him from being shot."

"Who you reckon shot him?" Roy Bean asked.

"I know who shot him. I seen them do it," Toussaint said, then snapped the reins over the mule's haunches and went on down the street on a morning so hot one could easily imagine devils lounging around on black settees drinking ice beer and complaining.

Doc Willis was seeing snakes crawling up the walls when Toussaint Trueblood knocked at his door. Doc Willis nearly bit off his tongue at the unexpected sound. But thank god it made the snakes disappear. He opened the door to see Toussaint standing there.

"What . . . what?"

"Got a man near dead in my wagon."

"Why bring him to me?"

"You're the only doctor in town."

Doc Willis blinked his eyes several times as though trying to discern what Toussaint Trueblood had just told him.

"Come on and help me carry him in."

Doc Willis followed Toussaint Trueblood like a zombie, took hold of the man's legs while Toussaint took his upper body and they carried him on in to Doc's house—a back room where the light was best thanks to a pair of ceiling-to-floor windows.

Toussaint pulled back the blanket to show Doc the bloody wounds.

"Who is he?"

Toussaint shrugged.

"Just some fellow I found out on the grasslands. I guess I done my part. See you around."

"Wait . . ."

Too late. Toussaint Trueblood went out the door, climbed aboard his wagon, released the brake, and snapped the reins, saying, "Step off, mule," and drove off toward a round house he kept just outside the town limits.

When the madwoman arrived at his place, Toussaint Trueblood was reading a Shakespearean sonnet: *Venus and Adonis*, one of his favorites. He liked the fact Venus pursued the young Adonis instead of the other way around. Seemed like it was always the man in pursuit of the woman, but not in Mr. Shakespeare's verse.

He looked up from the book to see the woman standing there.

"What you want?" he said. He recognized her as the blacksmith's wife.

She held something in her arms.

"Here," she said.

"What is it?"

"Here," she said again.

He had a bad feeling about her, the thing she was offering him.

"You go on, now," he said. "Go on back home." Said it the way he would tell a stray dog to go home to its owner.

She didn't move.

He set the book aside. Finding the man—watching him get shot—was a bad way to begin his day. He'd gone out looking for dreaming rabbits, knew that often he could find one or two down by the creek where they'd go for water and then sit in the pleasant sun and dream.

He was running out of bones he could sell to the travelers on Dunhill & Morgan's Stage line when they stopped in Sweet Sorrow for lunch and await a change of horse teams.

"What are they?" the travelers would invariably ask when he showed them the bones.

"Trigger fingers."

"Trigger fingers?"

"That one belonged to Wild Bill Hickok."

"No!"

"Bought it off the man who buried him, kept it for a souvenir but then he got sick and had to sell it to pay for his medicine."

"No!"

"I'm pretty hard up for cash myself, mister, otherwise I wouldn't think of selling it."

"How much you want for it?"

"It's worth fifty dollars."

"Maybe, but not to me it ain't."

"Like I said, I wouldn't sell it I wasn't so hard up for cash."

"I'd maybe go you five dollars for it if you can guarantee its authenticity."

"Got a hand-signed letter from the fellow I bought it off of."

And so it went each time, sometimes selling a few bones and sometimes not. And if not rabbit bones for fingers, then one of several rusty old pistols that used to belong to General Custer or Dick Turpin or Billy the Kid or any of a dozen other notorious desperados. Pistols were easier to sell than the bones, but harder to come by in such poor condition.

He told himself he should have just left that man be once he'd seen him shot; that if he had, the madwoman wouldn't be standing in his lodge trying to hand him something he was already sure he didn't want.

"You want me to take you on home, Mrs. Figg?"

She stared at him, her eyes as large and round as boiled eggs, her hair a nest of wild copper strands full of grass and twigs.

"Here!" she said again and stepped forward.

He took a deep breath and reached for whatever it was she wanted to give him. It was something wrapped in a piece of old blanket. And when she placed it in his hands he could tell by its weight and shape what it was and he didn't want to draw back the blanket to confirm it.

"No, you better take this back," he said, trying to give it to her.

She shied away.

He knew he had to be careful and not spook her more than she was or things could get worse.

"Look," he said. "I'm going to go put this in the wagon and then I'm going to help you get back home. Is that okay with you?"

Her face seemed to soften, to appear almost normal, and she looked around his lodge, at the shelves of books and the iron stove and the wolf hide tossed down on the floor for a rug. She began to mew like a cat hungry for milk.

He took a step and she stiffened again.

"Okay," he said. "Maybe you want to go on out first, ahead of me."

Then suddenly she started tearing off her clothes and he said, "No, no, don't do that now, Mrs. Figg! Don't do that now."

But in seconds she was completely naked and he looked away, trying not to see this overly large woman, fearing what she might try or do next, his thoughts rushing ahead of him to the near future: a lynch mob, the irate blacksmith with a pistol or a hammer trying to bash his skull in, possibly a long stretch in prison for molestation, maybe even hanging from a cottonwood without so much as a trial since there wasn't so much as a bit of law in the region except for two badass law dogs.

She sat on the floor and would not move. She closed her eyes and began to hum a child's lullaby. He cautiously placed the thing she'd given him in her arms and without opening her eyes she took it and sang to it and was still singing when he left and returned with her husband, the blacksmith, Junius Figg, explaining the situation on the way back to his lodge.

And later that evening, after the man had taken his wife away, Toussaint lay alone on his cot without even the benefit of the light from an oil lamp and looked up through the small window above him and saw the North Star. It seemed to be a distant eye staring at him.

What he'd seen that day had been foretold to him by his Mandan grandfather when he was just a boy ("Bad trouble will befall you if you stay among them white men"). Then his French daddy said afterward: "Don't believe what those Indians tell you, eh. They got strange beliefs, those guys. All you got to remember is Jesus will take care of you if you pray to heem."

Then his French daddy told him all about Jesus and miracles, and when Toussaint told his Mandan grandfather about Jesus and the miracles, his grandfather said, "I heard that story, too, but I don't believe it. I've seen lots of dead men and none of them ever got up and started walking around again. And that stuff about him walking across the water, ha! Charley Elk tried to do that once when he got drunk and almost drowned. Whites are crazy to believe that stuff. You better be careful what they fill your head with."

So Toussaint Trueblood kept his own council from that point forward, leaving open all possibilities, precluding none, knowing as he did, that the world was a strange and often tormented place, and men with two different kinds of blood in their veins were best off keeping their thoughts to themselves.

Still, it was overly troubling to have the blacksmith's wife show up at his lodge and try and give him her dead infant. He couldn't get the child's face out of his thoughts, and that night he had dreams of dead children in an old schoolhouse singing his name over and over again.

Roy Bean wandered over to Doc Willis's office upon having all the nits picked out of his hair by Birdy Pride. He was curious about the near dead stranger.

"Is he going to live?"

Doc's hands trembled like aspen leaves in autumn wind as he poured himself a water glass of bourbon, offering Roy Bean a glass as well. Roy Bean said, "Just a little, Doc, it's Sunday, you know."

Doc Willis just looked at him.

"None of his wounds are fatal, most hardly more than flesh wounds and the one that did him the most damage went clean through him like a hot poker through butter. He'll live unless he decides he don't want to."

"It'd be nice if we had us some real law in the area besides Bob Olive and that fool deputy of his, Teacup Smith," Roy Bean said, shaking his head. "I've always believed in justice and the law—but it is lacking in this far-flung buffalo wallow."

Doc refilled his glass, the tremors easing now.

"It's always been a mean and violent place, these plains, Mr. Bean. And it takes mean and violent men like Olive and Smith to stave off other, more mean and violent men. They're just the best of the worst is all. Where the hell you been, down some gopher hole not to know that much?"

"Have any idea who he is?"

"None. Nor do I much care. I don't know why that

damn Toussaint had to bring him to my door and disturb my peace."

Roy Bean looked close at the fellow.

"Maybe he deserved what he got," Doc said, glancing over. "Maybe he's nothing more than a rapist or murderer himself. He could have committed terrible depredations and someone caught up with him and settled old scores."

They heard the church bell ringing, went on drinking.

It wasn't long before the blacksmith arrived, his face gaunt.

"Things is bad," is all he said. "My woman's gone mad, smothered our baby. Jesus Christ, but things is bad."

2

❖❖❖

HE OPENED HIS EYES. Heard snoring. Turned his head and saw a man sitting in a chair, his head bowed, his arms hanging slack at his sides, an open book lying on the floor. It was a nice room, flocked wallpaper, a carpet, soft curtains that lifted and fell and lifted again with the warm breezes coming through the open window.

He went to sit up unaware of exactly where he was or how he'd gotten there. That's when everything inside him felt busted. He groaned, the eyes of the man sleeping in the chair opened, looked at him. One of the slack hands rose and wiped slobber from his lips.

"It lives," the man said rising from his chair and coming near. The man drew back the sheet to reveal the bandages, some of them tinged with blood.

"They shot the shit out of you, son, but they weren't very good at it or you'd be out yonder in the local cemetery."

The man looked down at the bandages.

"It hurts like hell."

"I'm not surprised."

The man's gaze took him in, measured him head to chest.

"You know who it was that shot you?"

He thought about it, trying to bring the events into focus.

"I don't know," he said at last. Things were blank, shifted out of time.

"Don't know, or can't remember?"

He shrugged, even that hurt.

"Who are you?" the wounded man asked.

"I was going to ask you the same thing. I'm what serves as the local medicine man—Woodrow Willis is the name."

He noticed how the man's hands shook.

"I'd be curious to know who you are, son."

He started to say Tristan Shade, then remembered why he'd been running.

"Jacob Horn."

"Well, Mr. Horn, you won't die—at least not yet and not because of your wounds, if that's any comfort to you."

"How'd I get here?"

Doc Willis explained about Toussaint Trueblood bringing him in off the grasslands.

"How long ago?"

"Three days."

He heard something, looked over at the window, saw that the wind was blowing dust against the glass, soft little taps of dirt. Doc Willis went over and closed the window and the curtains fell slack.

"You feel up to eating?"

Horn nodded and when the physician left the room he thought hard trying to remember everything.

It came back in broken pieces, like looking at a shattered mirror.

In one piece, he saw himself riding across the grasslands on his way to the Canadian border to take refuge in the house of one Jake Horn—a misfit and black sheep uncle on his mother's side. He remembered the sound of running water, saw the fragment of a creek he'd paused by. In another fragment he saw the two men ride up. Remembered some of their questions. Saw in a sliver the way they sat their horses, their rough faces; the faces of dangerous men. It was a bit of irony, considering he himself was a wanted man and considered a dangerous criminal. Words exchanged, then a blinding light filled the rest of what he remembered. But now he knew that they had shot him and left him for dead. Thankfully he didn't remember the getting shot part.

Doc Willis came back into the room with a tray holding a soup tureen, a glass of whiskey.

"You like turtle soup? One of my patients brought it over this morning. I'm not overly fond of it myself, prefer a good steak. The whiskey's first rate, though."

Days passed. He began to heal. Got well enough to dress himself and go to the privy alone, go for walks.

The wounds ached at first, then started to scab over and itch. He knew he was healing.

"How much do I owe you for the care?" he asked toward the end of the second week.

Doc Willis looked at him, said, "Hell, whatever it is, you can't afford it. You came in here stripped of everything but your drawers and bloody shirt."

"I'll pay you, just tell me how much."

"I know a lost cause when I see one, son. Not to worry. Any man who practices medicine on this frontier ain't doing it for the money."

"I'd like directions to the man's place who brought me in."

Doc Willis gave him a fresh shirt, pair of trousers, and a pair of dress shoes he hadn't worn in years and had no prospects of ever wearing again. Luckily enough they were men of similar size. Then he gave him directions to Toussaint Trueblood's lodge.

Toussaint Trueblood was stringing together a necklace of rabbit bones when he saw the man approaching.

"Hello," Jake said.

Toussaint watched him warily.

The man came close, offered his right hand.

"I'd like to thank you for saving my life."

"You look a little bent out of shape."

"I'm still listing some from those bullet wounds."

"You remind me of a man my father told me about."

"Oh, who's that?"

"Some guy he said got killed then came back alive again. A miracle worker."

Sun baked the earth and not even a little wind blew across the heads of the wild grass now. In the stillness they could hear bees working in the wild clover and nearer by a yellow jacket worried the purple thorn of a bull thistle.

"I've got some ginger beer if you're thirsty," Toussaint said.

"I couldn't ask anything more from you. I just wanted to come and thank you personally for what you did."

"You wouldn't be interested in buying something valuable, would you?"

Toussaint held a rabbit bone in the palm of his hand.

"It's the trigger finger of Dick Turpin."

"It looks like the bone of a rodent."

Toussaint closed his hand around it. Here was a man who obviously knew his bones.

"Besides," Jake said. "I don't have any money I could pay you with anyway."

"I know—they robbed you after they shot you."

"What else do you know, Mr. Trueblood? About the men who shot me?"

"I know you don't want to be around here when they come back."

"How do you know they'll come back?"

Toussaint Trueblood acted as though he hadn't heard the question, fixed his attention on the rabbit bone necklace again.

"Even if I wanted to leave here, I'm afraid I've got no means to leave—no money, no horse."

"Then you're in some fix."

"I guess that I am."

Toussaint watched the man turn and walk slightly leaning to his right back toward town and thought to himself, *This should get pretty interesting when Bob Olive and Teacup Smith get back to town.*

Roy Bean was soaking his feet in a pan of cold water out front of the Rosebud when he saw the shot stranger ambling down the main drag of the town. Roy had been waiting for Birdy Pride to rise from her late sleep and come join him for lunch, thinking that after they ate, he and Birdy would ride out toward Cooper's Creek and fornicate under the shade of the trees along its bank—something that gave him a great deal of pleasure and always left him inspired with a head full of ideas on ways to make something more of himself than a wandering man.

"Lo," Roy Bean said when the stranger drew even.

"Hello," Jake said.

"You're the shot fellow Toussaint brung in."

Jake nodded.

"I guess the whole town knows."

Roy Bean said, "Yes sir, gossip travels fast as lightning in these parts, though ain't none of us seen no lightning or rain neither in several months. I'm Roy Bean."

Jake introduced himself, still trying to adjust to his new self-given name, figuring his uncle Jake wouldn't mind so much having it used for the right purposes.

"Jake Horn," Roy Bean said. "I knew a Tom Horn down in Texas near got rubbed out by a woolly cowboy named Ligget. You wouldn't be any relation would you?"

"No, I don't think so."

"Ligget shot old Tom front to back, as I recall. Didn't kill him, either. Must be you Horns is hard to kill."

"Maybe so. You mind if I sit a minute? I think I pushed my luck walking out to Mr. Trueblood's place."

Roy Bean looked in the direction Jake had come from as Jake took a seat opposite him.

"Toussaint's, huh?"

"Yes."

"An enterprising fellow."

"You wouldn't know where a man could find a job in this town? I'm busted flat and need to make a little money—enough so I can continue on my way."

"Where was you headed?"

"West," Jake said, preferring to be cautious with information.

"In there, maybe, if you ain't too proud to swamp."

Jake looked at the false-front, the double doors.

"I'm not too proud to do anything, down on my luck as I am."

Peg Leg Watts looked over the fellow, then said, "It don't pay much, but meals are included and there's a shack out back you can sleep in if you don't mind mice and scorpions crawling in bed with you on occasion."

"I don't mind. When do I start?"

"Now's as good a time as any; those spittoons are near full to overflowing. I've been short a man since last week when Curly took off after Johnson. I don't suspect neither will be back soon."

Jake wasn't interested in knowing who Curly or Johnson was or why one had taken off after the other, so he didn't ask.

Peg Leg Watts explained about how it was important to keep the spittoons empty, showed Jake where he kept the mop and bucket and said, "She's all yours. That means cleaning up blood spilled and puke as well. You still interested?"

"I am."

"Go to her, then."

"I'd like to get paid at the end of each day."

Peg Leg Watts looked at him suspiciously.

"Because I'd like to get a shave and a haircut, a few clothes."

"Pay's once a week. Been my experience you pay a man daily, you'll be hiring a new one nearly every other day; such work ain't exactly what draws the professional types, if you know what I mean. But you go on over to the barber's and the mercantile and tell 'em you're working for me and to give you a line of credit."

End of the day Jake took his leave and headed for the barbershop.

"You're the shot fellow," the barber said.

He nodded.

"Cheerless Carl is what they call me. You want that beard shaved off?"

Again he nodded.

He sat there in the barber chair getting his hair cut, a shave, and made his plans while Cheerless Carl talked about President Garfield getting shot.

"Imagine that," he said several times. "A man just walks up to the president and shoots him. Ain't nobody safe anymore. But then I guess you'd know what that's like: somebody just walking up and shooting you."

Jake didn't reply. But yeah, he knew what that was like—getting shot.

Afterward he went back to the Rosebud and asked Peg Leg Watts if he was needed further.

"Come round this evening when things get rolling—work till closing."

He went out back and inspected the shack—found the previous occupant's cot, a dusty blanket, took it outside and shook it out, then finally eased himself down, surprised at how exhausted he felt. He slept, awakened to a growing darkness, rose and went back into the Rosebud.

The place was alive with customers—men in dungarees standing under flop felt hats, standing along the bar drinking, sitting at tables playing poker, gathered around a roulette table betting. He saw Roy Bean sitting alone with a bottle and looking forlorn as his gaze followed the pert Birdy Pride who was in the company of other men.

He went over and said, "Thanks for the tip about the job here."

Roy Bean said, "You want a drink?"

"I probably better keep at emptying the spit pots."

"Women," Roy Bean said.

"What about them?"

"They'll bust a man's heart every time."

Yeah, that was something he already knew about, too, and the reason he was on the run—a woman. A very clever woman with the wiles and charms of Salomé.

A fight broke out, one man battering another with his fists until Peg Leg Watts came around from behind the bar and cracked the bully across his shoulder bone with a wooden club then gave them both the bum's rush out the front door, saying, "You want to bash each other's brains in, do it down at Skinny Dick's—I run a peaceful place here!"

"A lawless place," Roy Bean bemoaned. "What this place needs is law and order."

"You mean there isn't any?"

"Oh, there's some, if you can call it that. But what law we got here is the lesser of evils."

It was something of a relief, Jake thought, to not have to worry about the law, possible wanted posters.

Roy Bean's gaze fell on Birdy Pride who was sitting on the lap of a rancher he knew to be married with a wife and a passel of kids. His anger and jealousy rose together in his whiskey-warmed bosom. Then he realized that he himself was no better than the sodbusting rancher, that he, too, was married with a passel of kids.

Oh hell, oh hell! he thought miserably.

A woman burst through the doors screaming. Everything stopped: the laughter, the loud talk, the turn of the roulette wheel.

"It's my husband, Bill!" she screamed. "It's my husband, Bill!"

Sitting silently outside his lodge watching for shooting stars, Toussaint Trueblood could see in the distance the lights of Sweet Sorrow's nighttime businesses—could hear faintly some of the nighttime activity.

And farther out on the grasslands he heard a wolf call.

Then an owl flew across the moon.

It was a bad sign. Somebody was dead.

He saw it then—the dancing lights—and thought maybe it was Jesus coming for him.

He sure hoped it wasn't Jesus.

3

THEY MARCHED OUT in the dark with lanterns. Toussaint Trueblood stood watching what he thought at first was dancing lights, but realized soon enough was a bobbing line of torches heading away from town. He didn't want to know where the torches were headed but he could not stem his curiosity either and went to follow them.

The torches and the men carrying them came to the homestead of Bill Blankenship.

What could it be? Toussaint wondered. Bill Blankenship was as stout and robust a man as could be found anywhere around Sweet Sorrow. Toussaint worked his way to the head of the crowd. He could hear Bill's wife wailing. It caused the hair on his arms to stand up.

The men with the torches stood in a semicircle along the side of the house, their yellow flickering light bringing to bear the tragedy. Bill Blankenship's upper half was submerged in a barrel of rainwater. It was as though he'd been bobbing for apples and never came up for air.

Roy Bean stepped to the fore and said to some of the others, "Well, let's get him out of there."

Nobody rushed to help, so Toussaint stepped forward.

Together, he and Roy Bean pulled the lifeless man from the barrel and laid him gently upon the ground.

"Somebody get a blanket and cover this poor soul up," Roy demanded. Somebody did.

Bill's wife continued to wail. Some of the men brought her forward. She stood shaking and looking down at the still form of her husband.

"How'd this happen?" Roy asked her in a kindly voice.

It took several times of asking before she settled down long enough to answer.

"He said he was going out to mess with the horses . . . and he just never came back in for the longest time . . . I . . . I came out to see if he was all right and found him with his head down in the water . . . He'd been acting funny all day . . . I didn't know what he meant *'mess with the horses.'*" Then she collapsed in a heap and some of the men carried her into the house and set her on the bed and one went to find Doc Willis. Somebody said he was probably drunk.

Roy Bean looked at some of the others; they seemed to shrink back when he did.

Everybody knew what everybody else was thinking: first it had been Emmaline Figg gone crazy, they all thought from grief of bearing a waterhead child. Now this—Bill Blankenship drowned in a rain barrel. Goddamn, goddamn.

A wagon was hitched, and Bill Blankenship put in it, and carried down to Tall John's.

Tall John was a former Confederate soldier who had one of his ears shot off in the fight at Petersburg. And when the fighting was over that day, he found his ear and wrapped it in a silk handkerchief, put it in his pocket, and walked away from the war and the killing, but hardly away from death itself. Death seemed to follow Tall John like a tick-hound pup following a rabbit scent.

Tall John hailed from near the town of Preatiss in Bolivar County, Mississippi, but saw no point in going home again a broken and sorrowful man for all his family to witness. And so he wandered for a time and somehow ended up the mortician in Sweet Sorrow. He felt uncommon grief for the dead, since he'd turned many a fellow from life to death himself. It came to him in his wandering that perhaps he could make matters right again if he was to care for the dead the way others cared for the living—with gentleness and kindness. Fact was, after he'd done it for a time, he preferred working with the dead over that of being around the living. The dead were silent souls, untroubled by a world full of trouble. They did not complain and bemoan their condition. They did not shoot or knife one another out of jealousy over a woman or a card game. The dead were peace loving and deserved a hand out of life just as they had deserved one coming into it.

Tall John hired an assistant named Boblink Jones and taught him about caring for the deceased: trimming their moustaches and combing their hair and seeing they had fine coats and lovely gowns and pretty shoes to wear to their eternal home. Though the children who infrequently were delivered into his care did make him sad to think of lives unlived—like the little baby that was brought to him yesterday: Emmaline Figg's waterhead baby. But he was buoyed by the thought that such were simply little angels God had called home so he could fix them right again and send them back to earth in different bodies.

So when the men knocked that night and delivered to him the body of Bill Blankenship, he looked gently on the still masculine face, its cap of wet hair plastered about Bill's head, and said quietly, "We'll see he's taken care of."

Of course everyone but Tall John and Boblink Jones went back to their drinking, this time in greater earnest than before the tragedy, seeing up close as they had, the mortal plane upon which they all were balanced so precariously. Drinking gave them strength to face down death, or at least not care that it was out there waiting for them. Liquor was also the oil that loosened the tongue and by which to prophesy and postulate reasons why a man would stick his own head into a barrel of rain and drown himself. It gave each man courage to speak his mind in the matter, which was all any of them wanted—to have some say in the matter.

Jake watched as they flowed back into the Rosebud, ordered whiskey and beer and cocktails. It had been peaceful for a time with the saloon empty, but the internal rage that drew men to gather and drink and become bawdy, seemed greater now that they had witnessed the strange death of Bill Blankenship.

Birdy Pride and her sisters were kept busy the rest of the night and clear up until the sky went from pitch black to a soft mourning-dove gray and the last of the drinkers and gamblers staggered home again— some to wives and others to empty rooms.

Peg Leg Watts fell asleep counting the night's take.

Jake looked at the pile of money and was sorely tempted, but instead he went out locking the double doors behind him and stood looking at the first of the sun rising out of the grassland.

"It always gives me a certain feeling to see it," a voice behind him said.

He turned to see Toussaint Trueblood standing there.

"There's something full of promise in a morning," Jake said.

"I got some good chickory coffee brewing over to my place," Toussaint said.

"Sounds good to me."

They walked out to Toussaint's lodge, two solitary men crossing the grassland between the little town and the earth house. Not a great distance, but great enough to suit Toussaint.

They settled on a plank bench outside the lodge where they could watch the sun come the rest of the way up, could see its light spreading over the grasses like golden water as they drank the chickory coffee.

They chose not to talk, but simply watch and keep to their own thoughts for a time. Then Toussaint spoke.

"You ain't him, are you?"

"Who?"

Toussaint cut his gaze to Jake.

"My old man used to tell me about this fellow . . ."

"The one who got killed and came back alive again?"

Toussaint nodded.

"Said he was supposed to come back and save everybody from their sins."

Jake smiled.

"Jesus, you mean?"

"Yeah, him," Toussaint said, nodding.

"No, I'm hardly him."

"Maybe you are and just don't know it."

"I think I'd know it."

"Maybe you would and maybe you wouldn't."

"What makes you think I might be him?"

"I don't know, just something about you doesn't equate."

"Equate," Jake said. "I'd say there's something about you that doesn't equate, either."

"I don't know what you mean."

"You're better educated than most, for one thing."

"You mean for a half-breed."

"I mean for someone living this far out on the frontier."

Toussaint let the comment pass.

"Trust me," Jake said. "I'm not him."

"You believe things you've heard about him?"

"Some, I guess. Hard to say. I've always been a practical-minded man—believe in what I see, what can be proven. The sciences, you might say, spiritualism less so."

Toussaint nodded again, said, "Uh-huh, me, too."

The sun warmed their faces.

Roy Bean felt restless and ill at ease, even with Birdy Pride in the bed next to him—someone who usually made him feel quite comfortable and relaxed.

"What is it, Roy? You ailing from something?"

"I surely am, but it's nothing man nor medicine can cure."

"Is it that you're missing your wife and children?"

Roy Bean tried not to think overly much about his wife and kids when he was with Birdy Pride. Her bringing it up only made him feel more uncomfortable.

"No, it's nothing to do with them, Birdy, and I wish you'd not bring them up in conversation when we're together."

Birdy seemed to pout, which instantly had a disconcerting effect on Roy Bean, causing him to feel all the more ill at ease. He climbed out of bed, his bare hams surprisingly small for a man of his bulk. Birdy tittered when she watched him pace the floor.

"What is it, child?"

Birdy hushed.

"There's something bad afoot in this place," he said.

"What, darling Roy?"

"I don't know, but something. First the blacksmith's wife took crazy in the head and now old Bill Blankenship has gone and drowned himself. Something's afoot, something evil possibly."

Birdy took on a fearful look when Roy Bean's words fell on her like a hard cold rain.

"Should I be afraid?"

He looked at her, at that lovely sweet little thing that she was—a child really, probably not more than sixteen or seventeen years old—not much older than his oldest boy Hector. Of course he was no longer sure exactly how old Hector was, nor even sure how old any of his other children were. His wife had been fourteen when he married her.

"No, my sweet, you should not be afraid. As long as I'm around, I'll protect you with my very life. Not to worry now."

But she could see that her lover was quite troubled by the wrinkles in his forehead and the way he could not stand still and the way he constantly looked out the window.

"Do you see a storm coming, Roy, is that what's troubling you?"

The sky was as clear as blue glass, but he did see a storm coming, just not the sort of storm Birdy Pride was thinking about.

"Listen, there's something I should tell you," Toussaint said.

"What's that?"

"Those men who shot you . . ."

"What about them?"

"I think they'll be coming back any day now."

Toussaint allowed time for his prediction to sink in.

"What makes you think so?"

"Because Bob Olive is hardly ever gone more than two weeks at a time. It's been almost that since I brought you in."

"Thanks for the warning."

"They're some mean bastards."

"Of that I've no doubt," Jake said, rubbing the healing wounds in his chest, feeling the hard puckering places left by the shooter's bullets; they were hard and the size of dimes.

"I think they would have killed you but for one thing," Toussaint said.

"What's that?"

"Bob always was a cheap son of a bitch, even when it came to his bullets; wouldn't buy store-bought ones, always loaded his own. Features himself as some sort of true gunfighter. Says a true gunfighter makes his own loads. What a crock of shit."

"This is good coffee," Jake said, tending to talk about things other than bullets and getting shot. "I guess I better get on back and get some rest before I have to go clean up the Rosebud again."

"You like that sort of work, cleaning up other men's spit?"

Jake looked at him as he stood. Morning sunlight had crawled all over the land and now reached the very edges of Sweet Sorrow, shrinking the shadows of the buildings.

"What do you think?"

"I think there are plenty of better ways to make money. I think what a man allows himself to fall to says a lot about the man."

"You're not looking for a partner in the bone-selling business, are you?"

"Hell no. It's skinny as it is."

Then Toussaint saw that the man was fooling with him.

"Oh, one more thing," Toussaint said as Jake turned to head for town. Jake didn't stop or turn around.

"Those men who shot you—Bob Olive and Teacup Smith. They're the law here. Just so you know."

Jake didn't look back but walked straight on toward the town, straight to the mercantile.

Otis Dollar was helping a woman pick out a nice gingham from a shelf bearing bolts of cloth when Jake entered.

Jake noticed the woman say something to the shopkeeper as he went straight to where Otis kept a display of handguns under glass.

He looked them over carefully, waited for Otis to finish with the woman.

When at last the woman bought her material, she lingered around the shop as though interested in other dry goods, but within hearing range. Otis came over and stood behind the counter.

"Peg Leg Watts said you'd float me a line of credit," Jake said.

"Peg Leg says you're good for it, I'll take his word, but only up to a certain amount."

"That matched pair of Schofields—the Russian models," Jake said, pointing to the pistols.

"Ah, these are very nice," Otis said, reaching in and taking each and setting them atop the counter.

Jake hefted first one, then the other, testing their weight and balance, working the mechanisms, sighting down the barrels.

"Forty-four/forties," Otis said. "Guns a man can trust to see the job done right."

Jake simply nodded.

"How much?"

"I'll take twenty each for them."

"That line of credit go as high as forty dollars?"

Otis rubbed his jaw.

"I reckon it could if you have something to put down."

"I've got nothing today but by week's end I'll pay you in full."

Otis nodded in agreement.

"I'll need cartridges."

"A two-gun man," Otis said, reaching for the shells.

Jake said nothing. Instead, he put the pistols inside his belt and took the box of shells. He saw the woman staring at him as she stood by a counter of notions. She was middle-age, not bad looking, better if she wore her hair loose, he thought.

Jake could feel her eyes and those of Otis watching through the store window as he crossed the street toward the Rosebud and the little shack in the rear and the waiting mop and the dirty spittoons.

He told himself this one thing as he placed the pistols under the pillow of the cot: *I won't be swamping out that place very much longer, one way or the other.*

4

TOUSSAINT TRUEBLOOD was out scouting for dreaming rabbits when he saw the riders coming, the sun low in the west now throwing their shadows long behind them across the grasslands.

He already had found two big jacks, said the proper prayers, then clobbered them in the head with fist-sized rocks. He was skinning them on the mossy edge of Cooper's Creek when he spotted Bob Olive and Teacup Smith. They rode along at a leisurely pace headed straight for Sweet Sorrow.

Toussaint finished up his skinning, then washed his bloody hands in the cool creek. It was a mile or two from town, near the same place he'd found the fellow, Jake Horn. Maybe he ought to get on back and see what would happen. It might be quite interesting.

Teacup Smith was by nature a loud rambunctious man, whereas his companion, Bob Olive was taciturn, withdrawn, and often surly. Bob Olive secretly thought someday he would probably fatally shoot Teacup Smith just as he had done several other loud-mouths. It always gave him a certain pleasure to silence forever a man who ran his mouth.

The pair was returning from a bank they'd robbed in Rolette County near the Canadian border. In their pockets was close to a thousand dollars, more or less the two hundred or so they'd spent on liquor and prostitutes along the way.

Teacup Smith was drunk in the saddle, carrying on about a woman he had once been in love with—someone named Jenny with pretty black hair he'd known down in Wyoming.

"I never should have left her," Teacup decried. "You find a good woman, you stick with her. Good women are as hard to find as chicken teeth . . ."

"Why didn't you stick with her then if she was so damn wonderful?" Bob said grumpily.

"I would have if I hadn't shot her."

"Too bad she didn't shoot you."

"What's that supposed to mean?"

"Whatever you want it to."

"Ain't you gonna ask me why I shot her?"

"No. I don't give a shit why you shot her."

"Reason I shot her was she was fooling around on me."

Bob Olive felt a headache coming on from so much talk. To him, Teacup's carrying on endlessly was simply noise and he hated noise. Noise reminded him of being in prison—the one at Huntsville most especially. The days and nights he'd spent there were nothing but head-splitting noise—men talking, yelling, screaming, never shutting up.

"She fooled around on me and I shot her and I shot him, too," Teacup said, then began to sob. Bob Olive could hardly believe his eyes when he looked over at his deputy and saw big wet tears staining his dirty face.

"Why don't you shut the hell up!"

"I shot 'em in the throes of passion! I shot 'em so bad the bullets went through them into each other . . ." Bob Olive detested any man who carried on like a woman.

Bob Olive saw Cooper's Creek glistening in the distance like a silver snake winding its way through the grass and felt relieved to be nearing the town of Sweet Sorrow again if for no other reason than to be shed of Teacup Smith for a while. He spurred his horse on ahead even as Teacup continued to carry on, sobbing and telling the sad tale of what he described as killing "the beast with two backs!"

The Dunhill & Morgan Stage had arrived just before the noon hour and several passengers disembarked to take a meal at the Fat Duck Café while the stage driver and his shotgun man changed teams of horses.

The stage driver was a man named Fuzzy Walls and he'd been driving for Dunhill & Morgan for almost five years. He had been shot twice by bandits, and once clubbed on the head by a rival over the affections of a hefty farm girl, a blow that left him deaf in one ear and plagued him with dizzy spells. He had once dreamt of being a sea captain and often made his way to the Rosebud during the hourly break to talk about sailing ships with Peg Leg Watts, who had been a sea captain for a number of years.

Peg Leg told Fuzzy what it was like to sail the China Sea and go around the Horn of Africa and what the Greek Isles looked like with their white houses littering the mountainsides like large pearls. It made Fuzzy Walls feel deprived.

"Why'd you give it up?" he asked Peg Leg.

"We got jumped once by pirates in the South Pacific. They threw us overboard and left us to die. Sharks et half the crew. One bit off my leg. Only thing that saved me was an empty rum barrel I grabbed on to and eventually floated me to an island had natives living on it. Such an experience was enough to make me want to never go in the ocean again. That rum barrel was an omen for me. I gave up sailing and come here in the middle of nowhere and not even close to an ocean and started this saloon. I never again have to worry about getting et by a shark."

Fuzzy Walls ordered a second whiskey and said, "I never thought about no sharks."

"Well, you ought to if you planning on going to sea. Sharks and storms and pirates makes the sea a contentious place."

Jake Horn was sitting on a chair outside the shed back of the Rosebud writing a letter to his uncle, the real Jake Horn.

Dear Uncle Jake. I'm down here in North Dakota Territory. It's a long and somewhat complicated story, suffice it to say I had to leave Denver in a hurry, was shot by some men and left for dead—which might have been some form of poetic justice considering what it was that brought me to this point to begin with, but more, I think it simply my string of bad luck continuing. I was on my way to see you, to seek refuge in your house for a time until I can sort things out and thought you wouldn't mind taking in a stray nephew once you heard my story. But now it might be awhile before I can get up your way, since the men who shot me robbed me of everything I owned including my boots. This country is by far the goddamn wildest place I've ever been. I hope you don't mind, but I'm using your name—temporarily at least—to avoid detection by the law and any others who might be looking for me. I expect more trouble yet.

I've fallen far from the young physician I was when you saw me last, very far indeed! But to let you know, I am innocent of all charges. And if you would, please write mother and tell her that whatever she hears about me simply isn't true, and not to worry. It's been a long time since she's heard from you and I'm sure she'd appreciate a letter from you either way. I'd write directly to her myself, but the less people who can trace me to where I am, the better. I'll be up to see you as soon as I can. Yr. nephew, Tristan Shade.

He finished, re-read it, nodded with satisfaction and slipped it in an envelope addressed: *Jake Horn, General Delivery, Winnipeg, Manitoba Territory,* then walked it into the Rosebud where he found the stage driver eating his lunch alone.

"You run mail on that stage?"

The man looked up at him with watery and red-rimmed eyes before nodding.

"I'd like to send this," he said handing him the envelope.

"Cost you a dollar's postage."

Jake handed him one day's pay—pocket money Peg Leg gave him from loose change left on the bar—then went over and helped himself to the buffet.

Jake was there toward the back at his usual place—away from the paying customers, as was his wont—when he saw two men who looked somewhat familiar enter the front doors.

The light was poor inside the Rosebud, the air heavy with cigar smoke. The two men went straight to the bar and ordered drinks. Jake studied them in that poor light. The one wore a battered stovepipe hat, the other a cowhide vest. He remembered that hat and the vest and where he'd seen them last. Then he knew who the two men were.

He left the remainder of his lunch and slipped out the back door.

He saw Toussaint Trueblood squatting on his heels outside the shack.

"Those men who shot you . . ." Toussaint said.

"I know; they're inside having a drink."

"You going to run, or kill them?"

"Yeah, one or the other."

"I don't blame you."

He went inside the shack and took the pistols from under the pillow, checked their loads, slipped a shell into each of the empty chambers under the hammers, came back out, a pistol in each hand.

"I guess you're not going to run," Toussaint said.

"Maybe later, after I finish some business."

Roy Bean had drifted into the Rosebud still feeling unsettled but thirsty for a drink, thoughts crawling through his mind like ants in a sugar bowl stirred up even more by the sight of Bill Blankenship laid out in Tall John's mortuary window draped in crepe. Bill Blankenship looked a lot like the wax figures Roy had seen in Madame Tussauds on a trip once to London—something he still dreamed about on occasion.

The other thing troubling him was that he missed his wife and children. To further compound his miseries, winter would arrive on the high plains in a few months—a season that always caused his lumbago to act up and his feet to ache. The thought of the warm southwest Texas sun was nearly as much a seductress for him as was the pert Birdy Pride. He had a lot to think about and maybe a cocktail or two would help clear his head as to what his next move should be.

He was sitting at a table near the door when he saw Bob Olive and Teacup Smith come in, their clothing so dusty it looked as though they'd dragged in a mile of road with them. They came and went as they pleased, without explanation to the citizenry whose taxes paid their wages. Most generally the lawmen did their drinking in the only other saloon, Skinny Dick's Pleasure Palace.

Bob Olive and Teacup Smith weren't much in the way of law, and in fact were probably just waiting for the day they could rob and kill every last person in Sweet Sorrow and move on to more prosperous climes, Roy Bean thought morosely. They were the type. The problem simply was that this far out on the frontier there wasn't any good law to be had. The only types who would serve the position were men like Bob Olive and Teacup Smith, and when replaced, were most often replaced by those much worse. Low dogs, every one, like the two standing at the bar.

Roy Bean heard them order drinks: whiskey with beer backs. Heard Teacup Smith spouting off about some woman he loved and missed along with a maudlin litany of her virtues—as though any woman of virtue would be caught dead with a skunk like Teacup Smith to begin with.

Bob Olive on the other hand drank in surly silence, hardly ever looking up from his liquor.

Doc Willis wandered in unsteadily, already a bit drunk, and went to the far end of the bar and ordered himself a bottle of Jamaican rum—a specialty of the owner's—sneezed while he was waiting and looked around until his gaze fell on Roy Bean, then looked away as though he hadn't seen him at all.

There were maybe a dozen others at the time Jake Horn walked in the back door and made his way to the bar. Behind him lingering along the back wall was Toussaint Trueblood.

"Hey," Jake said, standing a few feet away from the two at the bar.

At first neither Bob or Teacup acted as though they heard him, but some of the others there did and the silence spread like a fire through dry timber.

"Hey," Jake repeated.

It was Teacup Smith who turned around first.

Teacup didn't recognize the young man as anyone he knew. Having shaved off his growth of beard, Jake was left looking a different man from the one the pair had shot and left for dead. In fact, Teacup Smith had put the whole affair out of his mind right after it happened. He was now thinking about a woman he loved.

"What is it, mister?"

"You," he said to the back of Bob Olive. "Turn around."

Teacup elbowed his companion.

"He wants you to turn around, Bob."

The stout man turned slowly.

"What the hell you want?"

"I want what's mine."

The two lawmen exchanged looks.

"What the hell are you talking about?"

Jake raised the pistols, his resolve to see justice done fused in his brain and blood as one thing. His single-mindedness had gotten him through medical school and turned him into a fine doctor. It had also cost him dearly. These men with their bold presence simply made him mad as hell. He had done nothing to suffer their brutality, had merely been in the wrong place at the wrong time. They chose to set themselves upon him, to treat him worse than some animal they might have shot for sport. Well, now, the thing had turned itself around. He wanted to see how they liked it.

Neither man moved at the sight of pistols aimed at them.

"Bob?" Teacup Smith said questioning.

Bob Olive's eyes narrowed as he tried to make out this interloper, this visceral threat.

"Say it plain what you want!"

"Seems to me you ought to remember a man you shot and robbed and left for dead. But then again, from what I see, I doubt either of you would be troubled by such a thing. You look like you don't have the morals of a dog."

Then the two faces grew slack at both the insult and their understanding of who the threat was and what it represented.

But, Bob Olive was a cool customer and said, "Fuck you" and turned again to his drink sitting on the bar, exposing his back to Jake. Jake shot him in the leg, along the line of the hamstring in the meaty part, just inches above his knee.

Teacup Smith nearly jumped from under his hat, yelled, "Shit!" as Bob Olive toppled to the floor spitting a string of "goddamns" and "sons a bitches."

"What about you?" Jake said to Teacup Smith. "You want to turn your back on me, too?"

Teacup wore a long-barreled Peacemaker on his left hip.

"Mister, I don't have any idea what you're talking about, I swear to God."

Jake thumbed back the hammer of the Schofield.

"I know where to shoot a man that it won't kill him outright. Unlike you simpletons who shoot a man and hope he dies. Trust me, it's going to hurt like hell."

"Please, mister!"

"I want everything you stole from me, and I want extra for my medical expenses and my inconvenience. Give me that and I might let you live."

"Jesus Christ, 'at ain't a problem—except we don't have anything we stole from you—we sold your saddle, them pretty boots . . ."

"Shut up you idjit!" Bob Olive moaned.

"Then we have a problem," Jake said.

"No, we ain't got no problem, we'll pay you for the stuff we took off you. How much you want for 'em?"

"I don't want anything for them. I want what you took."

Teacup shook his head. He was at a loss for an answer.

"Why I'd have to ride back to Rolette and—"

"Dint I tell you to shut the hell up!" Bob Olive ordered, trying his best to stand, a string of oily blood coursing down into his boot.

"Take off your hardware and put it on the bar and step away."

Teacup took the Peacemaker and set it on the bar. Bob Olive followed suit with the gun he wore, only more reluctant in his compliance. Teacup helped him limp away from the bar.

Toussaint Trueblood observed the action with interest. He enjoyed watching white men fight with one another. The fewer of them, the more peaceful the world seemed. Doc Willis also watched the action. Bloodletting was nothing new to him. *Hell, let them kill themselves if they want, just don't come bleeding to him and expect him to patch them up. He was sick of the whole lot of them. Sick to death of every damn thing on these stinking plains.*

Roy Bean said from his table, "You've every legal right to self-defense if these are the men who shot you, Mr. Horn." Roy Bean had purchased a fat book of Blackstone's Law recently and had read several pages, thinking maybe a jurist was his one true calling.

"Nobody would find you guilty of a crime were you to shoot these two toads since it was they who filled you full of lead. But I'd like to believe that we here in Sweet Sorrow are of a more civilized nature and will let justice have its day."

Bob Olive glared at the mouthy man. He hated a mouthy man worse than he hated the pox.

As soon as Roy Bean gave his opinion on the matter, several others muttered agreement, but still others shouted with a certain glee: "Run 'em out of town!"

"Shoot the goddamn murdering bastards!" "Go on, kill 'em both!"

Public sentiment had turned on the lawmen—at least the public sentiment that occupied the Rosebud that day.

"Let's get a rope and hang 'em!"

Roy Bean held up his hand.

"No, boys. They deserve a trial, here and now."

The outcries against legalism, even in its hasty and unskilled form were loud, but Roy Bean being among the most sober of them prevailed with his sudden air of authority.

"We'll try 'em, and we'll find them guilty and set official and legal judgment on their fates. Who'll represent these two?"

Nobody answered.

It was silly of course, Jake thought. He just wanted what was his returned—and maybe a small measure of revenge.

Birdy Pride said, "I'll represent them. What do I have to do?"

Guffaws all around.

"Just say why you think they're innocent of shooting this poor fellow and leaving him for dead, and of robbing a corpse, even though he wasn't one exactly."

"Fine, I'll do it."

The trial was a farce, over in less than ten minutes; Birdy arguing that Teacup Smith had always been a generous patron of hers when he was drunk and always paid in cash for any of the girls who worked in the Rosebud, but that Bob Olive was a low skunk who took advantage of the girls and often abused them and demanded a line of credit, which he never paid.

"What the goddamn hell does that got to do with anything?" Bob yelled, as he tied his leg with his dirty kerchief to stem the bleeding, the bullet having gone completely through the fleshy part of the thigh and into the oak bar's facing.

"It goes to a man's character," Roy Bean said, playing role of both prosecutor and judge. "Any man who would abuse a soiled dove would shoot a man and leave him for dead, and further rob his person—dead or alive."

"Hear! Hear!" cried those in attendance. Peg Leg Watts was very much enjoying the proceedings, including the sudden surge in liquor sales such a spectacle caused.

"And as to his accomplice Mr. Smith being of good and generous nature, it has nothing whatsoever to do with this case, since the defense has attested to Smith's generosity being on display only when he is drunk—which he most likely was not when he shot Mr. Horn."

The defense quickly rested when Roy Bean asked Birdy if she had anything further to say on behalf of the defendants.

"No hon, I sure don't," she replied.

Guffaws again.

"Then I find them guilty as charged and submit

that they be hanged if they've not left town within the half hour."

"You goddamn son of a bitch!" Bob Olive said.

"The court further fines you whatever money is to be found on your persons. And any further remarks and this court will hold you in contempt. Meaning, you no-good scurvy dog, that you'll be tarred and feathered with one more outburst! Search their pockets, boys."

The search produced a little more than eight hundred dollars.

Even Roy Bean was surprised.

"Where'd a couple of saddle tramps like you get this sort of money?"

Neither man said a word.

"Mr. Horn, how much you figure the things these men stole from you were worth?"

"Two hundred ought to cover it."

Roy Bean counted out two hundred dollars and handed it over, looked at Bob Olive and Teacup Smith and said, "Git. And don't let the sunshine that falls on Sweet Sorrow ever fall upon your sorry hides again."

Local men with guns marched them to the door and watched as they mounted their horses and rode off toward the empty grasslands.

"Thanks," Jake said to Roy Bean. "That was quite a show even if it fell slightly short of legal."

Roy Bean winked, said, "Hell, I think I found my calling."

Doc Willis wandered off in total disgust.

Birdy sidled up to Roy Bean and said, "Damn, darling, that was a stirring performance. You want to go back to my crib with me? I'm feeling real rambunctious."

"Me, too," Roy Bean said.

Toussaint Trueblood was outside the Rosebud when Jake came out.

"You know you should have killed those two when you had a chance, don't you?"

"Right."

"You know they'll come back for you?"

"Yeah, I figure they will."

"You don't care?"

"I probably won't be around, to be honest with you, Mr. Trueblood. This wasn't my original destination."

"Yeah, I don't blame you there. This country isn't for just anyone. Some of us who live out here like the openness—some call it emptiness—others, it drives crazy."

Midafternoon that same day, Smiley Rivers walked into the kitchen of the Fat Duck Café with a hatchet and cleaved his wife's head nearly in two, causing her brains to spill and splatter over several pies she'd been preparing. Then he took the same hatchet and chopped off his own hand.

5

❧❧

J AKE WENT TO SEE the merchant to pay his debt.
Then he handed over a list of supplies he'd need to
finish the journey to see his uncle in Manitoba and
bought a new pair of boots, asking that the dress
shoes Doc Willis had given him be wrapped in paper.
After he finished at the mercantile, he stopped by the
livery—a place that advertised: BICYCLES & HORSES
FOR SALE & RENT. WAGON REPAIR.

"I need to buy a horse and saddle," he said to a
man pitching hay into a stall.

The man looked at him.

"You the one they shot, ain't you?"

Jake nodded.

"Got no horses for sale," the man said. "Might
have tomorrow if Karen brings me some."

"Karen?"

"Karen Sunflower—she and her boy Dex own a
place out east of here and they sometimes bring me
wild horses they catch and break. Piute ponies, she

calls 'em. She's due to come round any day I suspect, possibly tomorrow."

"Tomorrow, huh?"

"Might, might not. Depends if she and Dex has caught any since the last ones they brought in. But she's about due, I'd say."

"Well, I'll be around tomorrow. If she brings some in, save me one, will you?"

The man spat, wiped his wet mouth, went back to pitching hay and Jake walked up the street to Dr. Willis's office intending to pay off his debt and return the shoes.

Doc Willis was sprawled in a chair, drunk and muttering to himself, his front door flung wide open, flies buzzing against the window glass.

"Doc?"

He muttered something in the way of an acknowledgment.

"I've come to pay you what I owe you for the care you gave me."

Doc pushed his spectacles back up on his nose and looked at Jake.

"You should have killed those evil bastards," Doc said.

"I'm surprised you'd suggest it," Jake said.

"Why? Anybody deserves it, those two did. They're a bane on this community."

"I thought you were in the life-saving business, that's all."

Doc grunted his derision at such a suggestion.

"I'm just here waiting to die my damn self, like all the others," he snorted. "Because if the world's come down to men like Bob Olive and Teacup Smith and what they represent, who needs it. This world's gone to hell and if I don't get out of here soon, I'll be gone to hell as well. I'm nearly there now."

"Can I ask you something?"

Doc reached for the bottle that sat beside his chair.

"If you feel that way, what are you doing way out here in the first place?"

Doc took a long swallow from the bottle.

The old man shook his head. He looked over at a portrait—a reverse painting of a woman with dark sausage curls and painted blue eyes.

"She's what keeps me here and keeps me from leaving."

Jake did not want to pry into the physician's affairs even though he felt a certain kinship with the man, both of them having taken the same oath, having studied and practiced the same profession.

"Well," Jake said, taking a fold of money and placing it on a small side table, "For your work on patching me up, feeding me turtle soup, and lending me your dress shoes." Then he took the wrapping from the shoes and set them on the floor.

Jake looked down at the shoes, dusty now, and not at all befitting of a town such as Sweet Sorrow, he thought—they were way too fancy.

Doc Willis nodded, started to say something when a boy ran in the front door screaming, "Doc, Doc, you gotta come quick! Mr. Rivers chopped his wife's head off, then his own hand! There's blood every dang where!"

"What the goddamn hell . . ."

Doc tried to stand, stumbled, hit his head on the corner of a table and was out cold. The boy stood looking wide-eyed at the comatose man as Jake knelt to check Willis's pulse. A small gash had opened up just above the temple.

"Is he dead?" the boy asked.

Jake shook his head.

"He's got to come quick. They said Mr. Rivers is bleeding to death!"

Jake stood, looked around, found Doc's medical bag, and ran out again, calling to the boy to lead him to Rivers.

Once inside the café, he saw a small crowd of onlookers had gathered around the two bodies lying on the kitchen floor. A splatter of blood dripped down from a wall, over a counter with pies on it, and a pool of more blood had formed beneath the towel-covered head of a woman. There was a hand lying on the counter, its fingers curled, and a man next to the woman lay drawn up in a fetal position, his face blanched nearly white, but unlike the woman, still breathing.

Jake called for another towel and somebody handed him one. He did his best to cap the bleeding stump, saw that the cut was cleanly done, just above the wrist. A young woman stood calmly watching and he chose her to help him.

"Miss, I need you to hold this compress."

She didn't quarrel or decline but instead knelt and said, "Like this?"

"Yes, exactly."

He searched through the medical bag and found a small bottle of chloroform. The man was muttering something low and soft, his eyes rolled back. Jake asked if anyone had a handkerchief and someone handed him one and this he clamped in a ball over the man's nose and mouth, then spilled several drops of the chloroform onto it until the man's body went slack.

"Killed him," someone said.

"No, just knocked him out."

"I say he's dead."

Jake took a cauterizing iron from the bag, put it inside the stove where a fire still raged, held it there until its tip grew reddish, then cauterized the stump, filling the room with the scent of burning flesh, and even in a state of unconsciousness, the man's arm jerked back.

"You all right, Miss?"

The young woman looked at him. She had startling green eyes.

"Better than him, I'm thinking," she said.

Jake finished his care by sewing a flap of loose skin over the stump, then washing it with soapy water before bandaging it. He asked some men to carry the patient over to Doc Willis's place.

"Why didn't Doc come?"

"He had an accident."

"You a doc or something?"

"No, I just had some training in the Army."

The room fell to a hush once they'd carried Rivers off and Jake pulled back the bloody towel from the woman's face. The hatchet had split her skull open clear to the bridge of the nose. She looked to be about fifty years of age. There was nothing he could do for her. He laid the towel again over her face, saw in his mind the dead face of a man—a neat round hole through the center of his forehead. Jake knew that the last thing the man ever saw was the face of his wife just before she pulled the trigger. And the last thing this woman saw was the face of her husband as he brought the hatchet down. He wondered what that last moment must have been like for either of them— that split second of recognition that something terrible was descending on them by the hand of someone they loved and trusted.

The room cleared when the woman was taken away to Tall John's. The boy who'd come to get Doc in the first place began mopping up the blood-splattered kitchen. Zimmerman, the Fat Duck's proprietor, looked ashen.

"Mein business is ruined," he said in a slight German accent. "What is this ven you can just come and kill your wife, eh?"

The girl who helped Jake tend to the assailant said, "Would you like some coffee?"

Jake nodded.

"Only in the dining room, okay."

Zimmerman went and put a CLOSED sign in the

window and locked the door, muttering to himself how he should have stayed in Switzerland where such evils did not occur.

"Dis place!" he said repeatedly holding his head in his hands.

"I'm Fannie," the girl said.

"Jake Horn," Jake said.

"You probably saved that poor man's life."

"I'm not sure the folks around here will thank me once everyone hears what he did to that woman."

"His wife . . ." Fannie said. "She was his wife."

"You any idea why he would do such a thing?"

Fannie shrugged.

"There seems to be a craziness going around. First it was the blacksmith's wife, then Mr. Blankenship drowning himself, and now this. Some folks are saying it's the ungodly heat doing it. Some say it's because it ain't rained in forever. Some, like Preacher Poke, say Sweet Sorrow is another Sodom and Gomorrah and that the evilness here displeases God. Course Preacher Poke can be awful right-minded about some things."

"What do you think it is?" Jake asked.

She looked at him carefully.

"You mocking me, mister?"

He shook his head.

"No, Fannie. I just like to know what you think."

She was pretty in a rough, frontier sort of way, her dark auburn hair bundled atop her head and affixed with Spanish combs in a way that enhanced her somewhat broad face. She was tall, almost as tall as himself; a good strong woman, the sort of woman that could survive even the worst frontier.

"I don't know what it is," she said. "I only been here since the spring."

"Where'd you come from?"

A look of wistfulness came over her face.

"Indianapolis," she said. "I come out with Joe Boots."

"Your husband?"

"Lord, no. Just a footloose fool who convinced me into running off with him—someone he could take pleasure in on a long journey. I wouldn't have married Joe Boots for a thousand dollars."

"Why'd you come West with him, then?"

She looked at him as though he'd just asked her if she had wings to fly with.

"The adventure, of course."

He found himself smiling at that. She was an unusual soul—guileless, and he liked that about her.

"Well," he said. "It's a pleasure to meet you, Fannie, even if the circumstances aren't the best."

"It's a pleasure to meet you, too, Mr. Horn."

"Jake," he said.

"Jake," she said.

He walked over to the Rosebud and told Peg Leg he was quitting.

"Too damn bad, son. You was a good swamper. Let me buy you a drink."

Peg Leg filled them each a glass of rum.

"Heard you patched up Smiley Rivers, kept him

from bleeding out. Chopped off his own damn hand they say after he poleaxed his missus?"

Jake nodded.

"Got to be the heat. It's the only thing I know would make a man go that crazy."

"Well, I guess it keeps the undertaker busy."

"That's true."

The two men shook hands.

Jake went into the shack to pack his things, only there weren't any things to pack. The healing wounds no longer hurt enough to hardly remember he'd been shot. He thought about the men who shot him, his anger toward them gone now for some reason. What was done was done, end of story.

He decided to pay a last visit to Toussaint Trueblood and walked out to his lodge that sat alone like a hump on the back of the earth itself. He called in through the blanket that sufficed for a door.

"Hello."

Toussaint drew back the blanket.

"I thought you left."

"Just getting around to it. Waiting on the man at the livery to get a horse to sell me, might have one tomorrow."

Toussaint looked at the bloodstained cuffs of Jake's shirt.

"It's following you, ain't it?"

Jake nodded.

"I guess maybe it is."

"Some men are marked," Toussaint said.

"Perhaps so."

Jake took out twenty dollars and held it forth.

"What's this for?"

"Saving my life."

Toussaint took the money, like seed, he thought, money grew more money.

"I wish it were all that easy," he said. "Just going around the grassland picking up near dead men and getting paid for it. Around a place like this I might earn enough to buy a big house."

"Well, thanks again for what you did."

Toussaint looked at the money in his hand. It was about the most money he'd seen at one time in a year or two—ever since he'd gone to Bismarck and sold a human skull he'd found at the base of an embankment washed away by winter snows. He figured the skull belonged to some long-forgotten traveler, perhaps an Indian, maybe even an ancestor, though he didn't like to think he'd sell his ancestor's skull for ten dollars and lie about it, saying it was the mortal remains of Dick Turpin. He'd sold so many counterfeit bones of that ill-mannered gunfighter that if they had been authentic, the famed outlaw would have had to have been scattered all over the country two or three times. At last count, he'd also sold at least thirty-two Billy the Kid trigger fingers. The skull could have been anyone's. Toussaint chose to believe that it belonged to some no-account white man on his way to Alaska in search of gold.

"Getting out while the getting's good?"

"Something like that."

"I don't blame you. Here." Toussaint tossed Jake a rabbit's foot—long and boney under gray fur with the sharp nails still attached.

"What's this for?"

"Rabbit's feet are supposed to bring you good luck."

Jake examined the thing momentarily, then stuck it in his pocket.

Toussaint watched him head off toward town.

Whoever that man was, he told himself, he attracted trouble like a tree attracted lightning. Toussaint looked up at the cloudless sky thinking it had been a long time since it had rained, and therefore storm and lightning had been thrown down from the sky. It was abnormal for it to go so long and be as dry and hot as it had been. It was too hot to even hunt dreaming rabbits and that was never a good thing.

Toussaint went inside his lodge and stretched out on his cot, using the twenty dollars for a pillow and closed his eyes. That's when he saw Jesus again.

6

HEAT LIGHTNING SHOOK through the distant night sky in such glorious detail that it brought the citizens of Sweet Sorrow out of their homes and places of business to watch it. There against the purple sky the lightning ran horizontally—like flashes of gunfire in a room full of smoke.

"It's going to rain!" someone shouted hopefully.

"No, I seen this before—where it's raining we don't live," said a wag.

Emeritus Fly, the editor of the one-page newspaper, the *Grassland Democrat,* stood with his tongue hanging out hoping to catch the taste of rain, but all he tasted was a dry wind. Such a taste was remindful of the Arizona desert where he'd been a private and part of the great camel experiment of the United States Army. He'd fallen from the back of one of those strange creatures and broken a hip. It was such a terrible experience, that he vowed never again to ride a horse or anything that had four legs.

Even with the sun gone down, it was still uncomfortably hot.

Whores barely dressed and men went about with their shirtsleeves and pants legs rolled up. The more decent women cooled their skin with damp cloths they dipped into buckets of water carried from the springhouse, trickling the cold water between their breasts. Some young couples snuck off onto the grasslands and camped along Cooper's Creek and boldly stripped naked to splash and sit in the creek.

Horses nickered thirstily, and coyotes howled their displeasure. Snakes crawled slow in the night.

Jake Horn was taking his supper in the Rosebud, this time as a paying customer, but still seated off by himself. He half expected a United States deputy marshal to show up with a wanted poster looking for him, or a private detective hired by the family of Taylor Shaw, the man he was accused of killing. Only he and one other knew the truth. His innocence seemed simple enough, if he could only prove it—but he'd committed the fatal sin of *coveting thy neighbor's wife*. And it was she who accused him, she who'd set the trap, and she who'd pulled the trigger on her husband.

He recalled with a certain bitter irony the oath he'd taken upon completing his medical studies, which read in part—*Whatever houses I may visit, I will come for the benefit of the sick, remaining free of all intentional injustice, of all mischief, and, in particular, of sexual relations*—the Hippocratic oath.

She had come to him as a patient and the relationship had quickly turned intimate. She had that certain irresistible quality that could charm even the most resolute man, and he'd fallen in love with her in spite of his resolve, his reason blinded by his heart.

He could see her now, sitting on the edge of the bed rolling up her stockings that fateful day.

He'd decided it had to end and told her as much.

"Why does it have to end, Tristan?" she said.

"Because it's wrong in every regard. You were my patient, and you're married. And as much as I may regret losing your love, I just can't continue in a game I can't win." But the trap had already been set and she was moments away from springing it.

He'd learned in his medical studies something about the black widow spider and how the female of the species decapitated and ate the male after mating. But more important, he'd learned that it was the male who often enticed the female to kill him. Perhaps subconsciously in some strange way, he himself had tempted her to kill him, his reputation, and his life, in order to pay the price for his sin of loving another man's wife. He'd like to think he was smarter than that, but was he? For if he was, what was he doing sitting in a frontier saloon that very moment worrying about someone coming to arrest him?

Some of the Rosebud's patrons drifted back inside after having grown tired of watching a storm that was never going to bring them rain or relief. Their movements were listless; the heat was as much in their blood and brains as it was in the air.

Roy Bean had been outside with Birdy Pride watching the light show.

"It reminds me of dreams I've had," Birdy said.

"It reminds me of Texas," Roy Bean said.

"And your wife, too, I suppose?"

"Oh, let's not mention such unpleasant things," he said.

"Fine," she said.

Roy knew her to be prickly from the unrelenting heat—or at least that is what he attributed her prickliness to.

"I can't wait forever for you to marry me, Mr. Roy Bean."

"What's got into you, child? We've discussed this a hundred times already."

"You should know that there's others who would want me if you don't."

"Like who?"

"None of your business."

"Of course it is."

Silence.

"You want to go upstairs?"

"Too hot," she said.

"How about riding out to Cooper's Creek—we could shuck out of our clothes and swim natural as fishes and cool right down. And later we could sleep in the grass."

It was a tempting offer, Birdy said, but this time she had made up her mind that unless Roy Bean offered to marry her, she was through providing him the favors of her body.

"I got other plans."

"Like what?"

"You'll see."

He tried to stop her, but she went off in the dark by herself. His thirst was too great to follow her and he went inside the Rosebud to get an iced beer, the only salvation he could think of against such heat. He spotted Jake and brought his iced beer with him over to Jake's table.

"You want some company?"

Jake shrugged.

Roy Bean sat down, mopping the sweat from his face with a big red-checkered handkerchief nearly the size of a tablecloth.

Preacher Elias Poke was on his knees inside the small clapboard church praying mightily. But unlike some, he wasn't praying for rain, but relief of another sort.

"Sin's on me, Lord. It's on me like a chicken on a june bug. I swear that it is."

Elias Poke was a Tennessean by birth, born in Claiborne County near the hamlet of Tazewell. He had married a Kentucky girl from just over the line, a Daisy Flynn, who was short and skinny and had the fierce temperament of a rooster. Back then, he'd been a scratch dirt farmer trying to raise corn, sorghum, hogs, and making a little distilled whiskey when he could, selling it to the local men and drinking much of it himself out of glass jars and telling stories about women who left their backdoors open when their husbands went off to work in the fields or over to the nearby sawmill. Elias Poke was himself a backdoor man and had three or four such women to visit at any given time, which kept him plenty busy and plenty tired at night when his own Daisy would try and get him to rustle the shucks of their mattress. It all got to be too much at some point, the trying to be a farmer, a whiskey maker, a drinker, husband, and all the rest of it, Daisy's harping included. But what really did the trick and caused him to leave everything behind and head to the remote northern plains was a man named Ray Delgood whose wife Elias had been seeing via the backdoor.

Ray Delgood put a pistol under his chin one Sabbath morning and said, "I ever catch you sneaking in my backdoor again, I'll paint these walls with your brains. We clear?"

Immediately thereafter, Elias left a note for Daisy saying, *"Dere wife, cercumstance and misfortun forces me to leve you. I'm sur you will find another man quik enuf. Elias."*

And in his journey he met a preacher man baptizing folks in the Mississippi River just outside of St. Louis and felt the spirit move him to get in line. Something in the taste of that muddy Missouri water convinced him that God was calling him to preach the Word. So he bought a used bible and shucked off human desire like a ragged coat and ended up in Sweet Sorrow—a place that had no church and no preacher and it seemed about right—as though God himself had directed Elias's feet to stop there and take a stand. Which he did, and resolutely, raising funds and volunteers to build the little church where he preached about all manner of sin—sexual sin most especially—something he considered himself an expert on—both as its victim and its conqueror.

That was until he spied Birdy Pride one day out by Cooper's Creek where he'd gone to read Leviticus in quietude and she'd gone to bathe. Desire swept through him like a fire through dry grass, and he could not turn his eyes away from her lovely bare skin, dewy wet with the water of Cooper's Creek as she washed, turned this way and that so that he eventually saw every particular of her beauty and knew that he was in love and lust with her.

And thus it had been ever since and it was to this aim he now prayed, the hard floorboards pressing roughly against his bony knees while through the window he saw the lightning flash in the long distance of night. But the true storm felt as if it was inside him and not without. And as though by miracle, or by the devil's hand, Birdy appeared. She entered the little lonesome church with nothing more than a few candles to light the way and approached him, lissome in a thin dress that hardly hid any of her ample assets. He could not force his gaze away.

"Preacher, I've come to ask you something," she said.

Bob Olive said, "This goddamn leg aches worse than any bad tooth I ever had."

Teacup Smith passed him the bottle of liquor—the second one they'd worked on since getting run out of

Sweet Sorrow by Roy Bean and the liquored-up crowd in the Rosebud.

"We just gonna let them sorry asses run us off like we was dogs or something?" Teacup said. He'd been grousing the whole time, talking about how he was going to kill somebody soon as he got the chance, how he was going to "shoot 'em" and "cut their throats" and "drag 'em by a rope." All his grousing was an irritant to Bob Olive who was mighty irritable as it was, considering he had a bullet hole through the meaty part of his leg that left him feeling that he had a toothache down there.

They'd ridden until night drew over them like some invisible hand pulling down a shade and only then saw the lights of a small settlement they knew as Anna's Bloomers.

"I'm about ready to tear something up, ain't you, Bob?"

Bob didn't say anything, choosing instead to dwell in his own misery, a cocoon of pain and anger.

Anna's Bloomers was little more than a few shacks and one whiskey house of chinked logs owned by a pimp named Sally St. John.

"This is where they got that three-hunnert-pound whore, ain't it?" Teacup said.

"I don't give a shit about no whores. Shut up!"

They rode in, dismounted in front of the whiskey house, Teacup leading the way, Bob Olive limping in behind him.

They ordered food—beef stew and whiskey. The pimp Sally St. John remembered them.

"You two is the law over in Sweet Sorrow, ain't you?"

Bob said, "Keep the whiskey coming and leave me alone."

Teacup showed his teeth and said, "You still got that big fat whore?"

"Lady France? Yes, she still works for me. You want a go-round with her?"

"I might."

"She'll be free in a few minutes, she's out back giving some relief to a pumpkin farmer."

The pimp had boils along his neck and his face was pitted, eyes like a rat, Bob Olive thought. He hated a man who had eyes like a rat. He was in an especially hateful mood ever since earlier that day when that son of a bitch had shot him. What sort of man would shoot another when his back was turned but a low-life yellow-dog prick. Bob Olive's anger grew to the boiling point. And when the fat whore came waddling out from the back where she did her business, Bob Olive drew his pistol and shot her. When she fell, the room shook.

The pimp, Sally St. John, raised up from behind the bar with a sawed-off shotgun aiming to defend his business investment and Bob Olive shot him, too, and when he fell the shotgun clattered to the floor and set the triggers off—the loads tearing away most of the pimp's face.

The few customers in the place at the time—including the pumpkin farmer who'd been trailing Lady France into the room—ran for the door. Teacup

Smith had been startled by the sudden violence and fell off his chair. Bob Olive looked at him hard, his pistol leaking smoke.

Teacup held up his hands.

"Don't shoot me, Bob. Goddamn, please don't shoot me."

Then Bob lowered the pistol and went back to eating his stew.

"I feel some better now."

Teacup had wet his drawers.

"We got no law now," Roy Bean was saying to Jake Horn as they sat at a table in the Rosebud.

"Seems to me none is better than what you had."

"I would agree with you, but now it's every man for himself, which means the women and kids around here are going to be helpless."

"Why are you telling me this?"

"I was just thinking."

"About what?"

When Preacher Poke asked Birdy Pride what it was she'd come to ask him, she lowered her dress and said, "Do you find me desirable, Preacher?"

The question caused him to tremble.

"Please," he said. "Please go and don't tempt me so, child."

She stepped closer to him. The candlelight played on her skin like dancing golden fairies. She suddenly looked to him like the Madonna without clothes.

He tried to take his eyes from her—*If thine eye offend thee, pluck it out!*

"I seen you the other day—out at the creek. You was watching me."

She reached down and touched his face; his knees no longer felt the press of the rough boards; he felt as though he were about to ascend with the angels to a more heavenly place. Or, straight into hell.

"You find me beautiful, Preacher? I just need to know that even the good men around here find me desirable, and not just galoots, whoremongers, and drunks," she said. Her words were like those spoken underwater. He drew her hand to his mouth and kissed its palm.

"Oh, sweet child," he said. "Oh, sweet, sweet child."

Toussaint sat up and reached forth a hand, but the apparition was like a soft white smoke that he was unable to touch. When Toussaint tried, the smoke dissipated and re-formed on the other side of the room.

"Am I dead?"

"Not yet," the smoke said.

"What you want with me?"

"There are bad things going on here, I thought you should know."

"I know it."

"Evil things."

"I think I'm dreaming. I don't think you're real. I think I'm like those rabbits I knock in the head and eat and sell their bones—those dreaming rabbits."

"Maybe so."

Then the smoke was gone, the air inside the lodge blue-black with only the faintest trace of light from the stars and what little moon there was.

Toussaint looked around and didn't see anything. He went outside and all he saw was heat lightning way off in the distance. He remembered a man who'd been struck by lightning once—an old trapper hunting beaver along the Red River even though the beaver had all been hunted out sixty years earlier and all the old trapper caught in his traps were muskrats. Toussaint had come across him one day when he'd gone to the river to fish, which is something he often did instead of attending school because everything they tried to teach him in school he learned too quickly and easily and didn't see much point in continuing to waste his time every day.

It was a stormy day that particular day when he came across the old trapper who was sitting on a rock smoking a clay pipe and watching the river where he'd set some traps down among the cattails.

"Boy!" he called when he spotted Toussaint. "Come on over here."

"No sir."

The old man cackled menacingly, then a white-hot flash exploded and the old trapper lay sprawled out with smoke coming out of the soles of his moccasins, his head charred, his beard smoldering, and a black hole in his chest.

It was the strangest thing Toussaint had ever seen

until just a few minutes before when he saw what he was sure was Jesus in his lodge.

He went back inside and ate some cold rabbit he'd caught and cooked earlier, then went to sleep hoping he wouldn't have any more dreams or visions or visitors or thoughts about lightning-struck old trappers.

After Bob Olive finished eating his third bowl of stew he wiped his face with the frayed cuff of his shirtsleeve and said, "We'll lay around here until my leg heals up."

"Then what?" Teacup said.

"Then we're going to go back and kill that son of a bitch who shot me, and we're going to kill that goddamn Roy Bean and maybe a few others as long as we're at it. Hell, we might just kill the whole goddamn lot of 'em and start over."

Teacup Smith had earlier gone behind the bar and found a bottle of plum wine and had been working on it steadily to the point he was nearly cross-eyed drunk.

"Hell, I'm with you, Bob, you know that, don't you?"

Bob was drinking a bottle of green liqueur that had written on its label *The Green Fairy*—an absinth—and it made his insides feel warm and liquid and his brain believe he was capable of anything, any act, even mass murder.

"I feel like the Devil hisself! Powerful!" Bob declared.

"You know what I think?" Teacup said.

"What?"

"We ought to have us a turn with that whore."

Bob blinked, then said, "Why I shot her dead—she ain't moved so much as an eyelash."

"You did, Bob. You killed her." Teacup grinned that busted-fence grin. "I think it'd be interesting though, don't you, to try it just once?"

"You better run, you crazy bastard, before I shoot you."

Teacup Smith was halfway out the door when he heard Bob's gun fire again and felt the wood splinter of the jamb nick his face.

"You might make a damn fine lawman, son," Roy Bean was saying.

Jake wasn't sure he heard him right; the snakehead whiskey was buzzing in his brain. He thought Roy Bean had suggested that he become a lawman for the town.

"What did you say?"

Roy Bean grinned. He had a plan.

7

"WHAT I WAS THINKING," Roy Bean said, "was that maybe since you was the one mainly responsible for dispatching those two hellion law dogs, that you might consider the position for yourself. It'd have to beat all hell out of swamping saloons."

"I appreciate the sentiment," Jake said. "But I'm no gunfighter."

"Don't have to be, the way I see it. What we need is men with level heads, not pistoleros."

"But there will come a time when you will want the latter more than the former."

Roy Bean scratched his jaw. He was due a shave, something that generally Birdy Pride did for him, along with picking nits out of his hair. A shave and his toenails trimmed would make him feel like a new man. Where had that gal gone off to, anyway?

"A place like this practically begs for men like us," Roy said. "Decent, honest men with a true sense of justice. You got it in you, son, just like I got it in me; I can tell by the way we handled Bob and Teacup. Why we'd make something of this ramshackle little hog wallow was we to set our minds to it—me the magistrate, you the man doing the law enforcing."

Jake waved his hand.

"Come morning, Mr. Bean. I'm heading north. Thanks for the offer, but you'll have to find a more likely candidate to help you."

Roy Bean sagged in his chair. He'd hoped to convince Jake to help him run the town. He wasn't even sure why he himself was interested in such a far-flung settlement, except a man had to light somewhere sooner or later, and there were worse places a man could light than Sweet Sorrow—Roy Bean knew, he'd been to most of them.

Then, too, there was his growing affection for Birdy Pride. He sure didn't want to leave her to the rough hands of others if he didn't have to. His missed his wife and kids—some days worse than others—but Birdy made his blood weak and wanting in a way his wife never did whenever he was with her. Thinking about his dilemma, he felt like a horned toad caught between a rock and a wagon wheel.

"At least think about it, would you?" he said.

"No," Jake said. "I've got people expecting me."

Roy Bean sighed, reached into his coat pocket and took out a piece of paper folded into squares. He unfolded it and placed it on the table, turned it around with a forefinger so Jake could see what it was.

"Is this what you're worried about?"

Jake looked at the wanted poster. The sketched

likeness of him was a good one, copied from a daguerreotype of him right after he'd finished medical school. She must have stolen it at some point and given it to the federal marshal's office in Denver.

"If I said it wasn't me . . ."

Roy Bean quickly refolded the poster and put it back inside his coat.

"It came in with the mail today on the stage. I just happened to be out front and Fuzzy handed me the mailbag. I have a curious nature and besides I've been waiting for a letter to arrive from my missus when I came across this. I figured it was best that Bob Olive and Teacup didn't see it, nor anyone else."

"Why would you care to protect me?"

"I have a feeling about you, son, like I said, just like I have a feeling about them. I was right, too. If you hadn't shot Bob, he'd have tracked you down and killed you for the reward money. And this time I think he would have used store-bought loads just to make sure you was dead and stayed that way."

"Between us," Jake said, pausing for a moment, "I'm not guilty of what that paper says I am."

"You don't have to convince me. Far as I'm concerned this paper don't even exist. And as far as the law coming around—I mean the real law—I doubt it very much. The last time there was anything close to the real law it was a deputy U.S. marshal who came up this way more than a year ago, a fellow named Briggs looking for a colored who was said to have raped and murdered several white women down around Bismarck. Something that bad is the only rea-

son the federal boys would come to this far and away
outpost."

"I probably better grow back my beard, eh."

"Might not hurt."

"Nice talking to you, Mr. Bean. But I'm bound to
get some rest. I've got to get down to the stables early
in the morning and see if that livery man is going to
get that string of Piute ponies in he talked about coming."

"I wish you'd at least sleep on the notion."

"Of being a lawman?"

Roy Bean nodded solemnly.

"I think you better just start looking for another
man for the office."

"I can't think of a single one in all this town who
would qualify for the job."

"What about Toussaint?"

Roy Bean shook his head.

"Toussaint is a free bird, flies his own direction. I
sometimes get the feeling he wouldn't mind seeing all
us put under so he could have the place to himself."

Jake nodded, then turned and left.

Roy Bean watched forlornly as Jake walked out the
double doors of the Rosebud. He decided to try and
find Birdy; he could use some cheering up. Without a
lawman there was no point in trying to appoint himself as a judge. It seemed now like another idea that
turned out to be about as sound as a leaky bucket.

Doc Willis kept thinking about her—the woman
painted on the glass in the gilt frame upon his wall—

his Iris. He seemed ill fated when it came to women.
His first wife died of influenza after nearly twenty-
five years of marriage. Always healthy as a horse, and
then one bad winter something took her neither of
them could see and he buried her up in the cemetery
where he never went but that one and only time
because he couldn't stand the thought of her lying six
feet below the dirt in a wood box. And for a time he
stayed drunk almost constantly and only became
sober when there was a baby needed delivering, or a
wound needed stitched with a steady hand. Sometimes the patient had to wait until he sobered up. And
on occasion, the patient died waiting—like Bug Johnson when he got pitched out of his hay wagon and it
ran over him splitting his skull like a ripe melon.
Chances were that even sober, Doc told himself, he
couldn't have done a thing to save Bug; a crushed
head was a hard thing to fix. But, privately, he knew
he could have hastened Bug's death, and therefore his
misery, sooner than the twelve hours it took him to
pass on.

Woodrow Willis stayed in a state of near constant
inebriation until he met Iris—the daughter of old Forrest Hill, the local banker and richest man in
McHenry County as far as anybody knew. It was the
old man himself who pushed the courtship, knowing
that Doc Willis was a man of some breeding and education, and that he owned a large house—one nearly
as large as his own. The houses of the two men com-
peted for largest and most magnificent in the community, with Doc living at one end of town and Forrest

Hill living at the other. Between them, it was rumored, they had as much money as all the other citizens in the entire county combined. But in truth, Doc Willis had drunk most of his fortune away, and it mattered not to him until he met Iris.

She was comely with dark chestnut hair and china blue eyes. And she had lovely ways about her, having been sent off to a finishing school in Bismarck where she'd been taught manners, Latin, mathematics, and, unbeknownst to her papa, ways to please a lover (thanks in part to her more learned classmate sisters, who initiated her into sexual exploration, followed by a more complete education from the headmaster who took—as he put it—her "modesty and virtue with one swift prick of his lance"). But Forrest Hill was a cautious old duck who saw his daughter not so much as his offspring as he did an investment. He further saw the danger of letting a young woman become too educated and worldly, and so brought Iris home after only a year at the finishing school in order to get her married to Doc Willis—a man he'd had his eye on for some time since no other qualified candidate had landed in Sweet Sorrow. Iris at twenty wasn't getting any younger, and she was a bit of a flighty child and could stand the hand of an older man to guide her through the pitfalls of life that awaited a young woman of flighty tendencies. It would be quite a coup in the old man's eyes to have her marry a physician, even one that was much her senior and inebriated a good deal of the time.

"But, Papa, he's old," Iris complained when the father proposed the idea.

"He's still a vital man and can teach you much, dear child, as well as secure your financial future. The babies he gives you won't be old. I won't be around forever to watch over you. I won't have my fortune squandered by a silly girl who will fall in love with some wastrel."

But Iris cared little about her future, it was her most recent past that plagued her, for she'd already fallen deeply in love with the headmaster—one Umberto Vincenti, whose slate gray eyes she could still see gazing down on her from his dominant position there in his quiet office just off the school's library, with its must of leather and wood competing with Umberto's manly scent of sweat and shaving soap. He would often quote to her passages from Dante's *The Divine Comedy,* most specifically the story of Paolo and Francesca and their fatal passion. It would always make her weak and willing to give herself to him to hear of such unbridled desire, and he taught her much in the ways of amore.

She'd continued to write Umberto letters upon her return to Sweet Sorrow, and he in return wrote to her stanzas of poetry that wooed her as nothing else could. But the headmaster was as poor as a church mouse and not considered by her father a candidate for husband, having said of him once: "Aside from the fact they are as immoral as weasels, you can never trust those people not to steal you blind, for one thing, Iris." Those people meaning Italian school-teachers.

And after much pressure, she was convinced to

marry Doc Willis, who had fallen almost instantly in love with her upon their first introduction and wooed her as he never thought he would woo a woman again. The elder Hill paid for the newlyweds to honeymoon in San Francisco. And over the intervening months, Iris had become as warm summer rain and bright sunshine to Woodrow Willis's wilted flower. He regained much of what he had lost in his vigor and vitality and became again like the man he had been when young. He even quit drinking in order to become more robust for his young bride.

And while Doc Willis flourished, Iris privately withered. Except for the secret correspondence she maintained with Umberto, she constantly contemplated filling her coat pockets with horseshoes and throwing herself into the deepest section of Cooper's Creek. It was Umberto's florid promises to someday come and steal her away that kept her from drowning herself. And he proved as good as his word.

Her only presence in Doc Willis's life now was the reverse-painting portrait of her hanging on the wall above the mantle, a thing that haunted him as much as any ghost.

That foreign son of a bitch had come and stolen her away after her father died and the act of betrayal had ruined him again, crushed his spirit, rent his heart. He finished off the bottle of bourbon he'd been working on and flung it at the beatific smile of his Iris as she stared down at him from the oval glass. The bottle missed shattering her lovely glass face into a thousand pieces. In fact, the bottle did not even break.

Symbolic, he thought, of his impotence. He closed his eyes and fell into a nightmare.

And as Doc Willis was falling into his nightmare, Toussaint Trueblood was coming out of his—or what he took to be a nightmare, for it wasn't really possible for Jesus to find him in his lodge out there on those grasslands. Was it?

The pre-dawn sky was the color of an old buffalo robe and the only sound he could hear was the wind whispering in the grass, a sort of rustling sound like someone walking through it. Hair stood up on the back of his neck and he reached for his knife even as he held his breath, expecting any moment to see a shadow come through the door of his lodge. He waited and waited. But no one appeared.

This place is making you crazy like it has others, he told himself, setting a fire in his little cast-iron stove to brew some coffee. He reached for the can of chicory and scooped some into the coffeepot and went outside and took a dipper and reached into the water barrel, tasting the water before filling the pot to make sure it wasn't fetid. It sort of was, because it hadn't rained in so long that what little water had remained in the barrel had grown mossy and had sticks and dead grasshoppers floating in it. He decided to hell with making coffee with bad water and walked into town instead and took a seat at a table inside the Fat Duck Café. It was an hour yet till daylight and he was the only patron.

Old James, the morning cook, was sitting alone

drinking a cup of coffee when Toussaint came in and took a seat at the table by the window. Old James limped over carrying the coffeepot and a cup, set the cup down and filled it from the pot.

"You want something to eat, too?"

"No, I don't want nothing to eat."

"Just the coffee, then?"

"I guess if I'm not going to eat, then it is just the coffee."

"Fine with me. Means I won't have to cook you nothing."

Toussaint put a dime on the table and Old James picked it up and put it in his pocket and went back to his place at the counter. Old James had once been a sergeant in the army and had fought Indians on the plains of Texas and elsewhere and been shot several times and still had a small arrowhead in his right hip where a Comanche had shot him in a fight at Palo Duro Canyon. Sometimes Old James was sure that the arrowhead moved around inside him, believed the Comanche had put a curse on it before shooting him with it, and that the arrowhead was trying to find a way to reach his heart and kill him—which Old James heard sometimes happened with cursed arrows.

Toussaint watched the dark morning and it felt like the most lonesome thing a man could do, for the sidewalks were empty, the storefronts without light in the windows, and nothing moved but the wind that whistled along the eaves giving only the faintest indication that anything was alive.

Old James coughed and Toussaint turned his attention to watch him as he sat hunched over his coffee studying a little leather-bound book open in front of him on the counter.

"What are you reading?" Toussaint called.

"My journal."

"What you have in that journal of yours?"

"I put things in it that's happened to me I can remember."

"What sort of things?"

"Things I done; things folks has done to me and things I done to them."

"You put in there about those Indians you killed in Texas?"

"Yes, I put it in here."

Old James tapped a finger on a page. "Right here is where I put some of it."

Toussaint looked back out toward the darkness and wished the morning would get there soon because he was weary of so much night that felt as if it had gotten into him, into his blood, like the arrowhead Old James said was in his ass trying to work its way up to his heart in order to kill him. Toussaint felt that was some of what the nighttime was like—if it got in your blood it would find a way to kill you eventually.

Old James would often say, "I've got to be careful about how I live my life from now on so when that arrowhead finds me and kills me and I go to meet my maker I won't end up roasting in hell for things I done since I knew enough not to do 'em no more."

Toussaint saw a little light come on in the window of the church there at the far end of the street down across from the café. It intrigued him. Then he saw a shape coming out of the front door of the church and watched it disappear into the shadows. This also intrigued him.

"I'll have a refill on this coffee," he said to Old James who dutifully and without question left his place at the counter and limped over and refilled Toussaint's cup.

"You hungry now? You want something to eat?"

"No."

"Just the coffee, then?"

"I guess if I'm still not hungry, it's just the coffee."

"Fine with me," Old James said and limped back to his stool at the counter and sat down on it and began writing something in his journal.

"What you writing in that book now?" Toussaint asked.

"Some things about me, what I've done to folks and what they've done to me."

Toussaint thought about this as he sipped his coffee, then said, "What the hell could anybody have done to you or you to them in the last five minutes? It's just us here and I ain't done nothing to you and you ain't done nothing to me."

Without looking up, Old James said, "I just remembered something that happened to me back some time ago I forgot to put in until just now—something somebody did. I don't always remember some things until later."

"Oh," Toussaint said and went back to watching the empty dark street.

They had awakened naked on the altar with little more than the night's light to hide them—which was enough to obscure Preacher Poke's vision of the lovely and nubile Birdy Pride, and her vision of him, though he remembered quite well what she'd looked like before he had put out the lamp, and remembered equally well what his hands had told his brain as they coursed over her bare skin. He lost all sense of time and place after their first kiss and she'd left him exhausted in her ardor. They'd fallen asleep on a donated Persian carpet that had been set on the altar to give some semblance of holiness to the otherwise plain and practical interior; its rough nap proved less uncomfortable than bare floorboards for the lovers as they rolled around in fits and starts of unbridled passion. And thus they also slept, awakening only in that last hour before dawn.

Elias Poke awakened with a start, his heart quivering like a chicken liver in a pan of hot grease. What if he had not awakened in time and someone had walked in and found the two of them naked, entwined in each other's arms? He quickly awakened Birdy and had her get dressed as he stumbled into his pants, shirt, socks, and shoes.

"You must leave before it gets light," he whispered.

"You ain't disappointed are you?"

"Only in my own behavior," he said.

"Fornicating is as natural as eating," Birdy said.

"Maybe so, but I never knew a preacher to get run out of town on a rail for eating," Poke said.

"I'd run with you if they was to run you out," Birdy said.

"I thought you were Roy Bean's sweetheart."

"I wish you wouldn't mention that name in my presence."

"I'm sorry," he said.

"I am, too," she said. "Me and Roy is quits. He had his chance and didn't take it. I'm not a woman who can wait forever." Elias wondered what it was Birdy was unwilling to wait forever for.

And once Birdy slipped away into the shadows, he knelt before the altar and prayed for forgiveness.

"I know I did the worse kind of sinning, Lord, right here in your house. I am weak and no good and I wish you'd just take me, send a bolt of lightning or something and take me now—for I am deserving of being *took*!"

He waited for his heart to stop, for his head to empty of all thoughts, for the end of everything he knew. He waited for a quick and terrible death, but none ever came, and half an hour more passed and he was still kneeling and waiting. Only his knees began to ache and so did his back, for Birdy had been a rambunctious lover and had turned and twisted him this way and that during the course of their passion. And he was thirsty and hungry as well.

"I guess you will come like a thief in the night for me when you're ready, Lord," he said in a final flourish to his prayer, "take me when I least am expecting it—which is only fair, seeing as to what I've done here in your house." He waited a few more minutes, then stood awkwardly and painfully, for he was no longer the young man he had once been, and went out and down the street to the Fat Duck Café where he found Toussaint Trueblood drinking a cup of coffee at a window table and Old James writing something in a small book.

Toussaint wanted to ask him who it was that had come out of the church first and slunk off into the shadows, but instead he chewed on the mystery as though it were a piece of good roasted rabbit—enjoying the secret only he and the preacher knew about. And maybe Jesus, if Jesus was still around watching things.

8

SEEMED AS THOUGH there ought to be rain for a
funeral, but it was bright and sunny and hot as hell
if hell was a place where there wasn't a cloud in the
sky and the wind was so dry you couldn't spit. Such
was the day they buried the unnamed infant child of
Junius Figg, and Kathleen Rivers, murdered victim of
her husband, Smiley, and so, too, Bill Blankenship.

Tall John and his assistant Boblink Jones finished
preparations for all three. The child they dressed in a
mourning gown of white linen; the babe was hardly
larger than a bisque doll. They also did their best to
give the woman some semblance of dignity knowing
that like most women, her modesty would not permit
others to see her with her head split nearly in half. But
there was only so much that could be done for her,
and so Tall John doubled a piece of white lace and
used it as a funeral veil to cover up the terrible damage; then, to assure no one would see her thus, he had
Boblink nail shut the coffin lid. There wasn't much

involved when it came to Bill Blankenship—"Just comb his hair and wax his moustaches," Tall John ordered Boblink.

It took every ounce of strength for them to lift the short but stout body of the woman into her coffin. It was a nice coffin as coffins went. Smiley had, in his disgrace and regret, declared cost no object for "Me poor Kathleen" ordering their small house put up for sale to pay the expenses. "I want it to be nice," he said to Tall John. "You know." The other coffin—the one for Bill Blankenship—was a simple pine, and that of the infant, was a simple pine also, built by the hands of the father who added small horseshoe handles and a coat of whitewash. With great care, the coffins were loaded into the back of the hearse.

Smiley Rivers lay in his cell thinking of what he'd done, knowing as he did this was the day they would bury his wife. He regretted now more than anything having ever left his home in Ireland—Tullamore, famous for its whiskey—and wished he'd stayed and taken up the trade of his relatives, that of whiskey maker. But instead he'd had a dream that if he came to America, he would become rich, possibly become a cattle baron and landholder and thus took his bride— a woman some fifteen years his senior—and together they sailed to the new land where they quickly found little more than failure and impoverishment—he as a boot maker, and she as a pie maker.

He couldn't say what had gotten into him the day he killed her. He had been drinking heavily sure enough in the Rosebud along with several others: Roy Bean, Otis Dollar, Fly, the editor, and Doc Willis. But beyond that, it was all a blank to him why he left out of there, went home and got a hatchet and killed Kathleen. And to chop off his own hand! Surely a madness had overtaken him, for he had drunk just as bad or worse on previous occasions and never came near to such mayhem.

He could hear the brass band playing a dirge, and by great effort, he lifted himself up to the barred window and looked out in time to see the cortege passing down the street on its way to the cemetery. He wept great tears and held on as long as he could before losing his grip and falling to the floor again. It was such a pretty goddamn day, he thought. Too pretty for a loving wife to be dead and her funeral held.

Trailing the wagon was the blacksmith, Figg, dressed in a dusty black suit, his shuffle raising dust. He was a man stricken with grief, for he'd lost everything—wife and child. Behind him, the widow Blankenship riding in a cab, her face covered in black lace.

Tall John said to Boblink, "Hold them reins steady, boy. Don't let the horses get away with you and embarrass us all."

The horses that pulled the hearse were a mismatched pair: a Percheron and a big bay. Both were easily spooked and once had run off wild with the mortal remains of Tasker Hair in the back when a piece of wind-blown newspaper flew in front of them.

It took nearly a mile for Tall John to head them in, turn them around, and pick up the boy who'd been pitched from the seat into the mud. This in the spring. Tall John was saving for a pair of better-behaved horses.

Boblink said, "Do you think they know what dead is?"

"Horses, you mean?"

The boy nodded.

Tall John took pity on the boy, whom he deemed somewhat slow witted and said, "Of course they don't. Only humans know what death is, except maybe elephants. I once read that elephants are near human in their thinking, so them I couldn't say for sure if they know what death is or not."

Jake was on his way to the livery to see if new horses had arrived, and paused to watch the passing of the funeral. He could see the polished black casket with its silver handles, and the other two as well, including the small white one inside the glass-sided hearse, and remembered the stark brutality of the woman's death. He could not imagine why a man would murder his wife with a hatchet. Or worse, why a woman would smother her child, or a man drown himself. But then he'd learned as a physician that death comes in many forms and it didn't matter in the end to its victims which way death arrived. He waited for the procession to pass before crossing the street.

The liveryman wasn't anywhere to be found,

within or without the livery. No new horses could he see, either. *Damn*!

He walked out to Toussaint's lodge, found him hitching his mule to a wagon.

"I'd like to hire you," he said.

Toussaint was just strapping up the halter.

"For what?"

"To ride me out to Karen Sunflower's; I need to buy a horse from her."

"I'm going the other direction," Toussaint said.

"Cash money."

"How much?"

"Ten dollars. Out and back if she doesn't have a horse to sell me."

"I wasn't planning on coming back today. Planned on camping out."

"Well, if I can't buy a horse, it doesn't matter when I get back."

"Why not wait until she brings them in?"

"I'd like to get a start on things—the sooner the better."

"You worried old Bob and Teacup will come back here and shoot you?"

"Let's just say I have to be somewhere."

"They probably will."

"You for hire, or not?"

"I only take silver."

Jake handed him ten silver dollars.

"Something you maybe should know before we go out there."

"What's that?"

"Karen and me used to be married."

"I don't see what that has to do with anything."

"She's never forgiven me for some things."

"Not my business."

"Might be your business."

"Why would that be?"

"Just the sight of me can set her off. She might not sell you a horse out of spite because you're with me."

"I'll take my chances."

"Don't say I didn't warn you."

They started off, took the road past the cemetery. A dozen or so citizens stood around the open graves. Preacher Poke stood reading a prayer in front of one of them. Folks were dressed in black. It was terribly hot. The men sweated. The women sweated. The kids fidgeted.

"That's too bad about that woman and that child," Toussaint said as they drove past.

"Yes, it was."

"Smiley's woman baked good pies."

Jake recalled the blood-spattered pies in the café kitchen that day. He wasn't sure he'd ever be hungry for pie again.

They rode on toward Karen Sunflower's place.

Waddy Worth was one of ten siblings raised on a scratch-poor patch of ground in Crow Wing County, Minnesota. Skinny kid with a drifting right eye that seemed to look everywhere but straight ahead. Maybe it was this defect in his appearance and the subsequent teasing that often led him to get into fistfights and gave him such a bad disposition. Or maybe it was something else. But whatever it was, Waddy Worth got into trouble early and often and so much so that his daddy ran him off after the boy beat up a local grocer and stole three cans of peaches.

"Well, goddamn you," the boy cried and turned his back on his nest of kin.

It didn't take long for Waddy to learn: what you wanted, you took.

He hooked up with a train-and-bank robber named Frank Moore, an aging alcoholic consumptive who knew his internal clock was ticking down and ticking down fast. They seemed an unlikely pair, the sixty-two-year-old man and the fourteen-year-old boy, but they had evil in common, and evil was enough to make them equals in a sense.

They robbed anything they could, banks, trains, mercantiles, stages, travelers, even a blind man once.

Frank taught Waddy how to drink bad whiskey and like it. Taught him to smoke and whore and shoot the buttons off a man's shirt at twenty paces. Frank Moore was an evil son of a bitch and Waddy Worth wanted to be just like him.

The partnership came to a sudden and violent end one night in a tent they'd pitched along the Snake River just east of Grand Forks. It was a cold moonless night, air like frozen iron and wind that fought the little fire, its flames licking valiantly at the blackness.

Off in the distance they could hear wolves howling and when the wolves weren't howling, they could hear ice cracking the tree limbs.

"Goddamn coldest son of a bitching night I've ever felt," Frank moaned. He'd been working on a bottle of Red Mustang bonded whiskey for the better part of the evening trying to fortify his blood. The boy was drunk, too, lying by the fire, his boots and mackinaw steaming.

"Shit, I knowed it to be so cold one time in Minnesota the horses froze," he said.

"Shit, I knowed it to be so cold once Montan' men's peckers would break off and fall in the snow," old Frank said, his laughter a crackle of phlegm from which he hawked and spat off into the dark.

The boy chuckled because he thought it was a funny image—frozen peckers in the snow.

They could see stars up above the tree limbs. They could see strange lights shimmering in the far distance.

"Look," the boy said.

"Northern lights," Frank said. "What they call Ore Alice Bore Alice."

"I know it. I seen them all the time when I was a kid."

"*Was* a kid!" Frank cawed. "Hell, you ain't nothing but a kid now!"

They passed the bottle between them until it was empty and Frank pitched it off in the dark where it landed with a dull thud. He reached into his saddle-bags and pulled out another and worked the cork free with his teeth and took a long pull, then handed it to Waddy who tried his best to match Frank in drinking behavior.

"Goddamn but I'm about drunk as a skunk," the boy said, his words soft and dull.

"Go on and drink some more," Frank said, "it'll keep your blood from freezing. You wouldn't want to die on such a night."

The boy drank until he couldn't feel his face any longer and his limbs became numb as well.

Next he knew he was crawling into the tent, nearly done for, feeling almost like he thought the dead would feel like. He closed his eyes and couldn't open them again and saw his mother weeping at a table with an oil lamp lit on it, the shadows playing over her sad face. He sure enough hated it that he had to leave her behind with his mean old pap. He felt as though he were tumbling down a well. Even the earth beneath him seemed to be spinning.

Somewhere in his stupor he felt that there was something wrong. It was like a weight bearing down on him, like something smothering him, and he fought it. And when he suddenly came full to again, there was nasty old Frank Moore atop him, rubbing his naked hairless body against him. And to his amazement his own clothes had been stripped away—even his boots.

"What! What!" he gasped.

"Shhh, lad."

"Get the goddamn hell off'n me!"

But old Frank was a strong son of a bitch for a

man his age and size. Skinny and hairless, with stinking breath like coal oil blowing in his face. Waddy
fought to get free. The struggle was violent and furious and the tent came down around them as Waddy's
feet kicked loose the tent pegs, but old Frank hung on
as though he was riding a young bronc he was trying
to saddle break, saying the whole time, "Shhh . . .
shhhh."

Somehow Waddy's hand found a pistol—his or
Frank's, he didn't know which, nor did he give a
damn. He brought it round, pressed the barrel into
Frank's hoary ear, and without a moment's hesitation
pulled the trigger.

A warm wet rain splattered the boy's face as the
old fellow fell limp. Waddy pushed out from under,
scrambled from the collapsed canvas, and ran off to
the edge of trees before he stopped still holding the
pistol in his hand ready to shoot Frank again if he had
to. He stood there until his shivering seemed as
though it was going to shake his bones right out of his
skin. He dreaded going back to camp, but if he didn't,
he'd freeze to death.

When Waddy found the lantern and struck a match
to it, he could see the lifeless lump under the collapsed
canvas. He carefully pulled it away and saw he'd
blown off the upper part of Frank's skull, that his
teeth were clinched into what could have been a grin
that seemed to still say, "Shhh . . . shhhh."

Waddy dragged the dead man off down to the river
by his bony ankles and left him lying in the shallow
crusted snow.

"There, you son of a bitch, let the wolves eat you."

He washed blood and brains from his face in the icy water and it near took his breath away.

He shivered like a dog as he repaired the tent, crawled in it, the pistol handy in case for some mysterious reason Frank decided he wasn't dead and might decide to return. And in spite of his weariness, the boy did not sleep the rest of the night, but instead listened to wolves snarling down by the river, their jaws snapping as though they were fighting over something.

Frank Moore was the first man Waddy Worth ever killed, but he wouldn't be the last by a long shot. He eventually made his way to North Dakota to do more robbing and killing, for he found he had a knack for it, and found he liked it a lot better than he thought he would. A gun made him the size of any full-grown man, and bigger than some. And now that he'd killed old Frank, he had two guns, which meant he could do twice the robbing and twice the killing.

9

KAREN SUNFLOWER was sitting on an overturned tub plucking a chicken, worried sick about Dex. Dex had up and gone off somewhere two days earlier and hadn't yet returned. It wasn't uncommon for him to wander off, but he'd never been gone more than a day before he returned. Karen Sunflower thought she'd give it one more day and if he hadn't returned by then, she'd go looking for him. She thought she knew where she might start looking for him too: the Kunckles. They were a family of Swede squatters who lived ten miles distance from her place up near the upper end of Cooper's Creek. A filthy bunch, the whole lot of them. A brood of wild kids, including one girl about fifteen who'd already come into womanhood. They were all towheaded, tall and skinny, with long narrow horse faces. Cheerless people who never smiled, most likely because of the hardship the prairies put on them. Inge Kunckle, the wife and mother of the brood, was an older mirror image of the daughter; she looked near fifty but was probably younger, and as worn out as a stone-washed bedsheet. All the other kids except for the girl, Gerthe, were boys of various ages and sizes. The boys would fling stones at you if they caught you out riding alone, knowing as they probably did you would not dare shoot them, even though in Karen Sunflower's mind, they were no better than wild varmints and prairie pests that deserved shooting.

One time she came across three of them trying to light a stick of dynamite. Out of concern that they might blow themselves to hell, she'd made the mistake of stopping to warn them of the dangers of fooling with dynamite.

"Hey you young'ns," she called. "You ought to be careful with that dynamite. That's enough to blow you all into tiny pieces. What you aim doing with it, anyway?"

"Fishin'" one of them said—a boy taller than the rest.

"Go on home before you kill yourselves."

They looked at her the way coyotes might look at a rabbit the moment before they attacked, then suddenly reached down and picked up stones and began flinging them at her. One of the stones struck the rump of her pony, which then nearly bucked her off.

She was so goddamn mad she was ready to light the dynamite herself and stick it down their coveralls. But they scattered like the little varmints they were and she watched them run off toward the Kunckles' shack.

She did not know what the elder Kunckle did to sustain his brood other than hunt and fish. But she had an idea he might be a thief, for every once in a while things from her place came up missing: an adze, a rope, a tin dipper. She had no way of proving Kunckle had stolen the items, nor did she care to confront him and those wild kids of his. And she wouldn't have paid them any further attention whatsoever if it hadn't been that Dex came in one day yapping about how pretty that Kunckle girl, Gerthe, was.

"You stay clear of that little tart," she warned Dex. "That old man of hers is liable to shoot you—or worse, make you marry her." But it was clear to see that Dex was struck by love the way a tree is struck by lightning—clean down to his roots.

She knew Dex snuck off at night to meet up with the girl, for she'd hear him walking across the one loose floorboard she could never get not to squeak no matter how she tried to fix it. She'd be lying there at night in her bed, half asleep, worrying about the day that had gone before, and she'd hear him. Then she'd get up and look out the window and see him going across the grass, past the tool shed, the corral, his shadow shrunk to nothing at all in the moonlight, heading off in the direction of the Kunckles. And several hours later she'd be awakened by that same squeaking board when he came in the house again.

What was she to do? Dex was near a grown man. Couldn't tell him nothing. He'd never been full right in the head to start with, something with the way he was born. Dropped out of her womb silent. Even when the midwife smacked his little bottom he didn't make a cry. He was a man in every way but his thinking. Good with horses, though, and a heart of pure gold; would give you the underwear off his ass if you asked him to.

She plucked the chicken with a certain pent-up fury, tossing feathers this way and that, dipping the carcass back into the other tub of hot water, then out again; its head lay over in the grass, the barn cat sniffing at it. Then she saw a wagon coming, saw the mule that was pulling it, knew who it was. She wasn't pleased.

"Goddamn," she said to herself. "What's he doing coming out here?"

"There she is," Toussaint said when he saw Karen off in the distance. "She's plucking a chicken. Woman loves to eat fried chicken worse than anything. Won't eat a rabbit if you put a gun to her head."

"Why is that?" Jake asked.

"'Cause she knows I like them. Anything to spite me suits Karen just fine."

"I'm sorry to have to ask you to bring me out here."

"You didn't ask, you hired me, remember?"

Toussaint drove up into the yard—what he considered a yard, the part where the grass was scythed down—and drew back on the reins, then put the brake on with his foot. He and Karen stared at each other.

Jake felt that he wasn't even noticed.

"What do you want out here, you damn savage?" Karen said.

"Savage," Toussaint said for Jake's benefit. "I was always a savage to her even if I can speak several languages and read."

She shifted her gaze to Jake.

"Who's this?"

"He came to buy a horse off you."

"I can speak for myself," Jake said.

"Then why don't you?" Toussaint said, jumping down off the wagon to stretch his legs.

"Nobody invited you to get down," Karen said.

"Goddamn, woman, will you let a man have some peace?"

"Please," Jake said, wanting to restore some civility with which to negotiate. "I was told by the liveryman in town you might be bringing him some horses to sell. I thought I might just come out and buy one direct off you. I have to be someplace sooner rather than later."

She was a well-built woman whose taut body showed through her clothes, showed she had known real labor and it had only enhanced the way she looked. She wore a man's shirt, sleeves rolled up to the elbows, and faded denims tucked down inside the shafts of worn brown boots. A bandana hung from round her neck—a blue one with white stars, and her russet hair was cut nearly short as a man's as well.

"Had some horses I was going to bring in but they run off a few nights back—bear or something spooked them, caused them to kick down the gate.

Probably still running out there somewhere." She looked off toward the west. "Otherwise I'd practically give you a damn horse just to get rid of *him*." Toussaint tried ignoring the comment. He was watching the cat pawing at the lopped-off chicken's head.

Cats were strange and cruel creatures; always killing something it seemed just for the sake of killing it: birds, ground squirrels, baby rabbits; dragging them up to a body's door and leaving them. He especially disliked this particular cat. Sometimes jumping on the bed when things were going good with him and Karen, like that one time in the middle of a rainstorm afternoon when that delicious feeling married folks sometimes get came over them and they shucked their clothes and went at it. Then that damn cat jumped in the bed and dug its claws into his back and he got mad and cussed the cat and flung it out the window. Then Karen got mad for him cussing the cat and flinging it out the window and cussed him, and just like that, the delicious afternoon was nothing more than a bad rain and their feelings toward each other turned from sweet to sore. He went out and found the liquor bottle he kept hidden in the grain bin and drank it till he fell down drunk into a muddly wallow and nearly drowned.

That's what Karen's cat reminded him of when he looked at it fussing with the chicken's head—nothing but pure misery.

The three of them stood there silent for a moment longer than was comfortable, then Jake said, "Thank you, Miss." And then to Toussaint, "We might as well go."

"Suits me fine," Toussaint said and climbed back up in the wagon. He took hold of the reins and released the brake and gave Karen one last glance. She was watching him as if he were some sort of thief that had come to steal the teeth out of her mouth. Then he saw the cat pick up the chicken's head and skulk off toward the tool shed. *Goddamn cat*, he thought.

Dex said to Gerthe, "I've got something."

"What?" she said.

Dex liked her smile in spite of the gap between her two front teeth. He liked her nearly white hair and freckles and the length of her neck and all the rest of her, head to toe. He liked her so much, about all he could ever think about was her anymore. When he was with her, and when he wasn't.

"Something that will make it feel better."

"It can't feel much better than it does," she said.

"I was told it could."

"Who told you?"

"Can't say."

"Why not."

"It's a secret, I swore not to tell."

"You can tell me."

"No, I can't."

She giggled, Dex did, too. They were like small children playing at something—a game they'd made up, one that only they understood the rules to.

"Show me," Gerthe said.

"You show me something first."

"Like what?" she said coyly.

"You know what."

"This?" she said, pulling down the top of her dress.

Dex stared in wonderment even though he'd seen Gerthe's small firm breasts a dozen times before. They were as small and round and hard as pomegranates. He couldn't get over how they felt, how warm and wonderful they were each time he touched them. They had tiny blue veins running through them underneath the freckles that dappled them. Their tips were like tiny pink buttons.

"Oh boy," he said.

Gerthe reclined on the grass. It was dry from lack of rain; dry and scratchy.

"You bring a blanket?"

"I forgot."

"I hate how scratchy the grass is, Dex."

"I'll get underneath this time."

"You're such a wild thing," she said, the sun already burning her pale cheeks to a cherry redness.

"I know it."

He took from his pocket a small tin and worked loose the lid, held it forth for her to look at. It was filled with tiny seeds.

"What is it?" she said.

"Just something a man give to me to make it feel better."

"What you supposed to do with it?"

"Eat them," he said.

"I ain't eating them."

"Go on, Gerthe."

"No, you eat them."

"I aim to."

"Go ahead then. I dare you to."

He put some of the seeds in his mouth and chewed then swallowed them down with some water from his canteen then put some more in his mouth and did the same thing. It had a strange taste to it, but not one that was bad.

"Your turn," he said.

She shook her head.

"Why should I?"

"'Cause it's supposed to make it feel better."

"It feels fine as it is. Ain't you happy with the way it feels, Dex?"

"Come on, Gerthe, please!"

She finally relented, and when she'd finished eating and swallowing the seeds, she lay back on the grass and let Dex smother her breasts with wet kisses waiting for it to *feel* better.

"It don't feel no different, Dex."

"Give it time," he said. "I think I'm starting to feel some different."

She opened her eyes and looked down and saw him working his way out of his clothes.

"Let's make a baby and get married, Dex. I hate having to live with my folks. I want to be your wife and go live in some city somewheres."

Dex grinned with pleasure. What was she saying, this crazy girl?

"What'd you say?"

"I want to get married and have some babies."

Dex giggled.

"I'm seeing things," he said.

"What sort of things?"

"All sorts of things, colorful things—it's like being inside a rainbow, Gerthe."

"Huh?"

Then she started seeing black fearful things coming out of the ground, things reaching for her.

Dex was above her doing something to her, something that felt terrible. Dex was chewing on her, biting her arms and legs and it hurt terrible.

"No, Dex! Stop it!"

But it was too late for all that. Much too late.

A letter came for Roy Bean. It was written in Spanish. It was signed by his wife; that much Spanish he understood. It was just a one-page letter. Not even a full page. Just four lines of writing in a very lovely hand. He scratched under his sombrero. Felt as if he had nits in his hair again. Nits were hard things to get rid of. You could kill them all day, squashing them between your thumb and fingernail, and you still couldn't kill all the nits in a single head of hair or a mattress if you worked all day steady at it every day for the rest of your life. Roy Bean hated nits about as bad as he hated anything. He'd rather deal with killers and thieves than nits.

He didn't know anybody in Sweet Sorrow who could read Spanish except possibly Toussaint Trueblood. Roy Bean walked the letter out to Toussaint's lodge, but Toussaint wasn't there—his wagon and mule were gone.

Well, that was surely something: to have a letter from your wife and not know what it was she'd written. Maybe something had happened to one of the children. Or maybe his wife was sick and dying. Or, maybe she'd met another man and was planning on going off with him. It troubled Roy Bean a great deal to think that his sweet dutiful wife might have met another fellow she liked better than him. He tried not to think of her with another man—the two of them lying in bed together and all that such entailed. He walked to the Rosebud and ordered an iced beer and sat by his lonesome studying the strange words as though by studying them, they would reveal their secret to him. This, about midmorning, but so hot already that hardly anyone was out on the streets and very few even in the Rosebud.

Peg Leg Watts stretched out on the floor after he served Roy Bean his beer. It was somewhat cooler on the floor and he didn't mind that someone might walk in and see him thus and wonder why he was lying there. Peg Leg Watts was not a man who concerned himself with the opinions of others, for he knew what sort of man he was and what sort of man he had been. And when you've been a man who has sailed all over the watery world and seen about everything there is to see—everything from men wearing rags on their heads who charmed poisonous snakes in baskets, to three-foot-tall pygmies who carried around shrunken heads on strings, and when you've had your leg et off by a shark—the opinions of others meant very little. Besides, lying on the floor of the saloon reminded him of lying on the deck of a ship, something he especially missed at night when he could look up and see the stars and hear the waves breaking against the bow.

"Why you lying on the floor?" Roy Bean asked him when he looked up from the Spanish letter.

"It's cooler down here."

"You don't know how to read Mexican writing, do you?"

"I don't know how to read any sort of writing, Mexican or otherwise."

"I got a letter here from my wife—she writ it in Mexican."

"Why'd she do that?"

"Because she's Mexican. It's all she knows how to write."

"Then I guess you should have married yourself an American gal."

"Down in the part of Texas I hail from most gals is Mexican."

"I'd just as soon we didn't carry on no conversation; it's too hot to talk."

"Fine by me."

Birdy Pride came in looking for all the world as though she was set to go off to Sunday church. She wore a dress of soft white cotton and her hair was washed and freshly combed. Trouble was it wasn't Sunday, it was Saturday.

"Hi, Roy, honey."

Roy felt distressed seeing her thus. She looked like the sweetest angel, and a little like his wife, who was probably this very minute cheating on him with another man—probably someone tall with a black moustache and charming ways and knew rope tricks.

"Why you all fixed up?" he said.

"No reason, except it's cooler dressing this away."

"Where'd you go last night?"

"I just went off is all. I went off to be by my lonesome."

"You don't strike me as being the lonesome type, Birdy."

"Well, I guess I can be whatever I want to be, Roy Bean, as long as I ain't nobody's wife."

It was a remark that cut deep, for Roy Bean knew her sarcasm was aimed at him. He knew that once a woman got on her high horse, she hardly ever got down off it again.

"As long as I ain't nobody's wife, I reckon I can come and go as I please," Birdy continued, quite proud of herself that she was putting "the boots" to her lover. Well, her ex-lover, as far as she was concerned, now that Preacher Poke was in the picture, so to speak. Roy looked like a fish dangling from a hook with those sorrowful eyes.

"It'd be hard for me to marry a gal with so much sass in her as you, Birdy Pride, even if I wasn't already married. It truly would."

But nothing could crush Birdy's happy mood. She felt like summer; only not the hot summer like it was outside, but more like the summers she remembered in Michigan there by the lake when she was just a child with the breeze running through her hair.

"I don't reckon you can read a word of Mexican," Roy Bean said out of sheer desperation.

Birdy looked at the letter in Roy's hand.

"I suppose that is a letter from your wife—the one you *did* ask to marry you."

"Oh, let's not get into all that now. Can you or can't you read Mexican?"

"No, I can't. And even if I could, I wouldn't read you no letter from your wife."

. And with that Birdy turned and left out of the Rosebud, nearly stumbling over Peg Leg Watts who saw for the blink of an eye what Birdy was wearing under her pretty summer dress. He closed his eyes hoping the image would stay with him for a long time, just like the image of the Nubian Amazon he'd met in Calcutta had. That's the thing with living a long and interesting life: it just all comes down to a handful of pleasant memories a man hopes to hold on to until the undertaker comes and gets him.

Waddy Worth came upon the young man strangling the blond girl. Sat his horse for a long moment or two and watched, not exactly believing his eyes. The girl was kicking and trying her best to break the fellow's grip from around her neck. They were both naked as jaybirds. The girl was covered in red marks. But still she was the prettiest thing Waddy Worth had ever laid eyes on, thinking about it as he was. The boy was barking like a dog and snapping at her, too.

I seen lots of goddamn things in my short unhappy

life, he thought as he watched the fellow strangling the girl, *but I never goddamn seen nothing like this.*

He pulled one of his pistols and shot the boy through the back of the head causing it to explode in a bright red spray of thick matter, like watermelon hit by a sledge.

The girl screamed and screamed.

"Shut up!" Waddy said.

It didn't seem to have any effect on her whatsoever. She screamed and screamed.

Waddy sat with his left leg slung round his saddle horn waiting for her to shut up. Finally she did.

"That's better," he said. "You're as pretty as a god-damn winter when the sun shines."

"What?" she said. "What?"

"You must be daft," he said. "But it don't matter to me none if you are daft or not. This is by far the lonesomest country I ever been in and I could use me some female companionship and it looks as though you will have to do."

"What? What?"

"That peckerwood ain't going to do you any damn bit of good no more," he said, looking at the corpse of Dex Sunflower. "Perhaps you ought to get some clothes on and come with me."

Gerthe was seeing butterflies. Millions of butterflies as she tugged on her dress.

Waddy Worth felt his pecker stirring inside his trousers as Gerthe climbed up on the back of his horse and put her arms around him. He had brief thoughts of taking the girl and laying with her in the grass, but it wouldn't pay if someone come along and found a murdered body and him wearing the only guns.

"You ain't going to eat me, are you?" she said somewhat sorrowfully.

"I might," he said with a grin so big it hurt his face.

He spurred his horse and rode off, Gerthe, nearly tumbling off, but getting a good hard grip on the kid much to his delight.

10

❖

THERE HAD BEEN a knock at the door. She'd been quick to go to it and open it. The husband stood there, his face flushed with anger, his eyes whiskey red. He pushed his way into the room and she didn't try and stop him—quite the opposite.

"What's going on here, Celine?"

She was just in her corset and stockings, the bed rumpled.

Her act was a good one: that of the victim of some terrible transgression. She swooned and sobbed and pointed an accusing finger.

"I was unwell . . . he, Dr. Shade . . . he took advantage of my condition . . ."

There wasn't any chance to tell his side of it: that they had become lovers, that she was a willing participant in their affair. Then a struggle: the two men grappling for a small silver pistol suddenly in the hands of the husband.

He had been able to knock the pistol free, watched

as it clattered across the floor. But the husband's fury demanded justice; his indignation at being the cuckold too much to contain, and too late to settle matters like gentlemen. And so Jake—Tristan Shade—struggled for his life, to keep the husband from grabbing the pistol again as it lay just out of reach.

Then came the shattering explosion, loud as a thunderclap that filled the room, deafening, as the husband fell limp, as blood dripped out of his hair onto the good doctor's face.

She stood there above them, smoke trailing from the pocket pistol. He couldn't be sure who it was she was aiming for until she offered him a half smile and said, "You see, lover, hell hath no fury like a woman scorned."

Where was the scorn? He'd simply told her he couldn't continue their relationship. Where *was* the scorn?

Then with all the calmness of an assassin she said, "You'd better go, Tristan. Run for your life, for I'd hate to see a hangman's rope knotted round your handsome neck."

"What am I guilty of but loving you?" he said.

"Exactly. You're guilty of loving another man's wife—a very wealthy and powerful man whose family will surely demand revenge. You're guilty of being made a fool of. And now it will look like you're also guilty of murder."

"And what about you?"

"Me? Well poor me, the grieving widow of whom the doctor took advantage, for even doctors are but mortal men, aren't they, dear Tristan? Well, I'll play the role of the grieving widow, of course, and I'll collect my husband's share of his family fortune, and eventually fade away—back to England, I suspect, back to where my now late husband found me in a very fancy bordello, I might add. Only this time I'll own the brothel. Like you, he couldn't resist such beauty, such lovely charm."

And so there it was. Run or be found guilty of murder.

She promised him an hour's head start before she sent for the police. He doubted truly she would give him that, even as she stepped forward, over the body of her late husband, and planted a seductress's kiss on his mouth.

"Run, poor Tristan. Run for your life. Don't be the fool twice and think you will convince anyone it was me who shot my unfortunate husband. I mean, why would I, really?"

It was still as vivid in his memory as the day it happened. The ruts in the road that Toussaint drove, the jaw-jarring ride, he'd hardly noticed. Then Toussaint said, "There's someone coming."

Doc Willis smelled the infection before he saw it. Smiley Rivers lay atop his bunk within the one and only jail cell, being watched in turns by various local men who'd volunteered to keep an eye on him until some sort of new lawman could be found.

Smiley, looking for all the world like a wounded animal, lay atop his bunk. Doc could see the red streaks going up the arm missing the hand. He peeled back the crusted bandage.

"It's bad, ain't it, Doc?"

Doc Willis nodded.

"It's bad, Smiley."

Their eyes held for a moment, Smiley's eyes questioning, but Doc had no answers for him.

"Why, Doc . . ." It was half a question, incomplete as though he had not the strength to ask everything that trickled through his fevered mind.

"Do you believe in God, Smiley?"

"Uh-huh? I reckon I sorta do . . ."

"Then you might want to make your peace with him."

Beads of sweat dotted Smiley's brow. Fever quivered under his skin.

"I'm burning up, Doc . . ."

"It will take you slow, the infection will. It won't be pleasant."

"Maybe they could get someone to haul me down to Bismarck, Doc. Ain't they an infirmary in Bismarck?"

"They couldn't do anything more for you than I can. It'd just be a hard trip in vain."

"Oh! Oh!"

"There is one thing I can do if you want me to."

Smiley's gaze once more met Doc's.

"What is it, Doc? What is it you can do for me?"

"I can make it easier for you."

Doc Willis could tell by the eyes of his patient that his patient understood his meaning.

"Will it be painful?"

"No," Doc said. "It won't hurt at all. Just a little prick in the skin when I put the needle in. Hardly anything at all. You'll just go to sleep."

Doc could see Smiley was struggling with the decision. He dipped a ladle of water out of a drinking bucket by Smiley's cot and put it to the man's lips; some of the water spilled over the sides of his mouth, collected in the hollows of his ear. Smiley swallowed hard, as though he were swallowing rocks instead of water.

"Go on then, Doc . . . Go on and do it. I'd just as soon get it done. Even if I was to make it through this," he said, holding up his bandaged stub. "They'd hang me for what I done to Emmaline. There's nothing good waiting for me."

"Yes, that's most likely true. I think this would be a better way to end it."

"Go on, then . . . go on and end it, Doc."

Doc reached into his medical bag and found the syringe.

The man watching the jail, Brewster Hatfield, was outside having a smoke. Most folks who knew him called him Rooster Hat because he had a fiery disposition, was a smallish man with a shock of flame-red hair, and would fight anything that moved if provoked. He didn't much care to be called Rooster Hat. The town committee had offered to pay him and the other volunteers a dollar a day to watch the prisoner. Thing was, he couldn't stand the stink inside the jail and was relieved when Doc had arrived to look at the prisoner.

Prisoner, he thought as he rolled a shuck and smoked it. *Hell, I knew old Smiley when he was a two-fisted whoring teamster before he married Emmaline Straw. Now she's dead and he soon will be, too. Goddamn but how life has a way of balancing out the good with the bad. Old Smiley wasn't nothing now but rotting meat; his buckaroo days all over now. He was a finished man.*

Brewster said hidey to Doc Willis when he came out of the jail. Doc nodded and went on down the street. Brewster smoked another two cigarettes before going back inside. And even when he did go back inside, he didn't go to look in on Smiley in the back because of the stink being so bad, and he couldn't hardly stand to look into old Smiley's sorry eyes and see what a thing he'd come to after having known him back in his buckaroo days. He never went back to check on Smiley until the supper meal was delivered by Gus Boone, the man set to relieve him. They went back together and found Smiley asleep.

"Poor bastard," Boone said.

Brewster said, "We oughter just let him sleep." Boone agreed and they set the tray of food just outside the cell, then went and played several hands of whist before Brewster left out and ended up drinking up his dollar's pay at the Rosebud.

The dead began to reek after a full twenty-four hours in the stifling heat and somebody said somebody should go bury the big whore, Lady France, and her pimp, Sally St. John. But there wasn't anyone willing to take on the task.

Bob Olive had fallen asleep on the pool table and Teacup Smith on the floor beneath the piano. And when they awoke the next morning it was Bob who said, "This place smells worse than some shithouse" and Teacup said, "It's the stink of death, Bob."

And so they went out into the growing heat where the air didn't have any stink of death to it. A small crowd of the locals, curious as to what had taken place inside the whoreman's whiskey den, had gathered in front and were talking over the situation.

Bob Olive looked at them and said, "I hope you all ain't thinking of calling for any sort of justice for them two inside."

"We was just talking about the stink," one old man wearing the shapeless clothes of a miner said.

"You could always bury them if the stink bothers you so much," Bob said.

The crowd of faces looked at one another.

"It was already suggested," the old man said. "Ain't nobody willing to do it."

"Then I guess you all are fucked." Bob took a certain delight in seeing the misery on their faces, of knowing they weren't anything but a group of weak sisters who could be cowed.

"This place never was much," the old man said. "You shooting the whiskey man and this town's only whore has pretty well deprived us of what little pleasure there was to be had in this place."

"Not my problem, dad."

"Yeah, it ain't our problem," Teacup echoed.

All those in the crowd but the old man looked down at the toes of their boots.

"It's a lousy stinking thing what you did," the old man said. "I seen plenty of rotten things done by and to others, but what you did was damn low down."

"Maybe I ought to shoot you and let you add to the stink," Bob Olive said.

"I guess I couldn't stop you. I guess nobody could."

"That's right, you old coon. You couldn't, so shut the hell up!"

Bob Olive was disgusted with this knot of low humanity that stood before him. He was disgusted that he wasn't back in his own bed in Sweet Sorrow and running things. He was disgusted that he had a bullet hole in his leg because somebody had the audacity to shoot him with his back turned—somebody that should have been as dead as those two inside that stinking whiskey den. Well, by god, he was in a killing mood, and achy leg or no achy leg, he was ready to go and kill that same son of a bitch he and Teacup had shot once already; only this time he was going to kill him permanent.

"Let's get out of this pig sty!" Bob said to Teacup.

"Where we going?"

"We're going to go kill that son of a bitch who shot me and take back our jobs."

Teacup hesitated in moving toward their horses.

"What?" Bob said when Teacup didn't move.

"I was just wondering if maybe we shouldn't just

move on and find another town to practice our profession in."

"Profession! Get on your damn horse or I'll shoot you and leave you here to help stink up this slop hole."

"All I'm saying, Bob, is, we done shot that fellow five times and couldn't kill him, what makes you think we can kill him now?"

"We made a fatal error in judgment—the one mistake a shootist should never make when shooting somebody."

"What's that?"

"We didn't shoot him in the damn head." Bob Olive tapped the side of his head with a forefinger. "We ain't gone make that mistake again."

"Oh," Teacup said. "I see what you're saying now."

Toussaint halted the wagon and waited for the rider to approach, only it wasn't one rider, it was two, riding double on a big gray gelding.

Waddy Worth drew reins. The girl clung to him. What with the heat, they felt stuck together with sweat and Waddy liked the feeling it gave him. He did not know what he eventually was going to do with the wild girl, but he figured he'd think of something. He had ideas already floating around inside his head. This girl was prettier than any of the whores Frank Moore had introduced him to in their short and violent partnership. Maybe he could teach her to rob banks and railroad trains, like old Frank Moore had taught him to do. Most certainly she'd be able to cook better than old Frank Moore. And if she wanted to climb on top of him when he was drunk, he wouldn't shoot her like he'd shot old Frank Moore. Waddy had a good feeling about the turn of events. He was in high spirits when he came across the two men in the wagon.

"How do," he said to the men.

He could see one of the men, the older darker one looking at the girl.

"You're the child of Kunckle," Toussaint said.

She turned her face away.

Toussaint said to the boy, "How is it you have that child with you?"

Jake had noticed the scratches and bite marks on her legs and arm, the sticks and grass in her hair. Toussaint had noticed it, too.

"I just found her back aways," Waddy said. "She was just back there wandering around like she was lost so I picked her up and put her on my horse. Doing the right thing by her, don't you see. Taking her to her kin. Just being a good Samaritan."

"You just found her?"

"That's right you goddamn redskin."

Jake felt Toussaint stiffen.

"She looks pretty roughed up," Jake said. "You know how she came to be like that?"

"I wouldn't know anything about that, mister," Waddy said, looking at the man sitting next to the redskin. Waddy figured they might have some money.

He looked them over good to see if they were armed. The redskin didn't look as though he was packing iron. But it was hard to tell if the other fellow sitting on the far side of the seat was or not; he could have an iron in his belt, maybe one down his boot.

"I think I'll have a closer look at her," Jake said. "We've got some water in a canteen we could wash those scratches with so they don't get infected."

"I reckon once I get her home, her people can clean her up just fine."

"The direction you're headed," Toussaint said. "It's not the way to her home."

It befuddled Waddy for a moment, not quite knowing which lie he should throw out next. This was a time when old Frank Moore would have come in handy. Old Frank Moore was a bona fide goddamn liar if ever there was one. Frank Moore once lied his way out of a hanging.

"I don't know nothing about it except what she told me where it is," Waddy said. "If I'm headed the wrong way, then I'll by god turn around."

"Let her down," Jake said. "Let's have a look at her."

Waddy shifted his gaze back to the man sitting next to the redskin. He saw the barrel of a pistol pointed at him.

"They ain't no call for you to draw a goddamn gun on me, mister."

"We'll get all this straightened out soon enough. Let her down."

Waddy worked his arm round back and nudged Gerthe to get off the rump of his horse. She continued to hold on tight to him. The ground looked as if it was a mile down when she looked at it. She thought if she got off the horse, she'd fall to her death.

"See, she don't even want to let go of me," Waddy said.

Toussaint had climbed down from the wagon and took hold of her. She was as light as a sack full of rabbits when he lifted her off the horse.

"Don't be afraid," Toussaint said. She looked at him with those startled scarecrow eyes. Clean her up and feed her enough to put some meat on her ribs and she might actually be pretty.

"What happened to you? How'd you come by all those scratches and marks on you, the grass and sticks in your hair?"

She did not speak.

"I think she might be in shock," Jake said, climbing down from the wagon, the canteen in one hand the Schofield in the other.

I'm gonna kill these interfering sons a bitches, Waddy told himself.

"Stretch her out on the grass," Jake said to Toussaint. "Here, pour some water on her face, shade her with my hat."

Toussaint did as directed, wondering how Jake knew so much about the girl's obviously unwell condition. Gerthe did not resist.

Jake looked closer.

"Those are bite marks on her," he said.

"Well I sure as hell dint put them there!" Waddy said. "I ain't no people eater."

Toussaint looked around, said, "I don't see no one else on these grasslands, boy."

Waddy felt panicky the way the two men were looking at him. If they thought he raped that girl, they'd hang him. He often thought about being hanged when he was running and robbing with old Frank Moore. He'd even once seen a horse thief hanged, had watched how the man kicked his legs and the sounds he made as the rope was strangling him. He saw how the man wet his britches. He sure didn't feature being hanged and pissing his pants in the doing. He suddenly put spurs to his mount.

"Shoot him," Toussaint said to Jake.

"No. He's just a damn kid."

Toussaint looked around on the ground, found a fair-sized stone, wheeled and flung it with the furious quickness of a snake strike. The stone struck the boy true and knocked him out of the saddle. He lay unmoving in the grass.

Jake looked at Toussaint.

"Can't just let him go around the country abusing young girls," Toussaint said.

"By the looks of him, he won't be abusing anyone forever."

"No, he's just knocked cold. A human skull isn't thin and fragile as a rabbit's. Rabbits got skulls like egg shells. It doesn't take much, but with humans I find you have to hit them pretty good to kill them."

The girl suddenly sat up and screamed: "Dex!"

"Oh shit," Toussaint said.

11

ELIAS POKE had spent the day in prayer, had felt as though boils were about to break out all over his body. Sin, he told himself. This is what sin feels like when it gets on you—like a rash, like a real bad rash. He hadn't had a drop of liquor to drink in nearly a year and a half, but ever since Birdy Pride had snuck off in the early morning hours, he had a great craving for something to drink.

I've fallen off the righteous trail and into the briars of sin and now my skin is itching terrible and my thirst for whiskey has come back on me ferocious. And the next thing I know, I'll be gambling and whoring like in the old times and I won't be worth a shit as a man.

He'd been fighting such bad feelings for hours now and he knew that all it would take would be a single sip of liquor and he'd be finished as a teetotaler—and once done, hell and damnation would be waiting for him.

He went not to the Rosebud for a drink, but instead to see Doc Willis. Doc was an intelligent kindly man who might somehow be able to help him, perhaps prescribe some sort of cure, an elixir that might take away his craving for whiskey and satisfy his thirst. For the Lord didn't seem to be in a listening mood that day—and maybe it was because the Lord had seen what he and Birdy had been about the night before and was more than a little unhappy and disappointed in one Elias Poke.

Doc was sitting on the shaded side of his east porch— the side that faced the main street of town, his feet in a pan of cold water, one empty liquor bottle floating in the water like a small glass boat, and another bottle not yet empty clutched in his hand, when Elias made his appearance. Doc had also tied a large bandanna around his head and looked somewhat like a washer-woman sitting there resting.

"Doc, I need help."

Doc looked at him through bleary eyes. At first Doc thought it was Smiley Rivers, for the two men were somewhat similar in appearance, and it startled Doc when Elias spoke to him and startled him from his reverie. And when he first looked at Elias he saw he had both his hands and he was alive and walking around and it took Doc's breath away seeing Smiley still alive and not dead with that frozen look of a question on his stony face. Then Doc realized who it really was. It wasn't Smiley Rivers at all, but that preacher, Poke, the shaman, the spiritualist, the seer. Doc would have no truck with the spirit world or those who would lead others to believe in such fantastic things as dead men risen and virgin births and cities with gold streets. Science was the only thing Doc believed in and he wasn't sure he believed even in *it*.

"Did you hurt yourself?" Doc said. "You look all right to me."

"No, I ain't hurt, Doc, at least in no visible way."

Doc felt as if he were floating over the grasslands, he felt like one of those air balloons he'd seen the Union Army use at Gettysburg. He liked the feeling. A lot.

"Office is closed," he said firmly. "No patients today. Come back tomorrow."

"I need something to cure me," Poke said.

"Cure you of what?"

"I don't know of what, that's the whole reason I'm here."

Doc felt the earth tugging at him. He did not want to descend.

"Go on, leave me alone, you damn false prophet!"

"You might be right about that," Poke said. "I won't argue the fact. I ain't sure any more of what I believe or don't believe."

"Well, an honest man. Have a damn drink."

Poke looked at the bottle, saw the label, and knew it was top-notch liquor Doc drank. The amber liquid sloshed around inside like temptation with a thousand loose tongues calling to him, trying to urge him to come and set them free, and himself in the doing. It felt, too, as though the devil were sitting on both shoulders, no angel anywhere to be found to help him fight the temptation. But he was resolved not to give in just yet.

"No! I can't," he said.

Doc blinked.

"What's ailing you, young man, truly?"

Poke tried explaining it while Doc worked at finishing off what was still in the bottle. Poke spoke of feeling as if his skin was afire and how his thoughts were twisted and sharp as barbed wire and that he needed something, an elixir maybe, to get him through the worst of his condition until he could figure things out.

"I feel like I'm going crazy, Doc."

Doc said, "Let me look into your eyes."

Poke leaned in close, his eyes wide and bulging.

"Just as I thought," Doc said after a few seconds. "What you got wrong with you is female trouble."

Poke's gaze dropped away, for he felt ashamed that his sin could be so easily detected.

"What you got for female troubles, Doc?"

Doc had been thinking of his Iris when Poke had arrived unbidden on his porch. Doc had his own female troubles, only his were gone now and probably forever from his life with Iris living somewhere—probably in San Francisco in an apartment with the foreign headmaster—that fey little bastard who came one day in a yellow checked suit and stole her away. His anger rose every time he thought about it. For such cruelty against him was undeserved. He had spent nearly all his life in the service of others, and what good had it done him? What was his reward for delivering babies and sewing up gashes and telling folks bad news like they had cancer that would kill them and trying to be of some moral support, but to be abandoned in his love. To him, the whole world felt yellow and cheap and venal.

Now this man who was supposed to be the rock upon which others rested their souls and sought nurture for their faith, this shepherd of God's flock, was here whimpering about his personal failures and seeking his own salvation. Doc Willis could hardly stomach the man.

Fix me, Doc, fix me, he wanted to mock in the man's face.

Instead he said, "I might have just the thing. Wait out here while I go inside and get something."

Elias Poke felt an enormous relief to realize that, indeed, he might yet be saved from himself. That he might yet find salvation.

And as he sat there waiting for Doc to return, the vision of Birdy Pride naked upon the altar, the memory of her supple flesh against his, her sighs and whispers, buzzed around the edges of his consciousness like a worrisome fly around a hot apple pie. He tried hard to push all thoughts of her away, just as he might swat at a fly, but with just as little success.

"Doc!" he called. "Hurry up!"

For he thought he saw Jesus walking down the street, coming in his direction, looking angry and put out.

* * *

Roy Bean had set forth a plan. He went to pay a visit to all the regular businesses in Sweet Sorrow to try and up the taxation on them for a town marshal, starting with Peg Leg Watts, owner of the Rosebud. A regular set price instead of a percentage of profits from only the liquor and whores. He wanted to establish legitimacy of some order, not another shakedown as Bob Olive and Teacup Smith had done. He explained his plan to Peg Leg.

"Who you figure is stupid enough to take the job?" Peg Leg asked.

"Well, if we can raise enough money, we won't have to hire anybody stupid or corrupt, the way I see it," Roy Bean said. "We can hire us a good man who won't abuse the privilege or be so cowardly as to run away from the first yahoo who challenges him to a fight."

"I could go maybe fifty a month toward it if you can get others to chip in."

"Fifty is a generous start," Roy Bean said, pleased that his plan to bring law and order to the town, with himself appointed as its judge, seemed to immediately sprout wings. "Of course we'd need to pay for a judge, too. Can't have a town marshal arresting people without trying them for their crimes."

"And that'd be you, I suppose?"

"Yes sir, yes sir. I'm the only fellow in town owns a law book and I've read most of it. Fact is, we might as well hold elections while we're at it. I intend to run for mayor as well."

"Well, I suppose it's time we began to get a little civilized around here. Count me in."

"Let's have a drink on it."

Afterward, even though it was a godawful hot day to be doing much, Roy Bean walked over to Otis Dollar's mercantile and got a commitment for twenty dollars a month from him. And so it went until he'd hit every establishment in town except for Skinny Dick's Pleasure Palace, which was hardly more than a tent with board walls around it. The place contained two rooms divided by an old ratty quilt where on one side a man could buy a ten-cent glass of snakehead whiskey, and on the other side fornicate with a whore named Mistress Sheba, who, when not so engaged in activities of the flesh, entertained the customers with song. Mistress Sheba was Hungarian and featured herself as something of a chanteuse. And when she sang, it sounded like crows being chased by a bobcat. But the local gents who found Skinny Dick's to their liking, men whom Peg Leg Watts would have deemed as low types, did not seem to mind Mistress Sheba's off-key melodies, and quite often became maudlin upon hearing them.

Nonetheless, Roy Bean figured to squeeze every last dime he could to finance his operation, and thus announce to the citizenry no more taxes, which he was sure would win him election as town mayor.

It being midmorning and with nary a soul in the place except Mistress Sheba and Skinny Dick himself playing gin-rummy for matchsticks, Roy Bean did not have to concern himself with hearing either Mistress Sheba's fake cries of ecstasy, or her terrible rendition of "Beautiful Dreamer," for which he was much grateful.

"Well, look what the dogs dragged in," Skinny Dick said glancing up from his hand of cards.

Mistress Sheba raised her jowly face as well; she was farsighted and had to keep her face inches away from the cards to read them, but could spot a randy cowboy riding in off the grasslands at up to a mile distance. Skinny Dick liked to compliment her by saying how she'd have made a class-A sniper during the War between the States—something he had been for a time until shot out of a tree by a Mississippi lad of fourteen with a squirrel rifle and thus causing him to abandon both the Union Army and the war altogether.

Roy didn't bother taking off his sombrero, for he saw no real lady or gentleman in the form of Mistress Sheba and Skinny Dick.

"You slumming?" Skinny Dick said, for he'd only once before seen Roy Bean in his establishment—the first evening of his arrival in Sweet Sorrow, looking for all the world lost and thirsty. "Or, are you horny as a woodpecker and come to call on Mistress Sheba, the best soiled dove in all the county?"

Roy Bean looked first at him, then at Mistress Sheba. He privately considered how bad off, drunk or otherwise, he'd have to become before even considering lying in a bed with her—and, for money! He could not conceive of such a time during his natural life. Still, he felt a bit sorry for her, being foreign and having but one natural talent. The grasslands were a hard country for anyone much less a gal of Mistress Sheba's limited means.

Roy Bean laid out his scheme over a dirty glass full of beer warm and yellow as dog piss.

"Law? Judges? Why this burg is just a crossroads to the some place other," Skinny Dick complained. "What we need with law and judges for? Next thing you'll want is to build another church and run off all the whores. I seen it happen in Kansas and Nebraska and even some parts of Colorado. No sir!"

"I never heard you complaining about the law when Bob Olive and Teacup Smith was running things," Roy Bean said. He noticed how closely Mistress Sheba was looking at him.

" 'Cause I didn't have to pay them nothing is why, except for free drinks now and then and a turn with the Mistress here."

"And you see what sort of law they turned out to be. I'm talking about true law. You going to chip in or should the law when it does get here ignore your future troubles?"

"I don't expect no future troubles," Skinny Dick said, pointing at a Whitney double-barrel shotgun propped in the corner like a snake ready to kill something.

"Oh, I could see a time when all sorts of trouble might befall a fellow like you," Roy Bean said coolly from there under the wide shade of his sombrero, his eyes glittering like pieces of fool's gold. "Troubles like you getting robbed, or some murderous ranchers and cowboys getting into it here in your establishment and nobody to take them in tow, or maybe this eyesore of a shebang getting burnt to the ground by some firebug—things like that."

Roy Bean could see Skinny Dick rolling such possible calamities around in his mind and thought it was probably about like rolling a marble around in a tin can.

"Five dollars a month is all I could see my way clear to—business ain't been good lately, what with this heat. Seems none of these local fellows want to fornicate in such heat and ain't been no strangers coming in except that shot man the Frenchy hauled in here a couple weeks back."

"Make it fifteen and I'm sure you won't have to worry about no firebugs," Roy said, stretching forth his palm.

When Dick went to get the money Mistress Sheba said to Roy Bean, "It's half off today."

"What's half off?"

"This, sugar," she said, cupping her bosoms. They were the size of muskmelons.

"No thanks," Roy said. "I ain't that drunk or lonesome."

She gave him a sour look. He didn't care. Her offer only made him more desirous for the company of Birdy Pride. And beyond his desire for Birdy lay his desire for his wife and children like a mirage wavering in desert heat. For Texas was a long way off and Birdy was right here in Sweet Sorrow. Somewhere.

*   *   *

Bob Olive made Teacup hitch his horse to a fine little cabriolet that belonged to the now deceased pimp. It had nice new wheels and silver trim to go along with the horsehide seat.

"Why you look just like a politician, Bob," Teacup said once he'd hitched up Bob's horse.

"Politician, huh. Well, let's go do some politicking and cancel a few votes against me."

Teacup mounted his own horse and rode alongside the buggy.

"I'm glad to be shed of this town, ain't you?"

"I'll be more glad when we get our business finished and I'm back in my own bed," Bob said. "I feel like somebody's tossed me down a damn well and threw rocks down atop me. Remind me never again to go to sleep on a billiard table."

"I will, Bob."

"Oh, shut the hell up."

"Well, if you're going to be that way, I'll just ride on ahead so's not to disturb you further."

"Fine by me."

And so they rode off toward Sweet Sorrow, joyless in the doing.

12

ONCE THEY HAD the boy tossed in the back of the wagon and the girl, Gerthe, seated between them, Toussaint turned the wagon back around toward where the boy had come from. Gerthe remained silent as stone.

Jake said, "We going someplace in particular?"

"He didn't just find this child wandering around in the grass," Toussaint said. "She's the apple of Dex's eye. She wouldn't be out here alone. I'm guessing Dex was with her."

Sun blazed in their faces and they had to lower their hats to keep it out of their eyes. The girl sat with her head down, her eyes closed, the sun golden on her pale skin. She hardly seemed to breathe.

"Can I ask you something?"

"Sure."

"Is Dex your boy?"

Toussaint kept his gaze straight ahead on a line directly between his mule's ears.

"I'm not sure. Karen never said and I never asked."

"I guess the way folks do things out here is different than the way they do them in other places," Jake said.

"Faute de mieux."

Jake shrugged, he knew too little French to understand.

"Means, for lack of something better," Toussaint said.

They found the boy's body just off the trail. Toussaint sensed rather than saw it, the way he could sense a dreaming rabbit before he saw it. He turned his gaze just enough to see the grass pressed down. Halted the mule and got down slow. Jake said to the girl, "Don't run off" as though she might, but she never so much as lifted her head. Jake hopped down too and followed Toussaint to the body.

He saw the way Toussaint looked at the boy: a pained expression etched his face as though he'd been struck by something small and sharp. Toussaint's jaw muscle twitched and he didn't go any closer to the boy for the longest moment, then slowly advanced, walking careful so as not to step on the grass where blood had dried, or anyplace where part of the boy's skull had been scattered by the big-bore pistol.

"There's a tarp in under the seat of the wagon," he said, without asking Jake to get it. Jake went and retrieved it and came back to where Toussaint now knelt in a clean unstained place next to Dex who was lying as though asleep, one arm flung out to his side, his boots crossed at the ankles.

Jake could see how terrible the wound was, had seen such wounds before. It reminded him of the death of the man he was accused of murdering—his lover's husband. He cut his gaze away, then slowly back again. The left side of the boy's face was exposed: smooth and nearly hairless except for silky soft whorls of black hair thin as thread along the cheek and some over the lip.

Toussaint stretched forth a hand and touched that face gently, his fingertips barely brushing the flesh, extended forth to close the eyelids, which were partially open.

"I need some time alone," he said, and Jake handed him the tarp.

"I'll be over by the wagon. Call me when you need me to help you," Jake said.

Jake stood by the wagon looking up at the girl—so wan and youthful yet so sad in every aspect. His gaze shifted to the boy lying in the back of the wagon— even younger than the dead boy, a knot swollen to the size and color of a plum just above the ear where Toussaint had struck him with the rock. Perhaps Toussaint had damaged him in a way he'd never be normal again. He looked down at the pistols they'd taken off him and placed beside his hat. Jake reached down and took each one and checked its loads and saw one shell had been spent. He ejected the remaining shells then placed the pistols up under the seat just near the girl's feet.

He looked again at her and said, "Did he shoot Dex?"

She did not answer, did not look up, but Jake could see the truth in the way she shifted her body, could see the sunlight bleeding through the thin dress so that it showed the outline of her lithe body. The wind felt hot on his skin as it brushed his face and skipped suddenly through the grass.

He didn't know how long he'd stood there before Toussaint came carrying the boy wrapped in the tarp. Jake lowered the tailgate of the wagon and helped Toussaint put the dead boy in next to the living one— murderer and victim—as they once were in life, they now, at least one of them—were in death.

Toussaint's hands were bloody and there were bloodstains on his shirt and on the tarp.

"You want me to drive the wagon?"

"No," Toussaint said. "I need to take him home to his mother."

"I could wait here until you've done what you need to do."

"No. It will be all right."

Karen Sunflower had been listening to the wind sweep the dry grass—like a broom across wood planks. Anxious was she for Dex to return, for them to go find the missing horses. Times were poor, the cupboards nearly bare with but a few cans of beans, peaches, potted meat. They'd rounded up a good herd—nearly twenty horses that ran wild, or had once been saddle broke but unbranded and loose again, had returned to their wild nature. Mares, colts, and two stallions. She hated like goddamn hell to have lost them. Rounding up wild horses wasn't the easiest work there ever was.

"Where'd you get off to, you little peckerwood," she said aloud, for it was her custom to talk to herself when no one was about. Toussaint used to say to her, "Woman, they put people in the crazy house down in Bismarck for talking to themselves and they'll surely put you there too someday if you keep it up."

Of course Toussaint would walk ten miles out of his way just to irritate her. She never could figure out what it was about him she saw that made her agree to marry him in the first place. Except, he was an unusual man in many ways, the least of which was that he was smarter than most men and she admired brains in a man as much as she did a horse with fire in its eyes. She liked, too, that he was of a dark mixed blood and not one thing or another—not a goddamn Swede or Italian or German like so many who'd come to settle the grasslands. His mixed blood and his intelligence made him interesting. Well, at least in the beginning.

And it was true that for a time they'd gotten along well enough together.

Almost dreamily she'd catch herself sometimes thinking about those rainy afternoons when Toussaint found any excuse he could for them to get in the bed together and make love; she always put up a fuss as though she had better things to do, but never too much of a fuss to dissuade him. Afterward they would listen to the thunder and rain falling on the roof. He wasn't lazy, just that he took every opportunity to get romantic with her and find ways around tedious labor. And though she never admitted it openly, she adored him for such unbidden desires and his far-flung dreams. He was as wild and untamable as a wild horse; you could get him used to the saddle, but not much.

Still, when they weren't lazing about on rainy afternoons, which came all too infrequent it seemed with each passing year they were married, she and Toussaint rarely saw eye to eye on anything.

"I have nothing against horses that would make me want to go chase them," he said the first time she told him her idea of how to make extra money.

"We can sell them; there are always folks wanting a good horse. It's a living."

"You catch them, somebody has to get on their back and break them. I don't like riding even a broke horse much less one that's not broke."

Toussaint had no particular skills upon which to make a living—even if there was a living to be made in a place like Sweet Sorrow other than gambling, whiskey peddling, or whoring. The only other way to make money was to own something—a barbershop or mercantile or livery—all of which were already owned, even if Toussaint had been the type of man to work indoors, which he wasn't.

The man would as soon exist on rabbits he knocked down with stones or fish he caught from Cooper's Creek, or wild berries and roots, as he would go to work for another man. And being of an independent mind herself, Karen took up the profession of horse catcher and horse breaker, and when Dex was old enough, she took him with her. The boy had a gentle nature and horses seemed to understand him as much as he did them. Dex was the defining moment of their relationship. It still struck her as odd that when she began to show, Toussaint never asked her if it was his child. In fact he never said anything at all about it. And by the time Dex was born, Toussaint had gone off to live by himself in a lodge he'd built on the edge of town. She thought at first he'd gone his own way because he *did* suspect her of infidelity. And, it wasn't all that hard to see why he'd think that: Otis Dollar had come around often that long hard winter when Toussaint had gone off to see some of his people on the French side who lived in New Orleans. And of course a place as small and intimate as Sweet Sorrow held few secrets, and surely Toussaint heard about the visits and saw the stocked cupboards upon his return in the spring.

"Well, what did you expect me to do for food when you left out of here and didn't leave a nickel behind?" she said angrily upon his questioning glances. She wanted him to be jealous.

"Sounds like Otis got the better part of the bargain," Toussaint said counting the cans of beans, knowing as she did he was toting the cost at a dime a can in his head. "There can't be more than ten, twelve dollars worth of goods in these cupboards."

She threw a pot at him and he went out and packed a few things and left and that was that. She had Dex that spring and only once or twice did Toussaint come around on the pretense of needing a tool or whatnot he'd left in the shed. But she saw him looking toward the cradle out in the yard where she kept Dex while gardening, and once when she'd gone inside the house for something, she looked out the window and saw Toussaint standing over the child looking at him with that same soft look that he once got on those rainy afternoons after they'd made love.

Often, like now, she found herself thinking about it all again, wondering how things had got so wrong between them; telling herself she simply wasn't the type to be married to any man, just as Toussaint wasn't the type to be married to any woman.

She rolled herself a cigarette and looked at the burnished unrelenting sky that held no promise of rain to it. God, what she'd give for one more rainy afternoon there in the house, just the two of them the way it had been before Dex came along and before things went all to hell. Well, she might just as well wish for wings, or horns, she told herself.

And as though thinking about it so strongly was a force unto itself, she looked up and saw Toussaint's old mule and the wagon with three people sitting on the seat way off in the distance.

Well, thank God. He's bringing Dex home. She figured maybe it was time she had a talk with the boy and told him the truth about who his father really was; for even a somewhat soft-brained boy understood the shame of the rumors that still got whispered about whenever the two of them went into town and bought supplies at the mercantile. She was relieved

Dex was all right, though she'd show him a little anger for worrying her half to death before she'd show him kindness.

Roy Bean had gotten total commitments for two hundred and forty dollars a month to pay for a city marshal and a judge's wages. He sat inside the Rosebud drinking an iced beer and trying to tally which way to divide it up. The late day sun slanted through the front doors sharp and bright as a pair of knife blades that cut through the shadows. He figured half and half ought to be about right.

He was feeling very positive about the future and decided to write a letter to his wife, knowing that one of the neighbors—old Esparsa or, Harlan Doolittle, would translate it from English into Spanish for her—which was a sight more considerate than what she'd been by sending him a letter in Spanish nobody could translate—and tell her he'd be a while yet in Dakota Territory before returning to Texas. Oh yes, and to kiss the children for him and tell them not to forget their daddy. He'd place forty dollars in the letter as well, for food and geegaws for the kids.

He wrote the letter and folded the money inside and put the works in his pocket and ordered another iced beer. A mongrel dog had come and stood in the doorway where the light caused its fur to look ablaze. The cur whined and Roy called to it and watched as it cautiously came inside where Roy set his glass down and said, "You look like you could use a drink, try some of that."

The dog lapped up the beer and looked up at him with imploring eyes that made Roy think of how sometimes Birdy Pride would look at him when she wanted something real bad—like for him to marry her, or a silver brooch.

"Goddamn, I know it is hot," Roy said to the cur after it lapped up the last of the beer in the glass. "But I ain't one to get in the habit of buying beer for dogs, so you'll just have to find you someone else who is. *Adios*!"

Roy stood and walked out into the golden dusk that had begun to settle over the land even though the heat caused it to feel as if he were standing in front of an ore furnace. The dog followed him.

That's when he saw the preacher, Poke, running down the street stark naked, his body slashed in bleeding crosses.

"Son of a bitch," Roy said.

He watched the preacher run past him as though he was on fire and looking for a water tank to douse himself in. He watched the poor fellow run all the way through town and keep on running clear out of town, out onto the grasslands.

Peg Leg Watts came to the doorway and said, "What you cussing at, Judge?"

"Preacher Poke's either got the devil after him, or he's under the influence of some pretty bad whiskey."

Peg Leg stepped out onto the walk and looked in the direction Roy Bean was staring. He barely saw the butt cheeks of what had been up until that moment, the town preacher.

"Where's he going, you reckon?"

"Hell if I know."

"It ain't to church. Church is the other way."

"It sure as hell is."

"There's strangeness afoot, that's for damn sure."

"And Poke's afoot, too."

"You ought not make fun of a naked frightened man."

"Just an observation," Roy Bean said. "Just an observation."

13

❧❧

THE MAN WHO boarded the stage in Bismarck wore silver pistols and looked a bit like the former president, U. S. Grant—short, stocky, and with a thick dark beard. He smoked a cigar, too. Fuzzy Walls felt a bit foolish about asking the man if he *was* the former president, but he couldn't help himself.

The man simply looked at him when Fuzzy Walls asked him that question.

"You think I'd be riding this shit heap if I was the president of the country?" the man said, referring to the Dunhill Morgan stage. "Why those horses don't look strong enough to pull the hat off a man's head and that whole rig looks like it would shake your brains out."

Fuzzy Walls felt the burn of embarrassment in his cheeks.

"Well, I didn't really expect you as being him," he said apologetically, "but you sure look enough like him to be his twin."

"When is this shit wagon getting to where it's going?" The man pulled a pocket watch from his waistcoat and snapped it opened.

"We'll be in Sweet Sorrow sometime tomorrow morning if we don't break a wheel or one of the horses throws a shoe."

The man looked as though he'd just been told he had leprosy.

"Well, there isn't any other way I'm going to get there short of sprouting wings and flying," he said and climbed on board. "Let's get this circus on the road."

Inside the coach was a Chinaman, a woman who looked as if she had a pillow stuffed down the bodice of her dress, and two cross-eyed kids who tugged at her skirts.

The man squeezed in between one of the children and the Chinaman. The woman and the kids stared at him. He stared back.

The detective business often took him to far-flung settlements that required long and arduous travel and naught but poor accommodations awaiting him: hotels with leaky roofs, bedbugs, bad food and worse whiskey, ugly women, and men who'd kill you for a dollar or less if they thought you had a dollar or less in your pocket.

It was the sort of business that required a certain toughness, and if you weren't tough you had better find a different line of work—ranch house cook, hardware clerk, something along those lines. Prince Puckett was not only tough, he had a natural talent for being a manhunter. And in spite of the hardships, he enjoyed his work—especially the payoff.

Once rolling, he found his rhythm with the sway of the coach and settled in, he took from his pocket a flask and a small tin that had a painting of a naked woman on its lid. He admired the tin, had purchased it in San Francisco from a seafarer. The tin contained cocaine pills. He took two and washed them down with some of the contents of the flask. Soon he began to feel less edgy and the kids' yammering ceased to bother him quite so much that he no longer considered shooting them and pitching them out the window.

The Chinaman seemed to be asleep. You never knew what a Chinaman might be thinking, or if this one was really asleep or planning to murder you by slicing your throat at the first opportunity. But all in all, Chinamen were okay people in Prince Puckett's book. They were good purveyors of the dope trade and when it came to whores, Prince Puckett preferred Celestials over any other sort of whore. They had a certain graceful way about them and were clean as pins. They were artful in the ways of pleasuring a man as was no other sort of woman he'd ever paid cash money for.

"You a married man?" the woman across from him asked of a sudden.

Prince Puckett looked at her.

"What?"

"I was wondering if you're married?" she said.

He looked at those cross-eyed kids, one whose head lay in her lap, the other staring out the window of the coach yammering about when was he going to ". . . see some 'Injins'?"

"I don't believe we've met," Prince Puckett said sarcastically.

"I'm Sophie Merriweather," she said. "Widow and mother."

"Oh," Prince said and turned his gaze toward the opposite window of the one the child was looking out, hoping upon hope he might see a few *Injins* himself—something to shoot at and divert the unwanted conversation.

Sophie waited for him to answer whether or not he was married.

"No," he said finally, when he saw out of the corner of his eye she was still staring at him. "My occupation does not allow for much time to be married."

"Oh," she said. "And what is it you do?"

He reluctantly turned his gaze back on her. She was nearly as big as an ox and looked as if she probably had spit out those kids like a man in a melon-eating contest would as easily spit out seeds.

"I'm a ferrier," he said simply because it was none of her goddamn business what he did.

"Ferrier," she said. "I see."

He knew she had no idea what the word meant. Just as well. The less conversation the better.

"Well, isn't that interesting," she said, "being a ferrier." She reminded him of a watch wound too tight—wouldn't run down.

He took two more pills and another hit off the flask, the last few drops, in fact.

"Are those something you take for an ailment?" she said of the pills.

She was a sure enough nosy old brute.

"Liver," he said. "Keeps my liver from turning over on me."

"Oh," she said.

The child who'd been staring out the window grew tired of the nothingness and twisted around whining about not seeing any *Injins*. The woman told him to put his head down and rest—". . . like your brother, Herman."

The first leg of the trip brought them to a small outpost for a change of horses—hardly more than dugout, a corral, and a well. Fuzzy Walls told them to get down and stretch their legs.

Prince Puckett was more than eager to walk off by himself where he found a bench on the shady side of the dugout. He lit a cigar and puffed on it. But soon enough Sophie Merriweather found him and sat next to him on the bench. She smelled of sweat and rosewater, a smell something like a bad cocktail, he thought. He could hear her children off on the other side raising hell, probably worrying the horses with sticks or something.

"My, but it is terribly hot," she said, fanning herself with one pudgy hand.

"What is it you want, lady?"

"Why, whatever do you mean?"

"Hell, you're sniffing round me like a dog in heat, only generally it's the male in heat and not the bitch."

Her thick neck turned scarlet. He didn't care.

Then she began to sniffle. He didn't feel one bit bad.

"I was just trying to be friendly," she said.

"Well, I ain't the friendly type," he said. "And if that offends you, so be it."

She shut up and he was glad of it. He smoked his cigar and thought of what lay ahead of him—to find a man and kill him. Fifteen hundred dollars was riding on it. The man he meant to kill was a fugitive from the law, but Prince Puckett wasn't in the law business; he was in the people-hunting business and it didn't matter what the rules were as long as they were *his* rules. "Wanted, dead or alive, but preferably dead," is what the man who hired him back in Denver had to say. And as long as the man was paying, the man would get his wish. "Cut off his hands and bring them to me," the man had further requested. Prince Puckett never questioned a request, even one so odd, as long as the pay was in gold; he didn't trust paper money.

"I must be honest with you," the woman said after a long few moments of peaceful silence.

He did not inquire as to what she needed to be honest about. He did not care.

"My children and I are penniless. I spent the last bit of money we had for the stage tickets. I think my husband is hiding out in that settlement Sweet Sorrow. I received a letter from him this spring telling me he was there working in a saloon and that he would be home in a month or two. But he ain't come yet and I ain't heard no more from him. I aim to find him and make him take care of his responsibilities."

She gave a great sigh, then said, "But he could also be as dead as a stone since I've not heard anything more from him. His name is Harold, but most just call him Curly. I've not a single dime left to feed us or to pay for our shelter."

"What does any of this have to do with me?" he said.

"I am a Christian woman. I just want you to know that."

He started to stand up but she grabbed his sleeve and tugged him back down again.

"But, I must do whatever it takes to feed me and those youngsters . . . so I'm offering myself to you. There," she said, pointing off to a thicket. "We could go there and you could have your way with me for just a few dollars—just enough to feed us and for me to rent a room once we arrive in Sweet Sorrow . . ."

He looked at her as though she was daft, and maybe she was for all he knew.

"Lady, I wouldn't go in that thicket with you even if you was to *pay* me!"

Her moon face crumbled. Tears cut streaks through the cake of powder and dust on her cheeks.

"If it were just me," she sobbed, "I'd starve before doing such a thing. But those poor little kids shouldn't have to suffer. We don't even have to go as far as the thicket, I'll pleasure you right here . . ." She started to reach for him but he slapped her hand away.

"Oh, Jesus Christ!" he said reaching into his

pocket and pulling out two dollars and shoving it into her hand.

"I'll pay you just to leave me alone for the rest of the trip."

She was still sobbing when he went out to the privy beyond the corrals and made water, but had stopped her tears by the time they were told to get aboard the stage again. The coach sank down on one side when Fuzzy Walls gave her a hand up. The Chinaman still slept. The kids started their yammering again.

Prince Puckett thought one possible solution might be if he put a bullet into his own brain.

Karen Sunflower saw the look on Toussaint's face and knew something dark and tragic had transpired.

"Where's Dex?" she said with a trembling voice.

He handed the reins over to Jake, stepped down and stood between her and the wagon.

"He's gone, Karen. Dex is gone."

"You mean you can't find him?"

"No, I found him, he's in the wagon."

Next he knew he was holding her back from the child he did not know was his or not, but certainly hers.

"No!" she said. "No! Let me go, goddamn you!"

"You don't want to see him like he is . . ."

But she fought him like a she cat and he let her go. And when she saw the strange boy lying next to a bloody tarp she was sure Toussaint was mistaken, had thought up some evil joke to pull on her, but she couldn't understand why he would do a thing like that.

She turned back in rage to face Toussaint, then realized Dex was wrapped in the tarp, some of which had fallen away from his rough old boots—boots she now recognized, the same ones she'd saved for and gotten him the previous Christmas because Otis Dollar had, out of long kindness and love for her, discounted them down to where she could afford them.

"Oh, Dex," she said. "Oh, Dex . . ." and fell to her knees, her hands grasping his boots. It took Toussaint and Jake together to get her into the house and keep her there. Toussaint found the bottle of rye whiskey in the cupboard next to the cans of beans and peaches and potted meats—the ones Karen had bought at Otis's store, or the ones he'd given her on a line of credit he never aimed on collecting—and he poured Karen a cup of whiskey and told her to drink it, and when she did, he poured her another, and kept pouring until the bottle was empty and Karen was so drunk she could barely hold her head up. Then Toussaint and Jake went out and got the girl and brought her into the house and set her on Dex's bed where she stayed without trying to move—like some brain-soft child.

Jake went back to the wagon and checked on the rock-struck boy. He was still out. It was quite possible he was in a coma. It was also possible he might not wake up again. The spot where Toussaint had struck him with a rock had grown twice the size it had been; blood swelling his brain. He'd have to relieve the pressure or the boy would probably die. He went back in the house and searched through the kitchen until he found a small sharp knife, some clean towels, needle and thread, then went out and performed a small surgery, crude but effective, and drained the blood, then stitched the cut closed again.

When he turned around Toussaint was standing there, having seen everything.

"I don't know why you troubled yourself with fixing him," Toussaint said.

Jake started to say why he did it, then realized it would do no one any good for the truth to be known: that he'd taken an oath that in part read, *I will apply dietetic measures for the benefit of the sick according to my ability and judgment; I will keep them from harm and injustice.* He could not renege just because he himself had become a victim of injustice.

Jake took one of the Schofields from his waistband and handed it to Toussaint.

"You want to kill him, go ahead. But at least be humane about it."

Toussaint took the gun, cocked and pointed it into the bed of the wagon, and pulled the trigger. Then he handed it back to Jake and walked out to the shed, went inside, came out again with a shovel.

Jake looked in the back of the wagon. A bullet hole had been punched through the floor next to the boy's head. He was glad Toussaint hadn't shot the kid. He wasn't sure why he was glad, he just was, more for Toussaint's sake than for the kid's. He walked out to the shed and got a shovel, too, and followed Toussaint out to a small knoll that rose like a lump in the skin of the land and they began to dig without speaking until a grave was completed.

Elias Poke was sure the devil was chasing him. He'd gone home after his visit to Doc Willis's and taken the remedy Doc said would make him better. Not long after, bright colored lights burst in his head and the Devil showed up, said to him straightaway, "You're a goddamn son of a bitch and a fornicator, Elias Poke, and I've come to take your soul."

"My soul?"

"Price you have to pay for fornicating with Birdy Pride. We all seen it: God, me, the angels—both the good and bad ones. God's give up on you, sold me your soul for a can of beans and a parasol. Come on, let's go, I've got a good hot fire to toss you into."

"Can of beans? Parasol?"

The Devil's laughter sounded like pistol shots.

"I'll fight you tooth and nail!" Elias exclaimed.

"Come on then, let's get to fighting, you evil bastard!"

So they went at it, Elias grabbing a kitchen knife and the Devil baring his fangs. They tussled and fought all through the church, up and down the pews, on the very altar where he and Birdy had been intimate. But Elias knew he was getting licked good, could feel it every time the Devil tore into him, saw blood spilling from his flesh. That goddamn Devil was a fighting son of a bitch. Elias knew he had it coming, but finally couldn't stand anymore and ran out the door and down the street—the Devil probably right behind him—knowing that if the Devil caught him, it would spell his doom.

Birdy Pride had come around the corner just as Elias had gone into the church. She still had it in her thoughts about what a wonderful night they'd spent the evening before and had returned just as dusk was settling over the land turning it a soft hazy brown, the sun sinking like a liquid ball of red water off in the west, way out beyond Toussaint Trueblood's lodge and the hundred or so miles of grassland. She aimed to someday go where the sun set just to see where it did. She thought the sun set in the ocean. Peg Leg Watts had told her many stories about the ocean—the *sea*, he always called it—and it sounded like the best place to watch sunsets.

She was determined now to ask Elias to marry her and make an honest woman of her, for she could easily envision a world of bliss with such a man. She knew Roy Bean never would marry her. Roy Bean was never going to divorce his wife in Texas nor leave his brood of kids for her. She'd hoped upon hope that he would, but he wouldn't. And now that she'd found a new lover, one that didn't have any wife or kids that she knew of, she'd seen her chance to get out of the whoring business and become respectable. Why the preacher could preach the Word anyplace, including where the ocean was, and she would be his good and faithful wife and sip tea on Sunday afternoons with the other church ladies and attend nice functions. They'd move far away and nobody would know of her tainted past.

She was about to slip inside the church when she saw through the window the most horrible sight she could imagine: Elias Poke was inside naked, dancing around with a knife in his hand and cussing like a wrangler. And worse still, he began slicing his own skin with the knife: little bloody crosses all over his body, yelling "Take that, you old Devil, and that, and that!" The way he was going at it, she was sure he might cut off some of his more important parts. She bit her tongue to keep from screaming.

Too late, too late. Maybe it was her scream that sent Elias running out the front door, bleeding, naked, running like something or someone was chasing him, but nothing or nobody was.

Had she given him the pox and it gone to his brain the way she heard it did some men who got it?

Birdy fainted to see her new true love do such a thing. It just stole all her breath to see him thus and to think she might be the cause of his insanity.

After the burying, the lot of them sat inside Karen Sunflower's house with a single lamp center of the table they sat around: Karen, Toussaint, Jake, the girl, Gerthe.

The stone-struck boy still lying in the wagon had not awoken.

Toussaint had been feeding Karen cups of hot black coffee he cooked on the woodstove. She drank without protest, her thoughts a scramble.

Finally she said, "How did it happen?"

"That boy out in the wagon shot him, is the way it looks," Toussaint said.

Karen looked toward the door.

"Why did he shoot Dex?"

"I don't know, Karen. Could have been they fought over this child. You know how wild and willful boys can be at that age," Toussaint looked at Gerthe. "She probably knows what happened exactly, but she hasn't said a word since we found her riding on the back of that boy's horse."

Karen turned her gaze to Gerthe who sat staring into the flickering light that danced in the lamp's glass chimney. She felt both contempt and compassion for the girl.

"She's in shock," Jake said. Karen and Toussaint looked at him.

"It's just a guess, I've seen it happen . . . during the war. Something traumatic happens and puts a body into shock."

"Goddamn, but how many times did I warn him about her," Karen said. Then she looked at Toussaint hard. "Men. Goddamn every one of you for your randy and violent ways. You see now what such has led to!"

"I'm guessing she didn't have a direct hand in it," Toussaint said.

"How do you know what she did or did not have a hand in? How do you know she just didn't lead Dex on to make that other boy jealous?"

"I've never seen that boy around here anywhere

about, have you? I don't think he's from around here. I think he somehow come up on them and for whatever reason killed Dex. I don't think there was any plan to it, Karen."

Karen knew Toussaint was probably right; she had never seen the boy in the wagon anywhere around this country, either, but she didn't want him to be right. She needed someone to blame, needed answers to all her questions.

"We'll take her back to her people in the morning," Toussaint said.

"What about him?" Karen said, cutting her gaze back to the door and what lay beyond out there in the yard in the bed of Toussaint's wagon.

"We'll take him into town, put him in the jail."

"And do what with him?"

"I don't know, Karen. There's hardly any law left. But one way or the other he'll pay for what he did to Dex."

She looked at Jake.

"You patched that boy up, fixed his head. How come you couldn't patch my Dex up? How come you couldn't?"

Jake excused himself and went out and stood on the porch and looked off toward the red streaks scratched into the sky just above the horizon; the rest of the sky was the color of unpolished silver and the hot wind had abated, but still the air had not cooled.

He stepped down and went again to the wagon and saw that last bit of evening light in the boy's eyes—open now, uncertain and looking around.

"Who you?" Waddy Worth said.

"Just somebody," Jake said.

The boy tried to sit up, but his head felt heavy as an anvil and he lay it back down again.

"Something's busted my head," he said.

"Surely has."

"I don't remember nothing. Have I been brain shot?"

"No, nothing so serious."

"You got a drink of water I can have, mister?"

Jake walked over to the well near the tool shed and a storm of swallows swept out from under the roofline and through the air. It seemed like an omen of sorts, but an omen of what, he did not know. Everything remained a mystery to him still. Something odd and troubling was going on in this place.

It seemed like the worst place a man wanted by the law could find himself in. I've got to get gone from here, he told himself. I've got to get far away from here and soon.

14

BIRDY PRIDE found Doc Willis drunk on his porch, nearly swallowed up in the night shadows. She approached him with a certain caution.

"Doc," she said. "Doc."

He hardly stirred, did not lift his head off his shoulder, but snored softly.

She came closer, then touched his shoulder and shook it a little.

"Doc."

He roused, opened his eyes, and looked up at her. At first, he thought it was his Iris.

"You've come home," he said, his voice cracking with dryness and despair.

"Doc, I need your help."

"Of course, my sweet. Of course, anything. You've come home."

He took her hand and held it to his lips and kissed it repeatedly until Birdy could wrench it free.

"Doc, what's wrong with you?"

"Huh, huh?"

Then he realized that it wasn't Iris at all but the prostitute, Birdy Pride, and realizing that it wasn't Iris was a crushing disappointment, for he'd been dreaming of himself and Iris together—dreaming that he'd long searched for her and at last had found her and the joy of finding her was overwhelming.

"Go away," he said once he realized it was Birdy.

"Doc, I need your help."

"Take some tincture of mercury if you got the pox," Doc muttered, for he was sick to death of treating whores and the men who frequented them.

"Doc, I ain't got no pox. I need you to come with me to help find the preacher—he's gone mad and cut himself to shreds."

Doc Willis blinked.

"Mad?"

"I seen it, Doc. I seen it all."

"Where is he now?"

"I don't know. Last I seen he was running out of town."

Suddenly Doc's attitude toward Birdy became solicitous.

"Of course. We must go and find that poor man and see he is treated for whatever is ailing him. Go and get my bag inside—there on the table in my office."

And when Birdy returned, Doc looked into her eyes and said, "Are you feeling all right, Birdy? You don't look quite so well."

"Tell the truth, Doc, I have been sort of flummoxed here lately."

"Perhaps I should have a more thorough look at you . . ."

"No, Doc, later, maybe. Right now we must go find Preacher before he brings more harm to himself."

Doc followed Birdy off into the night. Things were becoming quite complicated.

Morning arrived on a riffling little wind that blew up out of the south and slithered through the grasses finding its way into the yet still sleeping settlement. It came up Main Street along with the early light, sniffing into every doorway, crack, and crevice like a hungry dog looking for scraps, and found its way to the bare head of Gus Boone who'd carried the night shift at the jail, sleeping as he had in a chair just outside the front door.

He wiggled in his sleep. He'd been dreaming of a seamstress he'd known back in Cincinnati—a comely young woman who had long fingers and large feet. Gus had courted her when he wasn't riding the ore boats up and down the Ohio River. Her name was Martha Peace. He liked her better than rum. They would often dance on the rooftop of the building in which she shared an apartment with two other seamstresses, and sometimes on hot nights they'd sleep up there and watch the stars.

"It's near as close to heaven as I will ever get," Martha was fond of saying in a mournful way; for she was a woman filled, it seemed, with great sadness. Even when Gus did his best to lighten her burden and tried to make her laugh, her laughter sounded sorrowful. But such sorrow only made Gus more enamored with her and he was sure that someday he would marry her, and had begun to save his rum money to buy her a gold wedding band—one they'd seen in a jeweler's shop. But tragedy struck before Gus could buy the ring; it was as though Martha's penchant for sorrow finally became a prophecy realized. She and her roommates were trapped by a raging fire on the upper floors of the old warehouse where they worked. They were forced to jump to their deaths. It broke Gus's heart to learn the news and he went on a month-long drunk with his "ring" money.

Still, Gus dreamed of her at least once a week. Dreamed that she was alive and happy and that they still danced on the rooftop now and again, and when he awakened he would always feel a deep melancholy, as he did now when the wind touched his hair and the sun his face.

He opened his eyes and rubbed away the bit of slobber from the side of his mouth as he adjusted to the reality that Martha wasn't there.

"Hidey, Gus," Brewster Hatfield said as he came up the street carrying a breakfast tray for the prisoner, Smiley Rivers.

"Hidy," Gus said.

"How's our lad this morning?"

"I just woke up, haven't been inside yet to check."

"Well, maybe we oughter since we're getting paid to watch him."

"I guess," Gus said.

Smiley Rivers was still asleep on his cot in the same position as they'd seen him last, hadn't moved so much as a twitch.

"Wake up," Brewster called. "Your breakfast is here."

But Smiley did not move.

"You know what?" Gus said after several seconds.

"What?"

"I think old Smiley might be dead."

Brewster stepped closer to the bars.

"Smell that?" Gus said.

"Uh-huh."

"That's death."

"Uh-huh."

They unlocked the cell door and stepped inside and Gus said, "Touch him, see if he moves."

Soon as Brewster touched Smiley he knew Smiley was no longer one of the living among Sweet Sorrow's citizens. Smiley was stiff as a starched shirt.

"He's gone. I reckon he just didn't have it in him to keep on living knowing what he'd done."

"Now what?"

Brewster shrugged. "I reckon nothing we can do but go get Tall John to come and take him. Shame, though, to just let that breakfast go to waste. You et yet?"

"No, you?"

"Un-uh."

"You want to go get Tall John first?"

"I reckon we oughter."

"Think they'll pay us for today?"

"I reckon I wouldn't pay no one to watch a dead man, would you?"

"I reckon not."

"We could say he was alive last night and just died this morning."

"We could, I reckon."

"Sure seems to be a lot of folks dying lately."

"I know it."

"You going to get Tall John?"

"Thought I might eat this before it gets cold. You reckon that's okay?"

Brewster looked at the corpse of Smiley Rivers.

"I don't guess it makes no difference to him."

They went outside where the air was better to eat.

Fuzzy Walls saw something up ahead of the stage—antelope he thought; big one. He handed the reins to his shotgun man, Sam Toe, and reached down under the driver's seat for his rolling block Sharps Big Fifty—a gun he'd used for a time on the Kansas plains to hunt buffalo, and before that, in the war, where he was a sniper with Brady's Independent Company Sharpshooters. He never kept count of how many rebel soldiers he shot in comparison to how many buffalo he shot, but if he had to guess, he would have guessed he'd shot more buffalo than men.

He told Sam Toe to halt the wagon and Sam Toe drew back on the reins of the team and pressed his boot down hard on the brake to bring the wagon to a skidding halt, raising a cloud of dust so thick it took several seconds for the air to clear enough for him to locate the critter running out across the grass-lands.

Sam Toe watched with interest.

From inside the coach they could hear swearing.

"What the goddamn son of a bitching hell are we stopping for?"

It was that fellow with the silver pistols, for Fuzzy knew the Chinaman hadn't yet so much as made a peep the whole trip. And it sure wasn't the woman nor those two brats of hers cursing.

The coach door swung open and Prince Puckett leapt down smacking dust from his coat and slapping his hat against his thigh and looking as if he wanted to kill somebody. He glared up at Fuzzy.

"Are you crazy, stopping out here in the middle of no-goddamn-where!"

"I aim to shoot that antelope yonder," Fuzzy said.

Prince Puckett turned in the direction the driver was pointing.

He didn't see an antelope; what he saw was a naked man running through the grass.

"Antelope! Why that ain't no goddamn antelope! That's a nekked man!"

"Huh?"

Fuzzy looked. His eyes had failed him a great deal since his sharpshooting and snipering days. A doctor in Bismarck told him he ought to consider wearing spectacles. But Fuzzy's pride was too great to consider wearing eyeglasses. He was a bachelor still, and kept hopes that someday he'd meet the right woman and get married and settle down and have a brood of kids.

A man with weak eyes might send off the wrong message: that other parts of him were weak as well, that he possibly had weak blood flowing through his veins and therefore would produce only weak and sickly children. And what woman would want to marry a man who couldn't provide her with robust babies?

Fuzzy lowered his Sharps.

"Naked man, you say?" Then looked toward Sam Toe for confirmation and Sam Toe nodded without saying anything.

"Naked man? Where?" the woman inside the coach said, leaning her head out the window. Her cross-eyed kids were staring as well. The Chinaman sat silent.

Fuzzy Walls felt surely the man with the silver pistols was mistaken, for what would a man be doing running naked upon the grasslands?

"Let's get this honey wagon rolling," Prince Puckett growled, "or I might mistake you for a antelope and shoot you."

"Yes sir, yes sir," Fuzzy said with an air of disappointment, for it had been a long time since he'd had a good antelope steak, and longer still since he'd shot something at such a great distance.

Waddy Worth said, "Where you taking me?"

Toussaint held the reins in his hand, his eyes fixed straight ahead in a line directly between the mule's ears. Thinking about Karen's sorrow caused him to feel as though he'd swallowed a handful of bullets. Listening to her mourn the night through, there in her room—a room that used to be his and Karen's room—made him realize that he still loved her in spite of everything. He'd longed to go to her and climb in the bed with her and wrap his arms around her, for he could have used some comfort as well. He wondered now more than ever if Dex was his boy, or had Dex been the result of Otis Dollar coming around during that long winter when he was down in Louisiana visiting kin? It was a question he would like to ask Karen, but now didn't seem the time. And besides, they had to deliver the girl back to her people before taking the young killer into Sweet Sorrow.

It pained him greatly to think that yesterday all he had intended on doing was going out to hunt dreaming rabbits, and now he had once again been visited by trouble. And for the first time since he could ever remember, life didn't seem as though it was worth much, that all the good he ever knew was either dead or grieving. He looked at Jake.

"I'd like to know something before you leave this place," he said.

"What's that?"

"The truth."

"Chickens are funny creatures," Teacup Smith said.

They'd been riding at a leisurely pace, Teacup on horseback, Bob Olive in the carriage. Bob Olive thought he could easily get used to riding about in a carriage as opposed to horseback. It somehow seemed more refined, more what a proper lawman should do. He could shoot a man just as well seated in a carriage as he could from horseback. It was also a lot easier on his leg and his ass, he determined.

"What the hell are you talking about chickens for?" he said sourly.

"I was just thinking about them is all," Teacup Smith said. "My mother used to have quite a few."

Bob Olive ignored such commentary.

"From now on, I'm going to ride around in a carriage," he said. "I'm through riding the back of a horse. It will mark me as a man of progress."

Teacup looked at him.

"I think that's a splendid idea, Bob. Why you'll probably be the only lawman in all of Dakota to ride around in a carriage. You'll probably set a trend for all the other lawmen. Quite stylish."

"And I aim to get a nice shotgun instead of wearing a pistol. I can do a lot more work with a shotgun than I can a pistol."

"You did some pretty fine pistol work back in Anna's Bloomers," Teacup said. "Shot that whore and her pimp like they were cans."

"Consider them my last pistol victims."

"So considered."

"When we get back to Sweet Sorrow, first stop will be Otis Dollar's place so I can buy me a shotgun—one of those new 20-gauge Spencers. Why hell, I can blow holes through walls with one of them."

"You'll be a force to be reckoned with, Bob."

"Damn straight."

"That damn back-shooting son of a bitch will know he's been shot good this time."

"Scatter him like milkweed fluff in a hard wind, we will."

"In a mighty *hard* wind."

"Jesus Christ but it *is* hot, ain't it?"

"Not as hot as where I'm sending that back shooter is going to be."

"To hell," Teacup said.

"Straight to it," Bob Olive said.

Toussaint tried hard to remember what exactly the color of Dex's eyes were. Damn if he could remember. He couldn't stop thinking about him. He couldn't stop thinking about Karen, either.

"I said where the hell you all taking me?" the boy called from the back of the wagon.

Gerthe sat quiet between Toussaint and Jake and still hadn't said a single word. When she tried to think of the events, her thoughts were all scrambled. She remembered Dex kissing her. She remembered riding on top of him for a time, the grass so dry it scratched her knees. She remembered seeing bright colors. She remembered sudden pain and being afraid. But she couldn't put it all together right in her mind what happened.

"We're taking you to jail," Jake said.

"To jail! What the hell for?"

Jake turned enough to look at him.

"I'd keep my mouth shut if I were you."

"Why you ain't the law—neither one of you. You ain't wearing no badges. You can't arrest me and take me to no damn jail."

Toussaint halted the mule. They all just sat there silent for a moment, the heat rising up like off a stove and it not yet nine o'clock in the morning.

Without turning around to look at the boy, Toussaint said, "You want to take off, take off."

Waddy Worth eyed him suspiciously.

"I do and you'll shoot me for trying to escape."

"Like you said, you little peckerwood, we're not the law. We've got no legal right to hold you. So if you want to go, go."

Waddy Worth looked around. In every direction all he could see was grass—grass and sky, sky and grass. He wouldn't stand a chance if he were to run.

"Go on, get the hell out of my wagon," Toussaint ordered.

Waddy did not move.

After a few moments more Toussaint said, "I hear one more word out of you I'm going to drag you out onto that grassland. You understand my meaning?"

The boy did not reply.

They rode on.

15

❧

OTIS DOLLAR could see a dark shape moving just below the green surface of Cooper's Creek. The sun-struck water looked like clear jade. Otis was hopeful.

Otis got the idea to go fishing from the calendar that hung over the coffee grinder in his dry goods store. On it was an illustration of one man fishing and the local sheriff peeking around from behind a tree upon which an advertisement for Arbuckle Coffee read: NO FISHING ON THESE GROUNDS! TRY ARBUCKLE COFFEE!

Well, why not? he thought. The heat was unbearable and no one other than Tall John had come into his mercantile all morning. Tall John had come in to ask if the new silk top hat he'd ordered had arrived yet. It had not. Tall John looked cadaverous, not unlike his clientele, and more so every day, as though his dealings with the dead were rubbing off on him.

His watery gray eyes looked as though they were always about to spill tears.

"Death abounds, Otis," Tall John had said. "Smiley Rivers is the latest to pass from this vale of tears. Died in his sleep at the jail. Better than having his neck broke by a rope, I suppose, but I wish business weren't so good. At this rate, the whole of the population of Sweet Sorrow will reside in our little cemetery. Funeral's this afternoon. I doubt many will show, considering Smiley's last human act upon his wife."

And when Tall John left his store, Otis felt a melancholy in the air that hadn't been there before the undertaker's arrival. Otis thought about the brevity of life—even a long life wasn't all that long compared to eternity. A man could live seventy years but once he was dead he'd be dead ten thousand years or more, as it said in that hymn. It caused him to ruminate about his life and how it had turned out—not exactly as he would have planned it if he'd had a hand in planning it at all.

He did not want to be a store clerk this particular morning. He did not want to be alone and thinking about his own mortality and a life spent that had pretty much come down to ordinariness. He thought in that glum moment that if he could start over again and become anything, it would be an artist, one of those famous painters who lived in Paris and painted naked women or bright flowers or bowls of ripe fruit that looked as if you could eat them.

He'd rise late in the day and go down to a studio

filled with sunlight and spend the day painting beautiful canvases. He'd eat smoked fish and cheese for lunch and drink wine, then take a long restful nap. And in the evening, he'd wander the streets of Paris and go off with beautiful and exotic prostitutes who lingered in dark doorways; they'd take him to their rooms with red curtains where he'd spend the night in revelry. He'd live like that and grow old so slowly he wouldn't even notice. And death would be a stranger who never came to visit his thoughts. And when he did die, he would die in the arms of a paramour, feeling fulfilled from having lived a robust and interesting life.

Otis was sure that if he'd gone home and asked his wife Lorena if he could go fishing she would have said no. She would have argued that their income was penury and that every nickel mattered and that she hadn't left a good home in Kansas, and he a good job with the KATY railroad, just to come and starve on the grasslands of Dakota. She would remind him that it was all his idea to go to some far-flung settlement and open a mercantile just so he could sell cans of beans and bolts of gingham and stare at a future that was hardly any future at all. And she'd remind him of his other failings as a husband and provider as well, and that taking the day off to go fishing wasn't going to put any money in their pockets. His asking her if he could go fishing would have turned her sour and their evening would have ended as it generally did in stormy matrimonial discord with him sleeping on a pallet in the summer kitchen and her in their bed.

That is why he did not go home and ask her, but instead rode straight out to Cooper's Creek with his fishing pole and a can full of grubs he dug up from under the springhouse, figuring he could be back to town before it grew dark and therefore home again without her knowing he was gone at all.

Fishing had a way of helping Otis forget the majority of his troubles. It also gave him time to think about pleasant things like Karen Sunflower, a woman he had been in love with for twenty years.

And as he sat there watching, the dark shape of the big fish moving back and forth beneath the water, he thought of Karen and what his life would have been like if he had married her instead of Lorena. Of course Karen was also married when he'd first met her. She'd come into his store with Toussaint True-blood, a man with a dark and mysterious countenance. They seemed an odd couple. Karen was tall and fair with thick wheat-colored hair and a cheerful manner. Toussaint was short, wiry, dark-eyed, and grim. Otis was sure that Toussaint was a very dangerous fellow and had probably committed unsavory acts at one time or another.

Then, not long after he'd met Karen and Toussaint, Toussaint went away a whole winter leaving Karen to fend for herself and she'd come into his store asking for a line of credit. He gladly let her have whatever she wanted and when she didn't come in for several weeks running, he packed a burlap sack full of foodstuffs and a salted ham and rode out to her place to check on her. He found her nearly too ill from a fever to stand.

"I can't accept such charity," she'd said when he stomped the snow off his boots and knocked it from his hat before entering their cold little homestead.

He insisted it wasn't charity, that he'd put it on her credit bill.

"Won't be able to pay you for all this," she said.

He lit a fire, chopped more wood, hauled it in, cooked her a nice warm meal, made a pot of tea and sat with her until the sky outside turned dark as a dead rose with the last of the sun glaring off the ice causing it to take on a blue quality.

She'd looked at him with suspicion.

He waved a hand.

"No need to worry," he said. "Take all the time you need to repay me. Main thing is to get well and back on your feet." He privately worried she would die alone and it caused his heart to ache.

And so he did return again and again to visit Karen that long winter, bringing her cans of potted meat and tins of sardines, flour, sugar, and coffee until she said to him one day, "You must stop this generosity, Otis. There is simply no way, even if I worked a hundred years, that I can repay you."

"You worry about things that don't matter," he said.

"But I simply can't accept all this."

He felt confused.

She tried explaining.

"Others will talk. You're married and I am too. My husband isn't here; it looks bad, Otis. You'll be the scourge of the town and I'll be its harlot."

How could he explain it to her, the way he felt, the feelings for her that had developed almost from the first moment he laid eyes on her. Secretly he was glad Toussaint had gone and left her. He hoped that Toussaint would stay gone.

"What will your wife think if she learns that you've been coming to visit me, that you're bringing me all these supplies knowing I can't ever pay you for them?"

"I don't care what Lorena thinks," he blurted out.

And even though it was late March, it had been snowing, a fresh white snow of brilliant beauty. And then the skies had cleared and turned a grand blue and the sun radiated a promise of spring soon to come as it shone on the snow causing it to sparkle as though the earth was covered in diamonds. A bluejay came and landed on Karen's windowsill, pecked on the glass with its black beak, looked in at the two of them sitting there in her living room, then flew off again.

Karen sighed heavily.

"You're lonely, aren't you, Otis? Even though you are married, you're a lonely, lonely man."

He nearly wept when she said those words, for he had been lonely, very lonely for nearly all of his life and he was nearing forty years of age and had never known a time in his life when he didn't feel lonely except when he was with Karen.

"With you I feel . . ." he started to say, but his emotions choked off his words.

She came and sat by him on the horsehair divan

and stroked his sparse hair very gently and said, "I understand, Otis. I truly do. Only lonely people like us can understand the lonely in others."

Then Karen kissed him a soft tender kiss that was not unlike the way one child would kiss another and it took Otis's breath away, caused him to tremble, for he'd never been kissed so tenderly. And the fact that it was Karen Sunflower kissing him, a woman he had until that moment only dreamed about kissing, made it seem all the more wonderful.

His face flushed bright red and his cheeks warmed.

"Oh," he said. "Oh . . ."

Karen stood then and took Otis by the hand and led him back to her bedroom. He went along as though a boy being led by his mother, for he felt inadequate in Karen's strong and sure presence, in the glow of her womanliness. And for just a fleeting moment as they kissed again, he thought of Lorena, that she was probably at home this very moment peeling potatoes or knitting something, that she would have a look of consternation on her face and be ill-tempered thinking about what a failure of a man she'd married.

And later, there in Karen's warm bed as he held Karen in that deep and wonderful afterglow of their lovemaking, he felt slightly ashamed that he had been unfaithful to Lorena even though he couldn't come up with one good reason why he should feel guilty while feeling as wonderful as he felt.

Then later still, with the sun lying low and spreading its brilliance out across the sparkling snow even as it threatened to slip beyond the horizon, Karen said, "We must never do this again, Otis. It was a one-time thing. I am not in love with you, as you might have concluded by my actions. I do love you for being a kind and gentle man, but I don't love you the way a woman loves a man she wants to spend her life with. I love only one man in that way. I don't regret what we've done, but you must understand that it is a one-time thing."

He felt at once miserable and happy on his trip back to Sweet Sorrow, his thoughts alternating between the most delicious moments of their time together and Karen's declaration that it would never happen again. Toussaint returned home the very next week.

And Otis recalled again those delicious moments as he dangled his baited hook in the water of Cooper's Creek. Years had since passed and still he could remember every wonderful thing about Karen Sunflower. And though he still saw her on occasion when she and the boy, Dex, came into town, they maintained a certain formality that often comes after such an intimate encounter, carrying within their souls their secret.

He tried hard to detect any resemblance between himself and Dex from the very first; for it was possible that Dex was his son and not Toussaint's considering the timing of the boy's birth. But Otis could see nothing one way or the other in the boy's features to lend a hint as to who his father was. He looked a lot like Karen.

Otis closed his eyes under the weight of the heat.

He did not care if he caught a fish or not. Life was better sometimes if you didn't get what you wanted, he thought. Sometimes it was better if you didn't catch the fish.

The next he knew, he was being pummeled by a naked man.

Toussaint pulled up short and stopped the wagon, his gaze pointed toward Cooper's Creek that ran a quarter mile in the distance.

"What is it?" Jake said.

"I don't know, but I heard something."

The boy in the wagon bed rose up and looked, too. The girl between them did not raise her head.

"Let's ride over there," Toussaint said, and turned the mule off in that direction.

Jake wondered silently if he was ever going to find a way to leave for the border. But he felt, too, that he owed a debt to those who'd saved his life.

As they drew near they could see two men fighting, one of them naked, bleeding.

"Crazy white men," Toussaint said.

"Isn't that the merchant?" Jake said.

"Otis Dollar, and it looks like he's getting his ass whipped one side to the other by the preacher."

"Maybe we should stop it."

"Yeah, I guess."

Toussaint looked round at the boy.

"You stay put. I knocked you down once and I'll do it again, only this time not so pleasantly."

Waddy Worth thought, *Go on you son of a bitch,*

just give me half a chance and I'll do you like I did Frank Moore. He didn't think he could get shot dead but he did and I'll sure as hell do you the same. But he didn't say a word in response to Toussaint's order.

Toussaint took hold of Otis while Jake took hold of the naked preacher. The man was wild, flailing his fists, kicking his feet. Rather than wrestle with him, Jake took one of the Schofields and cracked him behind the ear with it. All the fight went out of Elias Poke; he crumpled and fell to the ground.

Otis was bleeding from both nostrils, a busted lip, and half his right ear was bitten off.

"What happened?" Toussaint asked.

Otis's eyes were wild with fright.

"He attacked me! I was just sitting here fishing and he come out of nowhere and attacked me!"

Toussaint met Jake's questioning gaze.

Jake knelt and examined the slash marks on his body: small bloody crosses. Self-inflicted was his professional opinion. Pike sat with his legs out in front of him, his head lolling. Jake took hold of him and looked into his eyes.

"This man's doped on something."

"How do you know that?" Toussaint said.

"I've seen similar cases."

Toussaint made a mental note of Jake's observation.

At Jake's suggestion, they tied the preacher with a length of rope Toussaint kept under the wagon seat and set him in the back with the kid.

"Goddamn, but that's a pitiable thing to have to

look at," Waddy Worth said, staring at the naked man. "Why's he got to be back here with me? Why don't you just leave him for the coyotes?"

Toussaint glared at him until he ceased his carping.

"We must take this girl home to her kin," he said. "Then we'll deliver those two in the back to the jailhouse and figure it out from there."

"You going to be all right?" Jake said to Otis, who dabbed at his bloody nose with a silk handkerchief. He looked at Jake, then at Toussaint, remembering the winter Toussaint had left Karen alone, and that sweet lovely hour the two of them had spent with the snow falling outside her window and it seemed like a million years ago since, and he knew life would never get any better than it was then.

"Half my ear's been bit off, but I am okay enough to make it back alone."

Toussaint felt no compassion for Otis Dollar, for he too remembered that winter when he left Karen alone and all the stories he heard upon his return about Otis's visits to the house, and those stocked cupboards.

They rode into the sun, Toussaint, Jake, the girl, the boy, the crazy preacher.

Toussaint saying to himself as much as to Jake, "These are strange times."

16

·❧❦·

THEY REACHED THE Kunckle homestead at midday.
Two tattered quilts hung on a wire line like dead
butterflies. A pile of rusting cans rose like an anthill
just off to the side of the small shack. A corral. A
privy beyond the corral. Not much else.

"You're home, girl," Toussaint said. Gerthe still
did not make a move nor act as though she understood a thing.

Several boys were chasing an old hound around the
house. They stopped and stared at the wagon and the
men with their sister seated between them.

"Ain't that Gerthe?" the shortest of the boys said.

"Hey Gerthe, what you doing with them men?" a
taller boy said.

"Hey Ma, Gerthe's out here with some men," the
short boy called back over his shoulder.

The front door of the house was open, or perhaps
there wasn't any front door, it was hard to tell.

A woman appeared, shading her eyes as she

stepped out onto the rickety porch. She had a ladle in her hand but looked starved, thin as a wisp of smoke.

"Look Ma," the boys said in unison, pointing at their sister.

"Get down, child," Toussaint said. "There's your ma and people."

"Gerthe," the woman called. "What you doing with them fellers?"

The girl looked up at the sound of her mother's voice.

"What you fellers doing with my child?"

"Nothing," Toussaint said, stepping down from the wagon and reaching for Gerthe. "Come on girl, get down."

She did not move and when Toussaint took hold of her, she screamed.

"God Lord!" the woman shouted, "they's attacking my girl baby!"

The kids all stooped and began picking up rocks, then flinging them at the wagon and Toussaint. Far out in the distance, Jake could see a man trotting through the grass, a scythe balanced over his left shoulder.

"Leave my child be!" the woman shouted. "Leave her be!"

The rocks were small, and without much sting to them because of the distance between house and wagon, but they were worrisome, like hornets.

Toussaint let loose of the girl and turned and when he did a rock struck him just above the brow and warm blood trickled into his eye.

The woman's shrieking seemed to spur on the boys flinging the rocks and they flung at a furious pace. The man with the scythe came running in past the corral where an old swayback gray stood, its ears alert at the sound of the woman's screams. The man swung the scythe down in front of him.

"You goddamn sons of bitches! Leave her be!"

Jake drew one of the Schofields and fired it into the air. It sounded like a thunderclap.

"Everybody calm down."

Toussaint stood wiping blood out of his eye.

"We found this girl and brought her home," Jake said. "Toussaint here brought her home. Instead of acting like crazy people you should be thanking him."

The Kunckles stared at this stranger in their midst. They knew of Toussaint Trueblood already. They'd heard Gerthe talk about him, and had seen him wandering across the grasslands in hunt of rabbits. They thought him to be the father of the boy Gerthe had been sneaking off to see. But the man with the gun they did not know and thus gave him his due because out in this country you always gave a man with a gun his due.

"What's he done to her, your boy?" the old man said. He had hair like straw. "I know he must have done something to her, or why else would *you* be bringing her home?"

"He's not done anything to her. If anything, she's done something to him."

Jake said to Gerthe, "Get down now and stop this nonsense. You're home safe."

Without so much as a word she climbed down and walked past father, siblings, and mother into the house.

"You keep her home," Toussaint said, pressing a knuckle to the small gash above his eye. "You keep her home from now on lest she cause more trouble. If I have to come back here again, I'll clean out the whole nest of you."

"Boy those little peckerwoods is going to grow up to be some mean bastards," Waddy Worth said when Toussaint had turned the wagon around and headed back to Sweet Sorrow.

"Shut up," Toussaint said.

Doc and Birdy had searched throughout part of the night with no luck in finding Elias Poke. Exhausted, Doc walked Birdy back to her crib—one of several maintained by the prostitutes along a back alley, even though all the town's prostitutes had left for other more profitable climes except for Birdy and Mistress Sheba.

"I appreciate your help, Doc," Birdy said.

"Whatever it was that caused Poke to act like he did I'm sure is merely a passing madness," Doc told her. "It isn't uncommon for men who take up the practice of religion to become filled with strange fervors. I knew of such types back in Kentucky that even take up speaking in strange tongues and drinking poison and handling rattlesnakes."

"Is that where you're from, Doc, Kentucky? Why

you and me were practically neighbors. I'm from Darke County, Ohio. I suppose you never heard of it?"

Doc shook his head.

"No, I never heard of that place in particular but I have visited Cincinnati several times and thought it a nice town."

"Why, Cincinnati is right close to Darke County. Ain't it something you and me are from nearly the same place, Doc?"

They could hear laughter from the Rosebud. The laughter sounded lonely to Woodrow Willis. He stood unmoving, caught up in the moment of melancholy.

In spite of her exhaustion, Birdy felt sorry for the old man, for he seemed as lonely as the stars when she looked at him. His white hair glowed in the moon-light.

"Doc, would you like to come inside for awhile? I've got a little peach brandy."

Woodrow Willis looked at the shadowy face of Birdy Pride, looked at the darkened door that led to her crib. He thought about the induced madness spreading through the town, and he thought about Iris, off somewhere with a man half his age but not half his equal. On such dark and hopeless nights all he could ever think about was Iris. It was only natural to think that at this very moment she was probably giving herself to the school teacher. It felt like a knife wound to his heart to think that she was.

"Doc, would you like to come in?" Birdy repeated.

"Yes," he said so softly Birdy could barely hear him.

She opened the door and he followed her inside.

"I'll just light us a lamp," she said.

"No," he said. "I'd prefer you left it dark."

There was just enough moonlight inside to see by, shadows of things: the walls, a chair, a bed in the corner.

"I think the bottle of brandy's over here," Birdy said, starting to move to one side of the room. But he took hold of her wrist and wouldn't let go.

"What is it, Doc?"

"Just stay here by me a moment," he said.

They stood that way. Birdy could hear his breathing, how it had grown rapid and she knew the sounds of a man who had been deprived of the flesh of a woman for too long. She prided herself in understanding a man's needs, and knowing how an educated man like Doc Willis felt made her feel all the more sorry for him.

"You want to get undressed, Doc, and lay with me?"

"I . . . I . . ."

"It's okay, Doc. I know how lonely it can get for a man without no woman out here on these grasslands. I have known lots of lonely men. I'm in the lonely business, Doc. Even a working girl sometimes gets lonely, in spite of all the men wanting to pay attention to her. Sometimes like tonight, I miss my folks terrible and wish I was back there with them instead of way out here on this frontier."

Doc's passion overtook him. He pulled Birdy close and kissed her hard, trying to believe as much as he could that she was Iris returned to him. Birdy tried pulling away because she didn't like rough treatment very much, having suffered her share of it from the cowboys and the ranchers and farmers. But Doc held her tight, said, "I'm sorry, child, I'm sorry . . . It's just that I need so much to . . ."

"Go easy, Doc. We don't have to be in no hurry."

He settled himself on the edge of the bed and began taking off his shoes. Birdy undressed there by the window where the mercurial light of the moon shone on her and his eyes watched her movements. She could have been Iris, undressing for him. They were about the same size.

"Oh, Iris," he said.

"Do you want me to pretend I'm your wife, Doc? Your Iris?"

He felt the straight razor in his pocket.

"What would you know about a woman like her?" he said harshly, his mood quickly changed.

"I don't know nothing about her, Doc. I bet she was a real sweet gal, though. I bet she loved you."

The smooth hard handle of the razor was made of mother of pearl; his fingers encircled it.

"Come closer, child. Come let me touch you."

"You promise not to rough me up, Doc?"

"Yes, I promise. No more rough stuff, Birdy."

"I'm so tired. Maybe I'll have to sleep some before we do it."

"Yes, whatever you like, my love."

Birdy sagged down on the bed next to him.

"I'm sure enough worried about Preacher," she said, her voice trailing off.

Doc brought forth the razor from his pocket. Birdy's soft little snores came swiftly. He gently found the soft curve of her throat with his fingertips.

"Sleep, sleep, my drowsing child, let dreams take you to faraway places that are clean and pure and without sin. Let thy sleep renew you and make you whole again. Let thy sleep bring back the virtue you lost along the way to your final rest. And let not another man steal one more beautiful thing from you and leave you less than you were when you first arrived upon this desperate earth."

He placed the blade to her delicate exposed skin knowing how easy it would be to bring her final and eternal sleep. She would never know another moment of distress, of heartache, of wanting or longing or needing. He could make an angel of her in an instant, just as he should have made an angel of his Iris before she grew wings and flew away.

The razor's blade snatched a sliver of moonlight as he moved it a fraction of an inch and saw the first drop of blood appear in its wake.

He brought his mouth to hers. Her lips parted even though she was yet asleep, out of habit, he supposed, from so many men kissing her. And then knew that he could not end her life on such a hot still night, for her innocence in that moment was greater than her sin. He closed the razor and put it back into his pocket and chose instead to curl up against her, for he was ever so weary, too.

"Iris," he whispered. "My lovely sweet Iris . . ."

* * *

Roy Bean had been coming out of the Rosebud just as Birdy and Doc turned the corner to go down the alleyway that led to Birdy's crib. Roy Bean had started to call out to them, then realized that he would only seem like a desperate man if he did. Instead he watched with feeble thoughts as Doc followed Birdy into the alley, into the darkness, knowing where they were going and what they would be doing once they got there. Roy imagined that it was likely Birdy had taken up with Doc in her search for a husband. And why not? Doc was a single, if aged man, with plenty of financial resources to care for her. He had that big empty house. Yes, he could imagine Doc and Birdy as a permanent item and himself cut completely out of the picture. Boy, oh boy, he told himself. While I was standing in line buying a ticket, that's one train that's left the station. He felt an abiding sadness to think of his Birdy picking nits from Doc's hair and doing for Doc what she'd once done for him out of love and adoration. It left his stomach sour enough to want a drink.

Roy Bean looked and saw the moon and it made him think of his wife and children in Texas, for they seemed as far away from him now as the moon did.

I don't know why nothing's ever worked out right for me. I've been a good man, mostly. I always tried to do right by others. I believe in the law and justice and I believe in the Lord Jesus Christ. What more can anyone expect of a man than those things?

Something nudged him.

He looked down.

It was that beer-drinking dog.

"What you want?"

The dog didn't answer.

"Okay then, but just one, then I need to go get my rest."

The dog followed him back into the Rosebud.

"Two beers," Roy Bean said to Peg Leg, neither man knowing that by breakfast the next day Peg Leg would be shot and bleeding near to death by what used to be the law in Sweet Sorrow.

Peg Leg looked at the two of them.

"Next thing I know, folks will be bringing bears in here to eat the buffet."

Roy looked down into the cur's miserable wanting eyes and said, "I know exactly how you feel, old timer."

Toussaint halted the wagon along a thin stream—a feeder that ran off from Cooper's Creek and no wider than a garter snake.

"Mule needs water and a rest."

Both men had sweated through their shirts, turning them dark and causing them to stick to them like a second skin. The boy in the back said little, forewarned as he had been to keep his mouth shut. Preacher Pike had fallen into a sleep, a well of jangled dreams wherein he was tumbling through a field of colored glass.

"We best put him under the wagon," Jake said. "The sun is frying his skin."

They lifted Pike down and put him in the shade the belly of the wagon provided.

"What about me?" Waddy said. "I'm about burnt to hell, too."

"Crawl in under there if you want," Jake said.

Toussaint watered his mule from the feeder then let it crop the tender grasses along the piddling banks.

"How far are we yet from town?" Jake said. "All this land looks the same. A man sure enough could get as easily lost out here as he could in a forest of trees."

"In the winter it's nothing but a plain of snow and just as disorienting," Toussaint said, unfolding some dry rabbit jerky from a cheesecloth he pulled from inside his shirt. He offered it to Jake who took a piece and said, "What about them?"

Toussaint looked at the two men under the wagon; the preacher was snoring, the boy looking at him like a stray dog.

"Hell with him," he said. "I don't feed killers."

Jake handed him back the jerky. Toussaint looked at him, shrugged, and chewed silently staring off toward the nothingness.

"I'm sorry about what happened to Dex," Jake said.

Toussaint did not reply.

"I've been thinking about something," Jake said.

Toussaint removed his hat and ran a sleeve over his forehead then settled his hat back on his head again. He didn't ever recall such a hot relentless summer as this one. It was a mean time, everything about it was mean and it made folks mean and it made some of them crazy and led some to commit murderous acts upon themselves and others. The boy's name kept repeating itself in his head: *Dex, Dex, Dex.*

"I've been thinking that it's not merely coincidence that things are happening as they are," Jake continued.

"What do you mean?" Toussaint said as he checked the mule's traces.

"The craziness that seems to have hit people around here. The man killing his wife, the one drowning himself, the woman who brought you her dead baby—the preacher there. Something's causing it, or someone."

"You ever seen anything like it before?" Toussaint asked suspiciously.

"No, nothing on the same scale, individual cases, but nothing like this—widespread."

"Individual cases, huh?"

"I was an orderly in the war. I've seen lots of troubling things happen to people."

"Well, it has nothing to do with me," Toussaint said. "Let's get these fools into town."

But Jake wasn't convinced that the madness had nothing to do with Toussaint. The possibilities were endless, but he'd been thinking about it for a while because his physician's curiosity would not let him not think about it. Medical mysteries were always challenging. Medicine itself was a mystery half the time. No, he did not think that what was happening to the folks in Sweet Sorrow was at all a coincidental event, nor a random one, either. And he hadn't forgotten the bite marks on Gerthe's arms and legs. They could have been the young killer's, but he asked himself why he would do such a thing, then be so protective of her? There was one other possibility: it wasn't the boy who attacked the girl, but Dex who had. Maybe the boy was defending her and shot Dex in her defense.

A hot dry wind followed them all the way back to Sweet Sorrow.

17

❦

SUN GONE NOW, the darkness on them, they could see the lights of Sweet Sorrow in the distance.

Home, thought Toussaint disdainfully. What is home? He was weary, bone weary, as tired as he'd ever been. It wasn't the heat, nor the long travel, but the weariness of a man with a heavy heart. He told himself that tomorrow he'd go see Karen, take her something—a gift or flowers—the things that it was said a woman wanted, things she needed to cheer her. Karen needed to feel like a whole woman again, needed to know she wasn't alone in the world. Maybe he needed it, too. Maybe he needed it more than Karen did.

In the back, Waddy Worth had been doing little more than planning his escape.

Dying was one thing, how you died was another. If he had to die, he'd rather die trying to live than to let himself be hanged like a dog. If they shot him trying to escape, then they shot him. At least it would be quick, he told himself.

Elias Poke was muttering to himself, still feeling the effects of whatever it was that had put the craziness in him. His flesh stung like a thousand bee stings. He tried his best to hide his nakedness from the boy's curious glances. He tried figuring out how he'd come to be trussed up and knocked around in the back of a rough wagon. He didn't recall much, his head felt like a bucket of mud.

Jake was wrapped in his own thoughts.

So much death, such strange events. Was his world to be forever this way? Had he, as Toussaint suggested, been carrying a curse with him? He was a man of science more than one of spiritualism, but it was possible that anything was possible the way things were turning out. And in spite of everything, he knew he still loved the woman who had betrayed him. That was the worst part.

They pulled up in front of the little jail. It was dark.

"Let's take them inside and lock them up," Toussaint said.

Jake stepped down from the wagon and helped Toussaint get the two men out of the wagon and inside. The interior of the jail was hot as an oven. The one cell and its cot empty. No one around to watch the place.

They found a key lying atop a small handmade table.

"Look at this," Toussaint said, picking it up. "Some jail they got here."

He opened the cell door and shoved the boy in. Jake cut the rope from around Poke, said, "Go on in, Preacher."

Elias Poke went in meekly as a sheep, naked as a newborn.

Toussaint closed the door and locked it.

"Now what?"

"I imagine they could use something to eat and drink," Jake said.

Toussaint snorted, walked out the door, Jake on his heels.

"You do what you want with them," Toussaint said. "Me, I'm going to my place."

Jake watched him climb up on the wagon, take up the reins and snap them lightly, telling the mule to "step off," and watched as the wagon rattled down the street.

He looked down at the hand holding the key, realized he still wore two pistols in his waistband. All you need now is a badge and you'll be just what Roy Bean wanted you to be, he told himself: a lawman. It was a damn foolish thought.

He went to the Rosebud and found Roy Bean there drinking beer with a dog.

They acknowledged each other. Jake stepped to the bar and said, "Any food left over from the buffet?"

Peg Leg Watts shook his head.

"It was all ate up, like usual. These local big spenders come in, pay a dime for a beer, and eat three dollars' worth of luncheon meats, pickles, boiled eggs, and every damn thing else that don't jump off the plate. If you're hungry, try down to the Fat Duck, Zimmerman might have something left over."

"I've got two men in the jail," Jake said. "One's a kid who we think shot Dex Sunflower dead. The other's your preacher."

Roy Bean looked up.

"What he do? The preacher?"

"Nothing that I know of outside of beating hell out of Otis Dollar."

"Preacher?"

Jake nodded.

"Me and Peg Leg seen him running out of town last evening, naked as a skinned rat," Roy Bean said.

"That's how we found him," Jake said, explaining the rest of it, about the fight, finding the Kunckle girl, Dex Sunflower's body.

"Devil has put a curse on this place," Roy Bean said, his eyes as troubled as the dog's.

"I don't know anything about that. I need to get those men something to eat and the preacher a blanket, then I need to find Doc Willis."

Roy Bean said, "I'll go get them some grub, then I'll find Gus or Brewster to watch over them until we can decide what needs be done with them."

"What happened to the one-handed man, Rivers? I didn't see him in the jail."

"Dead. Found him dead yesterday. This town and the folks in it are keeping the undertaker busy, sure enough."

Jake started for the doors.

"Hold up," Roy Bean said, joining him outside the Rosebud.

"What is it?"

"I know where you can find Doc. I just didn't want to say anything in front of Peg Leg is all."

Jake figured Roy had his reasons for the secrecy.

"He's down the alley with Birdy Pride in her crib. I seen them go there earlier. Might be a bad time to disturb him if you've ever been in a similar deal."

"I guess I can find him in the morning just as easily," Jake said.

"'Less you want me to go disturb him for you?" Roy Bean said, thinking that if he did go on Jake's behalf, he might still stand a chance to win back Birdy's loyalty.

"No. It'll wait until tomorrow."

Jake went down the street to the hotel where he'd rented a room. He opened a window hoping somehow the night would draw the coolness from wherever it was hiding these days. He poured water from a pitcher into a pan and brought handfuls of it to his face, neck, and chest. Christ, he hadn't felt so dragged out since the war, when there was never any real sleep to be had.

He sat on the side of the bed and pulled off his boots, then stripped out of his trousers and lay back hoping for the merest whisper of a breeze to float in through the window. He could hear noise coming from the saloons—one at either end of town. He closed his eyes, tried to sleep. But sleep wasn't any easier to come by than cooler weather.

Then there came a knock at the door. A soft knock. His muscles knotted thinking it was someone who'd come for him—a lawman or a private detective, maybe several. He reached for the Schofields he'd placed on the chair next to his bed. One in each hand, he thumbed back the hammers, stepped to the door and listened.

The knock came again.

"Who is it?"

"Just me. Fannie. From the café. Do you remember?"

He took a deep breath, then opened the door an inch and saw through the narrow opening the face of the woman. He waited for her to say what she was doing at his door at night.

"I just got off from my job," she said. "I wondered if you wanted some company."

"Why would you wonder that?" he said.

Her face showed she was a little confused by the question, perhaps a little disappointed.

She shrugged, said, "I just thought since you were kind of new in town, maybe you didn't know anyone. You seemed like a nice man the way you helped out Mr. Rivers . . ."

He stepped aside, realizing how rude it must seem to her to keep her standing in the hallway. Then when she stepped inside, he realized he was standing before her wearing only a pair of short cotton drawers. He started to cover up, to turn and reach for his shirt and pants that were lying in a heap on the floor, but then realized that it was way too late for such modesty.

She didn't look away either.

"I caught you in bed already," she said.

"Maybe I should put something on," he said.

"If that's what you want. It's not like I've never seen a man naked before."

He pushed the door closed behind her. The room grew instantly dark again. Just enough night light that they could make the other one out—their shadows. She stepped in close to him.

"I just thought if you didn't mind some company, I didn't mind, either."

"No," he said. "I don't mind."

"I ain't no whore," she said.

"I know you're not, Fannie."

"It's just I sometimes get lonely. But most of the men around here are married, or types you wouldn't let lay down with your dog. Decent men come through rare and when they do, they don't stay long . . ."

He put his fingers to her lips.

"You don't have to say anything," he said.

And when she touched him, her hands felt cool and healing and suddenly nothing mattered, not the past, not the present, not the future.

Later, when he rose from the bed and went to the window, the night was quiet, cloaked in darkness, slumbering, for even the land seemed exhausted from the on-going heat. A few wispy clouds drifted across the moon that shone silver, then drifted away again. He stood there for a long time simply feeling alone in a world where nothing moved, where no life seemed to exist but his own and that of the sleeping woman.

He turned at last and slipped in the bed next to her and closed his eyes.

That night Prince Puckett shared a bed with the Chinaman at the way station along the trail from Bismarck to Sweet Sorrow. It was either share the bed with the Chinaman or sleep on the floor. The Chinaman smelled strange. Through the curtains he could hear the woman and her children snoring. Prince Puckett couldn't sleep. He was all keyed up. He rose and pulled on his boots then went outside in just his drawers and hat.

Seemed awful hot and dry for being so far north.

He thought about Denver, the coolness of the mountains, the feel of the first snow upon his face when it came. He'd gone to Alaska once looking for gold, but by the time he'd gotten there, all the gold had been taken. Later he'd gone to Arizona, where he heard they had silver mines, but the mines all got flooded and to get the silver you needed lots of equipment and manpower, neither of which he favored very much. Then he'd gone to the killing fields of Kansas to hunt buffalo because he heard a man could make some real money with good gun. And he killed plenty of buffalo but the money wasn't all that good and it was nasty hard work. And soon enough all the buffalo got shot out and that was the end of another dream and so he moved on. Became a policeman in El Paso, but didn't care for the work and the low pay. Finally he went to Denver and began hiring himself out as a private detective with thoughts he could turn his business to that the size and scope of Allan Pinkerton's.

But the plain truth was, he wasn't much for keeping books and organization and dealing with employees and so decided to refine himself as a manhunter extraordinaire and charge top dollar for his services and it began to pay off for him when the wealthy elite began to hire him for discreet assignments, such as the assignment he was on now. He let it be known that there wasn't any type of assignment he would not take as long as the money was right.

The night was colorless except for the glow of the moon. Prince Puckett preferred to live in such a world all the time; a world where he could go about mostly unnoticed, a world in which he could be a living ghost.

He walked over to the well and winched up a bucket of water, dippered out a mouthful, and drank it. The water was barely cool and had a mossy taste to it.

Well, this time tomorrow, if my sources are correct, I'll be on my way back to Denver with a pair of hands in a kit and a little more in my bank account. Prince Puckett had plans of buying a big spread in Wyoming someday, possibly marrying a young sweet

Celestial gal. He didn't want any old maids or ugly gals. Lately he'd thought about maybe a mail-order bride he could order out of San Francisco where he heard there was a Chinaman who specialized in such gals. It was a long-held dream of a man who'd all his life been chasing one thing or another and never been hitched or otherwise occupied by a gal for more than the twenty or so minutes it took to consort in a bordello.

He was thinking about this when he heard voices.

"Oh . . . oh . . ." he heard someone mutter.

He looked around, didn't see anyone.

"Oh . . . oh . . ." the little soft cry went again.

The voice was coming from inside the station. He thought perhaps one of the children was calling out in its sleep.

"Oh . . . oh . . ."

He went closer to the open windows.

Looked in the room where the Chinaman was sleeping, for it sounded as though the sound came from in there.

"Oh . . . oh . . ."

It wasn't the Chinaman and it wasn't a child.

Prince Puckett tried to see who was making such noises.

He heard a rustling, the shuck mattress, bed springs, then it grew quiet for a moment.

"Okay," the Chinaman said.

Prince Puckett saw someone rise from the bed, a short squat shadow, saw the woman slip past the curtain again. Prince Puckett owed her a begrudging admiration for her resourcefulness, figuring she'd screw every man jack of them before she reached Sweet Sorrow if she had to to get her and her cross-eyed children shelter and food.

He walked off into the dark and made water, then went and slept in the coach. Maybe that old China-man was still a little randy. Better to not take any chances, you just never knew nothing about people. Prince Puckett grinned like a briar-eating goat.

18

※

W HEN PEG LEG WATTS would not say where Jake
was, Bob Olive shot him. Teacup Smith shot him,
too. Still Peg Leg didn't die, but was close to it. He lay
bleeding on the floor of the Rosebud.

Peg Leg had been reading about the shooting of
President Garfield in the latest edition of *The Grasslands Democrat*. The article described the great suffering of the man as he lingered on death's doorstep
from a gunshot wound to the belly.

Peg Leg had been contemplating what it must be
like to get belly shot and not die immediately but have
to suffer with the bullet lodged somewhere in the guts
when Bob Olive and Teacup Smith came into his
saloon.

"We're back and aim to kill that son of a bitch
who shot me," Bob Olive declared. "Where is he?"

Peg Leg didn't have to get bit by a rabid dog to
know the danger. And danger is what Bob Olive represented in spades. He was surprised the two of them

would return to a town that ran them off less than a week earlier.

"I don't know where he is," Peg Leg said with a shrug. "I ain't been assigned to keep tabs on him."

"You know, I never did like you worth a goddamn wood nickel," Bob Olive said.

Peg Leg knew that the sawed-off shotgun he kept was down at one end and he was standing at the other where the light was better for reading that time of day.

"Like me or not, it don't make me know where that fellow is . . ."

"Shoot him, Bob," Teacup said. "I never did like him, either."

Peg Leg scrambled for the shotgun but Bob shot him before he could reach it. The bullet went in between his shoulder blades, felt like a fist that punched all the wind out of him. He grabbed at the shelves of whiskey bottles to hold him up, but the bottles and glasses came shattering down around him as he fell to the floor, the glass like mean rain falling in his hair and cutting his face.

He thought, oh Jesus, oh Jesus, I've been killed by Bob Olive.

He waited for his life to flash before his eyes like he'd heard it did when a fellow was dying. He waited to see all those days of sailing the high seas and to smell again the salt spray, to hear the laughter of women in the saloons along the wharves in Singapore and Cape Horn, to hear the swaying creak of a hull full of sleeping men in hammocks. He waited for the light they say a fellow sees when he's entering heaven.

But all he saw instead was Teacup Smith standing over him looking down, pistol cocked and aimed.

"Here's to you, you one-legged son of a bitch."

The second shot didn't seem to hurt so much and he lay there with his eyes closed, unmoving, waiting for death. It wasn't so bad, he told himself over and over again. It wasn't so bad. And far off somewhere he could hear laughter, hear Teacup Smith saying to Bob Olive: "Well, we fried his bacon, I'm ready to kill this whole damn town, start fresh with folks who will appreciate us, ain't you?"

Peg Leg never heard Bob's answer.

Birdy Pride awakened with sun in her eyes. It took her a moment to remember.

"Doc?" she said. "Doc?"

Her crib was empty. She tried to recall if she and Doc had had relations. She couldn't remember.

She got up slow, went and washed herself in a pan of water, her face, neck, under her arms. She saw herself in the mirror hanging above the basin, a little hand mirror set in a tortoise shell frame Roy Bean had given her as a gift. She looked this way and that, saw the small cut on her neck, wondered how it got there; stared into her own eyes until it spooked her.

I ain't but nineteen but I look old. I feel old. I feel like some old woman worn out by time. I must have had me a hundred men by now. Having all them men has made me a lot older than I am. I'll look like a hag by the time I'm thirty.

She wept.

She didn't want to be in the whore business no more. She wanted to be somebody's wife. But whose? It surely seemed as though Preacher had gone crazy and therefore unsuitable for being a husband; she didn't want to be married to no crazy man who might kill her in her sleep. And Doc was too old; he might die on her during relations. Roy Bean was married already. So was Otis Dollar. Tall John wasn't a married man but she could see why. She'd not want to sleep every night in a bed next to someone who handled the dead. She wouldn't want those cold hands feeling on her. There was the boy who worked for Tall John, but Boblink Jones was just that, a boy, younger than herself. Then there was Peg Leg, but she couldn't feature herself marrying no man with just one leg, either. And finally there was Toussaint Trueblood—who might make her a good husband, but she was afraid of him—something about the way he looked at her whenever she saw him. He was a strange and aloof fellow and not someone she could ever feel comfortable around. She felt forlorn, knowing that there wasn't an eligible husband in all of Sweet Sorrow she would marry.

She went and reached under her pillow and took out the small flask of mercury she kept there. A sweet gal named Ellen, a sister in the whore business she knew back before she met Roy Bean, had given her the mercury, saying, "Birdy, sometimes things get bad for girls like you and me. They get so bad some can't take it no more. That day might come for any one of us if we don't find us a husband who will take us out of this life. And if such a day comes and you find you can't take it no more, drink this. It's surefire. It's what I aim to do if that day ever comes for me. I'm almost twenty-five and I ain't found a man yet who'll take me for his wife. Ellen was a very tall girl, well over six feet, and had mannish ways about her: a long horse face, short cropped hair, and a deep voice. She just wasn't very pretty, but nice enough all the same.

Well, of course, it seemed like a desperate thing to do, drink mercury, and she told herself she'd never get that desperate. But lately it seemed as if she was thinking on that possibility more and more often. The silver liquid was tempting, some days more than others, like today. She wondered what it would taste like or if it would cause her belly to ache and death would be painful and slow. All Ellen said was it was surefire, and Ellen was right, for Ellen had drunk it herself that very winter when she learned she had a bad case of the pox and no man would go near her once word got out.

Men saying: "You don't want to go nowhere near Ellen White. You'll be dancing when you piss, if you do."

Most of those same men had wives or sweethearts and they knew better than to carry the pox to them. And so Ellen was let go from her job in the saloons and had to take up being a crib girl, and the only trade she got were rough types coming in off the plains—trappers and teamsters and the like—men who didn't know about her having the pox and she gave it to them left and right—out of spite, she said—

until one teamster returned and cut her face for what she'd done to him. Her cut face ruined any last chance she had of attracting even the lowest form of man; not even Curly who swamped out saloons for a living would pay her for the privilege of having relations with her. Then the winter came on hard and she had no place to stay except for the kindness of Birdy who let her stay with her—two of them sharing the space of the small crib, sleeping in the same bed, sharing the same blanket.

This, until one morning someone found Ellen dead in a snowdrift, the empty mercury bottle still clutched in her hand, her lips blue as ink, her eyes half open and staring as though in that last fatal moment she'd seen salvation.

Ellen wasn't the only working girl Birdy knew to take her life from mercury poisoning. It was quite common among the prostitutes. Marriage or mercury, they often said, sometimes with humor, sometimes not.

She held the flask to the light where she could see the mercury roll from side to side when she tipped the bottle, then put it back under her pillow.

Maybe tomorrow, but not today, she told herself. She was hungry for flapjacks drowned in sorghum and went straight away to the Fat Duck Café.

Old James was sitting at the counter waiting for Zimmerman to come in and relieve him. He had already cooked up several skillets of eggs, bacon, and flapjacks, having opened the café well before daylight. And in between his cooking and serving he wrote in his journal, realizing as he did that if he kept remembering things, he was going to have to buy another book if he was going to put everything in.

"Hidey, James," Birdy said.

He turned to look at her. She was as pretty as brass. It roused something ancient in him to look at her. What would a young gal like that be like to have again? he wondered as he went over to her table to take her order. When she smiled, it was like feeling sunshine after a long winter.

She told him she wanted flapjacks and to smother them in sorghum, as though she even had to say what it was she wanted for breakfast. Old James remembered every little thing about Birdy Pride, from the color of her eyes clear down to the size of her tiny feet. And he remembered what she liked for breakfast.

Old James often thought about renting Birdy. He thought of it more as rent than as buying her, as some of the men who frequented her talked about doing.

"Think I'll go over and buy me some of that Birdy Pride," they'd say.

But Old James knew you couldn't buy anyone, whores included. All you could do was rent them for a little while, just like beer and food and anything else a man might acquire in his life. Getting on in years as he was, Old James knew that the life of a man and everything about it was just a temporary condition. But whenever he thought about renting her, something in him wouldn't let him do it, some vague sense that a gentleman never paid for the services of a lady he was in love with—that fornicating should be part of marriage and not done outside it. He knew he'd never ask Birdy to marry him—he was too old for her; she'd never agree to such a foolish notion.

"What you writing, James?" Birdy said once she'd worked her way through most of her meal.

James looked round at her, saw a few sticky droplets of sorghum on her lips and nearly swooned.

"Just some things I remembered has happened to me over the years, Birdy."

"I bet you was a regular firecracker when you was young."

He felt warm crawl up his neck.

"I don't guess I was nothing more than any other young buck. Just a rascal cowboy like all the others. Rode the Cimarron Trail and up the Belle Fourche several times. Trailed a lot of cattle, seen a lot of country, been witness to the unusual and the profane, as well as the beautiful things in this old world."

"I bet you was a real buckaroo."

Yeah, he had his days he had to admit to himself, but never to a sweet young woman like Birdy Pride. Her ears couldn't stand to hear the things he had to say if he was to say them.

"Nah," he said instead, and went back to writing in his journal a poem he'd been composing for nearly a month—one called, "The Blackest Night on the Lone Prayrie." It was a poem all about the hardships of a cowboy, and in it he had a stanza that dealt with river crossings, and another that dealt with lightning, and one about stampedes, and one about trail grub.

He was down to working on a stanza about cow towns, and thought he'd have to say something about drinking and dance hall girls and fifty-cent haircuts and sleeping under the stars, too, as well as horses and dreaming about sweethearts left behind.

Then he heard gunshots. Birdy heard them, too.

"Why, whatever in the world is that?" she said.

"That ain't good," Old James said. "Gunshots so early of the morning."

Roy Bean looked out the window of the apartment he and Birdy had once shared. He'd just been putting on his paper collar when he heard gunshots. Sounded like they were coming up the street from the vicinity of the Rosebud.

Now, what damn fool would be firing off his pistol this early in the morning? he wondered. Didn't whoever it was realize a stray bullet could kill some innocent—maybe a woman taking a bath or a baby sucking on its mama's tit? Sure enough do need to get some decent law in this town. Things is bad enough with folks dropping dead and acting crazy all over the place; now someone had taken to shooting up the morning. Good Lord, but it was nearly hot enough already to boil eggs.

Toussaint Trueblood had been harnessing up his mule when he heard the echo of gunshots; a sound like tree limbs breaking in the distance. He looked toward the town. The mule's ears twitched at the sounds as well and it shifted its hind feet. Toussaint gave it a sugar

cube. He had it in mind to go and find a gift for
Karen. The only problem was, most of the kinds of
gifts he could afford he could only buy at Otis's place
and he did not want to go and give the man who had
courted Karen his hard-earned money if he didn't
have to. But the only other option was to try and buy
something on credit at the jeweler's. A silver ring,
maybe. Though he worried that if he bought Karen a
silver ring and gave it to her she might get the wrong
idea and think he was asking her to marry him again.
Better he swallow some of his pride and go to Otis's
and buy her a dress, or a shawl—though it sure
wasn't the weather for shawls. Dress, he decided.

Bob Olive and Teacup Smith finished drinking
their whiskies as Peg Leg Watts lay bleeding out on
the floor behind the bar. Bob Olive said to the
Teacup, "Let's go find that back shooter and show
him what it feels like."

"We showed him once."

"Well, we're by god going to show him again, only
this time he won't be climbing out of the grave again
like he did last time. This time we'll shoot him in the
head like we ought to have done the last time."

Emeritus Fly, editor and owner of *The Grasslands
Democrat,* had been setting type in his shop in prepa-
ration of the latest news on the wounded President
Garfield. A telegram he'd received from a friend who
worked at the *New York Herald* described the president as being in great agony while a team of doctors

probed and poked their fingers in his gut wound trying to retrieve the assassin's bullet.

"The great man remained stoic throughout the almost brutal efforts of the medicos to find the onerous bullet and take it out. I was a witness to the act and I can tell you it made my nuts shrink just to watch. The weather is hot, the blowflies abundant. Negroes have been hired to wave a fan over the suffering president. They are talking about transferring him to the Jersey shore. More to follow."

Emeritus tapped the lead type in place.

Then the shots rang out and caused him to jump.

"What's this?" he said aloud, and went to the door and looked up and down the street.

It was early yet. Perhaps some kids shooting off firecrackers. Emeritus went back to setting type. The headline was to read: PRESIDENT GARFIELD VALIANTLY CLINGS TO LIFE. THERE IS HOPE!

Roy Bean saw Bob Olive and Teacup Smith come strolling out of the Rosebud. Saw them from his window above the dentist's office. Two mean bastards pacing. What now? There would be blood running in the streets, of that much he was sure. They hadn't come back just to get something they'd forgot.

He watched until they strode off down the walk toward Skinny Dick's Pleasure Palace.

What are those two dirty devils up to?

He quickly slipped down the back steps, up the alley, and into the rear door of the Rosebud.

Peg Leg Watts was mewing like a kitten as he lay in a pool of blood leaking out of him.

Roy bent low. Peg Leg opened one eye, then closed it.

"I'll get Doc," Roy said. Started to stand, saw Peg Leg's shotgun there on a shelf, took it with him.

I ain't no killer, but I might have to turn into one before this day's over, he thought.

He went out of the Rosebud the same way he came in, went down the alley to Birdy's crib, knocked on the door. Nobody answered. He looked in the window, saw the bed was empty and therefore the room around it. It was something of a relief to him that he didn't see Doc and Birdy having relations. Back down the other way he went—toward Doc's house.

Found Doc there eating an onion sandwich, and for once not drunk.

"Doc, those goddamn killers is back and they already shot Peg Leg Watts."

Doc looked at him, a mouthful of bread and onion.

"Bob Olive and Teacup Smith," Roy clarified.

"I thought you all ran them out of town."

"We did. But they're back now and looks like they're in a murderous mood. Peg Leg's about dead, but not quite. I wonder if you might go have a look at him and see if anything can be done for him?"

"Yes, I'll go."

"Good. I got to find Jake. They'll be after him, I'm sure. They'll kill him if they find him. Everybody in Sweet Sorrow could be dead by nightfall now that those bastards have the taste of blood."

"You go do what you have to. I'll go tend to Peg Leg."

Doc had a funny look in his eyes. But then Roy Bean didn't have any time to contemplate why.

Otis's wife shook him awake.

"Somebody's shooting a gun," she said.

Otis had lain in bed well beyond his usual rising time because of the whipping the preacher had given him. He came awake slowly, for he'd been dreaming that he and Karen Sunflower were living in Paris— that they had been strolling through the Luxembourg Gardens and it was a dream he didn't want to readily leave.

"Wake up you sad fool," she said. She was still angry at him for having snuck off from the store the day before and gone fishing. "You see what playing hooky got you?" she cried upon seeing him beaten and hearing his confession on how the beating had come to take place.

When he did awake, it felt as if someone had tossed him under a mule train. The beating would leave him bruised and scratched for a week, and his ego wounded for longer than that, for his wife wouldn't ever let him hear the last of it.

"Somebody's shooting a gun," his wife repeated.

"I don't hear nothing."

"Of course you don't, they stopped shooting."

Otis scratched his scalp. It felt tenderly painful.

"I don't see why you woke me," he said. "I can't do anything about somebody who wants to shoot a gun."

"Oh, there could be trouble. Somebody might break in and rob the store and steal us blind of every red cent we own. You better get some drawers on and go look. It ain't normal somebody shooting a gun this early in the morning."

Reluctantly Otis got dressed and found his hat. The sun outside was sharp enough to cause his eyes to water.

Who the hell would want to shoot a gun on such a hot morning?

Fannie was saying how much she enjoyed their night together when Roy Bean knocked on the door. She'd been sitting on the side of the bed rolling up her stockings in a way that was reminiscent of the way Celine had done the last time she and Jake were together—just before she sprung the trap on him. He turned his back on Fannie as he dressed just so he wouldn't be reminded of that fateful day.

"Jake!" Roy Bean called from the other side of the door. "Better open up if you're in there. I got some bad news for you!"

Jake opened the door.

Roy's gaze darted to Fannie then back to Jake.

"They're back."

"Who's back?"

"Bob and Teacup, and they already shot Peg Leg. He's probably dead by now. They're on the prowl like a pair of rabid dogs. Saw them heading down toward Skinny Dick's. Jake looked at the shotgun Roy was holding.

"This isn't your fight," he said.

"Hell, I don't reckon I got no more choice in it than you," Roy said.

"I was the one who shot Bob. It's me he wants to get even with. No point in getting yourself killed."

Roy thought of his wife and children down there in Texas still waiting on him, still counting on him to return—in one piece, to be sure. What would they think if word came he'd been shot dead in Dakota, or worse, if somebody sent his corpse home on a train in one of Tall John's homemade caskets?

"I can't let you go face them two alone."

"Hell, there's just two of them," Jake said. "It's not like there are a dozen."

Fannie said, "God, God, what's happening?"

Jake took up his pistols, checked the loads.

"Stay here with her, Mr. Bean. If they kill me and you're still feeling the need, then you can pitch into the fight, for then you just might have to."

Jake went out and left Roy Bean and Fannie together.

It was no time of course to be thinking such thoughts, Roy told himself, but Fannie wasn't a bad looking young woman. Not as comely or as young as Birdy, of course, but still comely and young enough if a man had his mind set on such a gal.

But all that would have to wait of course.

Until the killing was finished.

19

❖❖❖

SKINNY DICK was three dollars up on Mistress Sheba in a stud poker game between just the two of them when Bob Olive and Teacup Smith came in.

Mistress Sheba hadn't been able to concentrate on card games since she had come to conclude that very morning that she was pregnant. By whom, she did not know. She fretted as to who the father might be. Any number of men (by calculation, she reckoned the event would have occurred during the spring) were possibilities. And even though she'd taken great precaution to prevent pregnancy by taking regular cocktail mixtures of quinine, rock salt, and alum, she was sure there was another human growing inside her.

She'd been mentally running through a list of names as Skinny Dick won pot after pot off her.

One name that jumped out right away was that of a traveling douser named Calvin Cloud who had come through town beginning of April—April first, April Fools' Day—if she recalled correctly; and she thought she had. Mistress Sheba hoped it wasn't Cloud, a short belligerent fellow with a cat's curiosity. He barely stood five feet tall and had a raspy voice he said was the result of a burned voice box. He did not say how his voice box came to be burned. There were scars around his neck, and she considered the possibility that someone had tried to hang Cloud and that was what ruined his voice. Not only was he short and bellicose, he had suffered from a self-admitted wanderlust.

"Never can stand to be in one place too long," he said the evening of their encounter. "Me, I got to bug out soon as I do my work. There is always somebody needs a well witched. I probably doused a thousand wells across this country. I'm the Johnny Appleseed of well witchers." Mistress Sheba sure enough hoped Calvin Cloud was not the father of her child, or else the April Fools' joke would be on her.

Then there was that sometimes cowboy, sometimes post-hole digger, sometimes wagon driver, Will Bird. A big strapping boy about half Mistress Sheba's age, who spent every spare dime he earned on whores, explaining: "I just got a yen for you working gals. Can't get enough. Don't have to court you, don't have to bring you no flowers or candy or go on no picnics or rides with you in the moonlight. Don't have to meet your folks or think about growing old with you. All I got to do is wash my neck and come up with the money. It's the way I prefer romance."

Will came and went like the seasons—drifting all over the country in pursuit of work and whores, and she never quite knew when he would arrive or when he'd leave again. She liked Will Bird well enough. He had uncommon good looks and youthful ways—but Will Bird wouldn't make no kind of father or husband, either.

Then there was that damn Bob Olive who fornicated like a threshing machine—real quick and with about as much charm. Bob Olive had visited her on a regular basis all through the winter, spring, and summer until they ran him and Teacup Smith out of town. Now they were back—standing there big as life and she wondered if it were providence they were back, or just plain bad luck.

It was as though thinking about him had produced him. Mistress Sheba had something of a gift for the supernatural—a common trait among the Periwinkle women on her mother's side.

Skinny Dick looked up from his hand and said, "I thought they had run the two of you off."

Teacup said, "You want me to shoot him, Bob, or do you want to?"

Toussaint saw Jake coming out of the hotel—a pistol in each hand.

"You kill somebody, or about to?"

"Bob Olive and Teacup Smith are back in town. They shot Peg Leg."

"Dead?"

"Sounds like it."

"Where they at now?"

"Roy Bean said he saw them walking east, down toward Skinny Dick's place."

"Maybe you ought to kill them this time instead of just shooting one of them in the leg."

"Yeah," Jake said, "I was thinking the same thing," and walked on, staying close to the storefronts.

Toussaint watched him walk away, then snapped the reins and told his mule to step off, went half a block and pulled in at the mercantile. Otis was standing in the doorway, his galluses hanging down, his hair a small haystack on his head.

Their eyes met.

"I came to buy a dress," Toussaint said.

"I never featured you as the dress-wearing type."

"I'm not up for jokes."

"I got some new that came in this week. Nice gingham."

They let silence settle between them as Toussaint climbed down from the wagon.

"My wife shook me out of bed, said she heard shooting," Otis said, leading the way into the store.

"Bob and Teacup shot Peg Leg."

"Dead?"

"As far as I know."

"What's to be done?"

"Why ask me? I just came to buy a dress."

Upon hearing the pistol shots, Old James went back into the kitchen and came out again with a big

Walker Colt—one he used to carry when he was a fuzz-faced Texas Ranger. He hadn't shot the gun in years and years, but kept fresh loads in its cylinders and kept it wrapped in an oilskin and stored in the bottom drawer of his room for just such emergencies.

"What you going to do, James?" Birdy asked.

"Defend you if I have to, from killers and would-be killers."

Birdy tittered.

"How heroic," she said.

"I killed plenty of bad men with this here," James said showing her the hogleg. "I got all the names of the ones I killed written in my book. I ain't proud of the fact, mind you, but what is, is."

"You really think you have to kill men to defend me, James?" Birdy said.

"Hard to tell—but it ain't normal to hear pistol fire this early of the day. Something bad's going down. I can feel it. You stay inside here. Don't go out on them streets. A stray bullet could find you . . ." Old James's voice broke. He felt full of worry for the sweet Birdy Pride. He'd been thinking ever since she came in about that cigar box full of money he had stashed under his mattress. He hadn't counted it lately, but the last time he had, there was close to fifteen hundred dollars in it. Birdy might just be persuaded to marry him for that kind of money, he reasoned. He seen lots of folks do worse things for money. Old James knew he did not have much longer to live. He never went to a doctor—but he didn't need to go to a doctor to know his heart was bad. Sometimes he'd wake in the middle of the night and his heart would be flopping around like a chicken that's had its head twisted off. Sooner or later that chicken heart of his was going to stop flopping. It was possible he had children to leave his small fortune to—but who they were and where they were was impossible to say; he'd fornicated all over Texas. He had no known living kin. Birdy might as well have his fortune if she'd consent to marry him.

Birdy was touched by James's concern for her welfare.

Their eyes met. A moment of truth passed between them.

Birdy thinking to herself, *he's a kind man like my daddy was before I left him and Mama in Darke County. It's sweet of him to go out on the streets with a gun to defend me; but I swear I don't know, defend me from what?*

Old James made a big show of sticking the Walker into his waistband and strutting forth onto the streets, ready to take down whatever danger lay ahead, ready to be Lancelot to his Guinevere.

Toussaint nervously fingered the dresses Otis laid out for him to consider.

"That's a nice one," Otis finally said of a dark green number with velvet trim and bone buttons.

"You'd probably know better than me what Karen would look good in," Toussaint said. Otis was caught off-guard by the unexpected comment.

"I don't see why you'd say a thing like that?"

Toussaint looked at him, looked at the dress.

"Time we put things in the past," Toussaint said. "Dex is dead—murdered."

The news struck Otis like a lightning bolt.

"No. It can't be."

"Buried him yesterday out to Karen's. Got the boy who did it in jail."

Silence welled up between them again like a held breath and naught but the ticking of the Regulator clock above the shelves of dry goods and cans of peaches could be heard in the store.

"Anyway," Toussaint said stoically, "I'm not holding it against you what may or may not have happened that winter I was gone. Just thought that if Dex was your boy, you ought to go pay your respects to Karen. Only not today. I'm going out there myself today. I need to make peace with her. Wrap it up, I'll take it."

Otis wrapped the dress in paper, tied it with a string.

"How much?" Toussaint said.

Otis shook his head.

"I can't charge you for it if it's for Karen."

"How much, goddamn it?"

"Ten dollars; it's my cost on it."

Toussaint reached inside his pocket, took out the money Jake had given him to drive out to Karen's in the first place. He laid it on the counter, took up the package and walked out.

Word spread quickly about the shooting. Folks began drifting onto the streets. Jake told the ones he passed to go back inside. They did, then drifted out again once he passed on his way toward Skinny Dick's.

He could hear some of them whisper: "He going to face them alone?" "Ain't nobody going to help him?"

He wondered the same thing until nobody stepped forth, one old man with a big Walker Colt stuck down the waistband of his pants, who'd come out of the Fat Duck.

"You better go back inside," Jake said.

"I heard shooting," Old James said.

Jake quickly explained what the shooting had been about.

"Those filthy dogs," Old James said. "Somebody should have plowed them under a long time ago."

"They've come for me. Once it's settled, one way or the other, you and the others might not have to worry."

"I got an interest in this. You might as well not argue with me, son."

"I can't stop you, but I can't promise I can watch your back, either."

Old James snorted and clomped down the walk toward Skinny Dick's pulling the Walker as he went.

Jake caught up with him.

"When we get there, why don't you go around back and in that way and I'll go in the front."

"Suits me."

"Hey."

"What?"

"Just don't shoot me with that damn thing, okay?"

Old James looked as if he had indigestion.

* * *

Toussaint went out and got into the wagon, the packaged dress under his arm. He saw Old James walking in the street up ahead, a big pistol in his hand. Jake was sticking close to the storefronts. There would be more dead before this day was over. He took up the reins, held them a second. He really should go on out and pay Karen a visit, take her the dress and make his peace with her. It wasn't right she should sit out there alone feeling friendless.

"Step off, mule."

The mule did as ordered.

And just as quick Toussaint tugged back on the reins and the mule stopped, swung its head back around, confused.

"Hold on, mule."

Toussaint's gaze followed the progress of the two men.

"Shit," he said.

Bob Olive had ordered Mistress Sheba into the backroom.

"You going to kill me, Bob?"

"I might once I get finished with you. Get on back there."

She did as ordered, but once back there, fearful Bob was going to end her life, she blurted: "You wouldn't kill a woman carrying your youngster, would you, Bob?"

He looked at her strange.

"What the damn hell are you blabbering about? Hike up them skirts and let's get to it."

"I got a kid in me, Bob. Your kid, the way I calculate."

Bob was unbuckling his belt so he could tug down his britches. He never thought to waste time taking *off* his clothes, boots, shirt, hat. It wasn't his way.

"I don't want to hear no foolish talk, woman. Climb up on that bed and stop all this nonsense."

In the other room Skinny Dick said, "You got no call to shoot me. I never did you no wrong, Teacup."

"You never did me no right, either."

"I'll give you free liquor the rest of your natural days."

Teacup cocked his pistol.

Otis was still stunned over the news of Dex when Toussaint walked back in the front door.

"Give me one of those shotguns and a box of shells for it."

Otis took one down from the rack—its price tag still strung to the trigger guard—without asking any questions; he saw the look in Toussaint's eyes.

"This is it, isn't it?"

Toussaint broke open the shotgun as he waited for Otis to hand him the box of shells, then loaded each of the barrels and put the other shells in his pockets.

"Go on and get it over with quick," Otis said.

"What the hell are you talking about?"

"You've come to kill me over Karen," Otis said. "I just want you to know nothing happened . . . well, almost nothing. But she said—"

Toussaint snapped the breech shut.

"I didn't come to kill you, you damn fool. And I don't want to hear anymore about it."

Otis gulped air as Toussaint strode back out again.

"Go on around back," Jake said to Old James.

Old James slipped down the space between the Pleasure Palace and the jeweler's, Jake saying as he started, "I'll give it a count of twenty, then I'm going in."

Old James felt his blood up for the first time in years, felt a tightness encircle his chest, knew that it was his heart protesting the excitement. Well, goddamn, let it protest, he was about sick to death of serving up coffee and writing in a book about the things he done once. Anymore writing to be done, it would be about the things he was about to do.

He came quick enough to the back of Skinny Dick's. A narrow door with a porcelain handle stood there waiting his hand on it to turn it, to open it, and slip inside. He held the Walker at the ready as he reached for the knob. The pistol felt heavy as brick— a lot heavier than he remembered it being when he rode with the Rangers as a young buck.

Inside he went. Hell fire. Let her rip.

Jake waited at the front door, counting. Got to the agreed-upon twenty. Went in.

Two men there at the bar. The light inside bad. One turned. Jake saw the gun in his hand.

"Lay it on the bar," he said.

"Fuck, you say!"

Two shots exploded almost at the same instant. Gunsmoke filled the room.

Teacup felt the bullet go through him, and as it spun him round, he shot Skinny Dick in the face without intending to. Jake fired again and this time Teacup was carried off his feet, flung back over a table scattering cards, whiskey glasses, and poker chips.

One shaft of sunlight thin as a knife blade fell through a side window, and in it smoke roiled.

Toussaint had reached the front door just as Jake shot Teacup the second time. He saw through the smoke a man standing, couldn't tell who it was. Leveled both barrels and stood behind them ready to cut whoever it was in half.

In his haste to reach the front, Old James failed to notice the door to his left as he moved down the hallway. He passed it just as the shots rang out. The burst of gunfire startled him and when he swallowed it felt like a small apple was stuck in his throat. The hand holding the Walker trembled. He told himself he wasn't afraid. That he'd kill every goddamn son of a bitch that stepped into his sights.

He stood for a moment trying to steady his rickety heart. It rattled like a stone inside a tin can.

It was only when the woman screamed that he turned around and saw the man standing there with a gun aimed at him.

"Don't move!" Toussaint yelled, "or I'll cut you down."

Jake froze, said, "I thought you were going to Karen's."

Toussaint stepped into the room, saw the carnage. Teacup was still moving his legs, as if he were trying to crawl but wasn't having any success. Skinny Dick sat with his back against the wall as though he were having his lunch on the floor, only his face was a bloody wreck.

"Where's the other one? Bob Olive?"

That's when they heard the woman scream, followed by gunshots down the hall.

"The old man," Jake said.

They moved cautiously, a curtain covering the hall's entryway. Toussaint used the barrels of the shotgun to draw the curtain aside. Jake stood ready to shoot anything in his line of fire. Too late. Old James lay crumpled, leaking blood like a damaged pump, groaning.

They saw half his jaw shot away, white bone, teeth, bloody gristle. Air whistled through the wound each time Old James took a breath. The Walker lay clutched in his hand, the hammer down, the hand twitching.

Toussaint drew Jake's attention to the door that stood ajar.

They called in to Bob to give himself up. No answer.

"Last time we'll ask you to come out," Jake said.

They waited.

Nothing.

"You got the scatter gun," Jake said. "I'll kick it open, you kill him."

Toussaint nodded.

Jake kicked open the door as Toussaint stood waiting.

They found Mistress Sheba on the bed with her throat slit, her blood soaking into the carmine silk sheets, her worries about who the father of her child was now inconsequential. It could have been Calvin Cloud, Will Bird, Bob Olive, or even Skinny Dick. It didn't matter. Nothing did anymore.

The backdoor stood open.

20

DOC WILLIS SAID, "You poor unfortunate bastard."
Peg Leg moaned.

"I'm killed, ain't I?"

"Pret' near."

"Oh, god!"

Doc stood from his patient and pulled down a bottle of the bar's best whiskey from the upper shelf, took two glasses, and filled them each, then remembered how Peg Leg liked his rum and filled a glass with the bottle labeled Tropical Isle. Then he knelt again and propped Peg Leg up.

"Oh! Oh!" the shot man moaned. "It hurts like someone running hot pokers through me."

"Drink this."

Doc put the rum to Peg Leg's lips. The lips nibbled at first then parted for the rest. Doc spilled it into his mouth, then drank from his own glass.

"How's it feel now?" Doc asked.

"Not so good."

"Tell me what it's like," Doc said.

"What?" Peg Leg muttered.

"Dying."

Peg Leg's eyes fluttered.

"I . . . I, done things I like better . . ."

"I mean are you afraid?"

"Some . . . I guess . . ."

"But not terribly so?"

Peg Leg swallowed, once, twice, three times. Doc poured him another glass of rum and fed it to him; some of it spilled out the sides of his mouth and down his chin.

"It's like a light coming towards me . . ."

"Death?"

Peg Leg nodded.

"Feels like I'm drifting . . . like in a boat . . . towards that . . . light."

"Go on and let yourself go."

Again Peg Leg nodded.

"I'm trying . . ."

Doc poured himself a second glass of liquor and sat next to Peg Leg, there on the bloody floor, not minding that his clothes were becoming stained. He was trying to experience the death along with his patient. He truly wanted to know.

Time ticked slowly as it always does when a man is waiting for the unknown to happen.

Doc heard pistol shots off in the distance.

"Death is all around us, Mr. Watts. There's killing on the streets and in the houses and everywhere. You're not alone in your dying this day, Mr. Watts."

Peg Leg's head lolled.

"It's coming for us all," Doc said. "Sooner or later it will sniff us out and eat us, and then that will be the end."

Peg Leg's eyes fluttered again.

"It's closer . . . Doc. The . . . light is clos . . ."

"Go on to it, dear fellow."

Peg Leg slumped over.

"Ilicet," Doc said in Latin. "It is finished."

He closed his own eyes and saw Iris dancing on the moon, blood red as a great bowl of cherry juice, and he sighed at the thought of her. Soon I will join you, my love. Soon.

The Chinaman smiled knowingly. Prince Puckett knew why. He wanted to say to the fellow, I guess when a dog is hungry any scrap will do, but did refrain, for just the thought of seeing him and the woman together the evening before was one that caused his skin to crawl.

Prince Puckett said to the driver, "What time we due into Sweet Sorrow?"

Fuzzy Walls snapped open his pocket watch—one given to him by the stage lines to keep him as much on schedule as was possible, taking into consideration rain-swollen creeks, busted wheels, lame horses, highwaymen, and other disasters—and saw that it was nearly eight o'clock.

"We should arrive around noon."

"How about I ride on top?"

Fuzzy shook his head.

"Against company regulations. The only ones who ride on top is me and the shotgun man."

Prince looked at the shotgun man, a silent, droopy-eyed little fellow who had not spoken a single word to anyone since Bismarck.

"How about him and me change places—him in the coach and me on top, then?"

Fuzzy Walls looked over at Sam Toe.

"He wants you and him to change places," Fuzzy said.

Sam Toe was a man who sat under his big hat tugged down to the tops of his ears. He had a turkey feather stuck in his hatband—something he was told by one Cutbank Charley Warner would bring him good luck all his days. Cutbank Charley Warner was a former saddle pard Sam Toe had ridden fence line with in and around Big Piney, Wyoming Territory. Cutbank Charley wore a turkey feather in his hat and never so much as had a toothache. His wearing of a turkey feather in his hat convinced Sam Toe to wear one as well—and thus far, his luck had been as good as Charley's.

"Well?" Prince Puckett said impatiently to his offer that they exchange places.

Sam Toe cut his gaze down to Prince's.

"Nope," he said.

"I can ride shotgun just as well as you. Probably shoot better than you, if it comes to that," Prince Puckett said. "I've got lots of shooting experience."

Sam Toe looked at Fuzzy as if to say, You tell him it's my job. But Fuzzy just shrugged.

"You trading with me?" Prince said.

"Nope," Sam said.

"That's the most I ever heard him say," Fuzzy said.

Prince started up to change places. Sam pointed his shotgun at him.

"You better get down lest he shoots you," Fuzzy said. "Sam takes his job serious."

"I don't forget such insults easily," Prince Puckett said, slipping back down again, giving the shotgun rider a final hard look before climbing inside the stage.

The Chinaman hadn't changed expression. The kids yammered. The woman sat with her eyes closed and her mouth open, snoring. Three, four more hours of being cooped up with this lot and having every bone in his body jarred loose was going to be sheer torture, he told himself.

But fifteen hundred dollars went a long way to easing the pain of it all.

Fannie and Roy Bean heard the shots.

Neither said anything at first. Then Fannie said, "What do you think has happened?"

Roy Bean listened a time longer to the yawning silence that comes after gunfire has stopped.

"I guess whatever happened is over. I don't hear no more."

"I hope Jake isn't killed," Fannie said fretfully.

"I know this might not be a proper time to ask you this," Roy Bean said, "but in case things has gone bad for Jake, I was wondering if you'd consider my coming round to court you?"

Fannie simply looked at him for a full moment before saying, "I know you to be a married man, Roy Bean. Birdy Pride has told me so. I told her she was an empty-headed fool for letting herself be courted by a married fellow and I'd be just as empty-headed as her were I to say yes to your offer. So, I'm saying no."

Roy Bean looked sorrowful.

"I guess I've just a weakness for fine-looking young women," he said. "I sure didn't mean any insult by asking."

"None taken."

"You best wait here while I go and check things out. Danger could still be lurking on those streets out yonder."

"Come back quick and let me know if Jake is all right."

"Yes'm."

"What do you want to do?" Toussaint said.

"It's not your fight," Jake replied.

"Hell, anyone knows that, it's me. That wasn't my question."

"I appreciate the help," Jake said. "But you've done enough for me as it is."

"That's fine with me if that's what you want. There's just Bob now. All you have to do is find him and kill him."

"Tell me something," Jake said.

"What?"

"This place always been so damn trouble-filled?"

"Not until you came along."

"Believe me, I'd just as soon I'd never come along."

"Can't help what is."

"Where do you think a man like Bob Olive would run?"

"Wherever it is, it won't be far. Bob Olive's not the running sort. He'll ambush you, shoot you in the back, if you give him a chance. But then you already know that. The other thing is, he'll kill anyone who gets in his way."

Toussaint looked down at Old James. It was the one thing he wouldn't be writing in that book of his—his own death.

"Then I better find him before he does."

"You sure enough could steal you a horse and make a run for it. Nobody could blame you."

"Don't think I haven't thought about that already," Jake said.

"Maybe you ought to think about it some more before you go out that door."

"You know anything about cancer?" Jake said.

"Not much."

"If you leave it alone, don't cut it out, it spreads and kills everything it touches."

"Sounds like you know a thing or two about medicine," Toussaint said.

"It doesn't matter, does it—what I know about?"

"No, not to me. Nor any of these others, I expect."

"Good, let's just keep it that way."

Toussaint watched Jake eject the spent shells from his pistols and replace them with fresh loads, then slip out the same backdoor that Bob Olive had slipped out of earlier. He thought about the dress he'd bought Karen, sitting there on the seat of his wagon, wrapped in butcher's paper. He thought how nice she'd look in it if he could talk her into wearing it. Karen wasn't the dress-wearing type, but if she were, she'd look nice in it. He ought to ride it out to her.

He told himself two or three times, that is what he ought to do and let these people kill themselves if that was what they were so intent on doing.

That big Walker Colt of Old James's had blown a ragged hole through the side of Bob Olive—just below the ribs and above the hip, right side. He knew if he didn't get the hole plugged, he'd bleed out like a throat-cut hog.

There was only one place he could get the hole plugged—the big house at the end of the street,

Doc Willis had left Peg Leg Watts to his ephemeral future and gone out of the Rosebud with the remainder of the house's best whiskey sloshing in the bottom of the bottle he held in his hand.

Oh, it felt like a time to dance the dance of the macabre, for the souls were flying everywhere and the world seemed asunder.

Then, once home and prepared to drink himself into unconsciousness, he found instead a man waiting with a gun, blood soaking through his shirt and the man's name was one Bob Olive.

"Well, go ahead and pull that trigger, son, if that is what your intent is."

"You plug up this hole and you'll live to deliver more babies and fix more broken arms," Bob Olive said. "You don't and you won't see lunch."

Doc Willis couldn't tell if Bob's sweat was caused by the heat or his being shot.

"And if I refuse," he said, "we'll both die, won't we, Mr. Olive? Only you more slowly."

Bob stepped close and put the end of the barrel to Doc's temple and thumbed back the hammer.

"I guess we by god will."

Until that moment, Doc thought himself prepared to die. He'd even dreamt of it as a way to escape his ongoing misery and loneliness. But when the cold iron touched his skin and Bob thumbed back the hammer, the sound it made traveled down the whole length of the barrel and entered his soul. His resolve to accept death crumbled and he felt the flame of survival grow hot in his belly.

"Do something, you goddamn drunk! Patch me up or get ready to go straight to hell."

"Sit . . . on that table," Doc stammered. "Pull up your shirt."

Bob Olive sat with the gun pointed at Doc's skull as Doc set to plugging the hole in him. He felt ashamed of his weakness, he, a man who'd dealt with life and death nearly all his adult life, a man who had no truck with the spiritual world, now silently prayed to a God he didn't know or understand to spare his very life—to let him live one more minute, hour, day.

He was glad Iris wasn't there to witness such weakness.

Jake picked up the blood trail. Old James got one off. Good for him. The blood trail led up the alley and out the end, across the street. Jake could see Doc's house in the distance. It made sense Bob would seek medical help.

Toussaint watched from his wagon seat.

The street was filling up again with townsfolk, milling about, talking among themselves, peeking in the front doors of Rosebud and Skinny Dick's Pleasure Palace, women jerking their kids by the arms away from the murder places, men pointing, scratching their heads. He saw Emeritus Fly, the editor of the newspaper, scribbling notes in a ledger. He thought about Old James, that book of his he wrote in, how he'd do no more writing in it.

Almost without notice, he saw Jake emerge from the alley that ran back of the saloon and cross the street and head in the direction of the physician's house. Toussaint thought, you would make a good hunter of dreaming rabbits—you got the nose for it.

"Hurry up, you alky!" Bob Olive commanded.

Doc Willis had already dropped one bandage in his nervousness.

"I could go faster if you didn't press that gun to my head."

Bob Olive nudged him with the pistol barrel.

"There's a bullet in here with your name on it if you don't finish patching me up in about ten seconds." Bob Olive was a wary enough man to know there were those who would not let his murders stand. Whoever it was that had come for him—and there could be only one he could think of with the gall—wasn't about to just let him escape. He kept one eye on the door expecting any minute someone to come through it.

Doc finished his work as well as he could without the use of stitches. Bob Olive looked down at the bandage already tinged pink.

"Go stand in front of that door."

Doc did as ordered.

"Don't turn around."

Doc waited for the bullet to enter his spine or the back of his skull. He prayed that if it were to be, that it be quick, painless.

Jake slipped around to the side of the house, crossed the porch to a side door that was open, one that led into a parlor. He could hear voices coming from Doc's office. Doc sure as hell wasn't talking to himself.

Jake, with a gun in each hand, stepped to the edge of the entryway and made a quick check of the office. Doc was standing at the front door. Bob Olive was behind him, his pistol aimed at Doc's back.

"I guess when I finish round here, this town ain't

going to need no damn doctor," Bob said casually as he thumbed back the hammer.

Jake stepped into the entrance and as he did, the floorboards beneath him groaned with his weight.

Bob Olive spun round, and for a split second their eyes locked.

Jake was already pulling the triggers of both pistols just as Bob's finger clamped down on his.

The bullets from the Schofields slammed into the gunman: one dead center, the other just above the heart. He was dead as he was falling, his own shot, rendered by the contraction of his hand and trigger finger, tearing through Doc's Belgium carpet—the very one Iris had begged him to buy.

Doc cried out in terror, then realized he was not shot.

He turned to see Jake, the smoking pistols in his hands—a dead Bob Olive on the floor. Both men would have known upon an autopsy examination that the shot that killed Bob Olive had ripped through his aortic valve and exploded his heart.

It was either excellent shooting, or just plain luck.

21

❧❧

TALL JOHN FOUND four bodies in Skinny Dick's Pleasure Palace: two in the bar, two in the back.

Some pleasure, he thought, as he went from one to the other. Folks shot in the face, through the middle, jaws torn away, throats slit. Tall John's young assistant, Boblink Jones, said, "I'm going to puke," and ran out the backdoor and did just that very thing.

"You'll get used to it," Tall John said when Boblink returned.

"No sir, I never will."

"You're right, son, you never will. I just said that to try and make you feel better. Death is one thing, violent death is another."

"It's this woman that's got me the worst," Boblink said.

They'd found Mistress Sheba lying crossway on the bed, her skirts still hiked up, the slash of her throat like a bloody grin. Tall John went over and delicately pulled her skirts down and said, "I know, son.

Women and children are always the worst—especially when such violence is visited upon them. Bring the wagon around back—best folks don't see us taking these poor souls out the front door."

Once done, they loaded Mistress Sheba, John saying how ladies should always go first, even in death, then took Old James and placed him next to Mistress Sheba.

Finally they went into the bar for the other two.

"Pick up Skinny's legs," John said. Boblink grabbed the former bartender by his limp legs while Tall John took him under the arms. It was mean work, carrying the dead, even if they were skinny as Dick was.

It took a lot of effort to load all the bodies and by the time they were finished, both Tall John and Boblink were soaked with sweat, their clothes turning stiff with drying blood. It was while loading the last of the corpses—Teacup Smith—that they heard the gunfire coming from Doc's house.

"I don't guess our day's yet finished," Tall John said. "We'll probably be half the evening embalming and preparing them for their final resting place. I'll stand you to a cold beer, how will that be?"

"Anything to cut the stink out of my taste."

Boblink sniffed the air.

"Blood smells awful in the heat, don't it?"

Tall John nodded. The beer tasted like a blessing. Flies buzzed over the wet bloody puddles staining the floor.

"We best get them poor folks over to the mortuary

and fixed up for burying sooner rather than later," Tall John said, setting his empty glass atop the bar. "This heat won't do them any good, or us neither."

"I hope you don't mind my quitting soon as we get 'em all buried, Mr. John," Boblink said. "I just ain't cut out for the handling of the dead."

"You have a fine knack of dressing them and fixing their hair, waxing their moustaches, and such. I'd sure hate to lose a good assistant like you."

Boblink thought of the choices he'd made thus far in his young life. A Missourian, he had wanted to join the James-Younger gang who had made quite a reputation for themselves as bank robbers all over the Midwest. He'd even arranged to meet Cole Younger and plead his case. But the cold-eyed desperado just laughed around his cigar.

"We ain't in the whelping business, boy, we're class-A outlaws. We shoot people! If we have to, that is. We rob banks and trains and ride all day and all night and sleep in our saddles and eat grubs we dig out of the ground and drink muddy water. If we have to, that is. We fight with guns and knives and our fists. Sometimes we get shot and stabbed and punched by the folks we're robbing. Sometimes our horses get shot out from under us. Sometimes when we do sleep, we sleep in cold caves and wake up with snakes crawled into our blankets. And sometimes when one of us gets caught, and we ain't shot dead, they hang us! You still want to be a desperado?"

Boblink reckoned not. But after working almost a year with Tall John, he did not want to be an undertaker's helper, either. At least being a desperado had its rewards: bank money, fast horses, loose women, and never having to pick up another dead body.

He made up his mind as they were setting Teacup Smith atop of Skinny Dick for transport to the mortuary that he'd pack his things and head back to Missouri and find Cole Younger and tell him he was ready to become a desperado.

Toussaint waited to see who would emerge from Doc Willis's home, and when he saw Jake come out and stand on the porch, he knew it was over and told his mule to step off. He had a dress he needed to get to Karen's, some words he needed to get said.

Karen sat staring at the grass. She could not bring herself to look off toward the freshly dug grave. She had looked at it once and wept and could not look again.

She carried on a silent monologue: Nothing you can do about it. You did everything you could for him and you raised him into manhood, and once he became a legal man, there was nothing more you could do.

Still, she felt as guilty as if she'd been the one to pull the trigger on Dex.

She fought the angry feelings until it felt as though she would jump out of her skin. What was she to do without Dex? And what was the point of anything? Hate and anger filled her the way bad water fills a poor well.

Then she saw a speck of something coming across the grasslands.

Soon enough she saw what the speck turned into and her hatred became a bitter bile that rose into the back of her throat.

Toussaint halted the wagon just shy of the front door. Karen sat there staring at him.

He reached down on the seat and took hold of the package and held it forth.

"I brought you something."

"Take whatever it is and yourself on back to where you came from."

He set the brake, looped the reins around the brake handle, and stepped down.

"I spent good money on it," he said, walking the package over to where she sat.

"I don't care if you spent every cent you had on it. Whatever it is, I don't want it. And I don't want you here, either."

Toussaint set the package down near her feet.

"I need to ask you something," he said.

Her gaze shifted from the sea of grass to the man who had once been her husband.

"I don't see how it matters now," she said.

"To me, it does."

"You were never a father to him when he was alive, so why should I tell you if he was yours or not now that it's too late for him to know the truth? What right do you have to the truth when Dex never knew it?"

"I got no right. I just want to know."

Karen looked off to the grass again. A wind stirred

through it so that it bent and lightened under the sun, then shifted and darkened when the wind drew it back again. Sometimes when it was ever so quiet she could hear the wind talking in the grass—as though God's own voice was whispering down through it.

"Today is not the day to talk about secrets," is all she said.

Toussaint nodded, climbed back up on the wagon and took up the reins.

"When will be the day?" he said.

Karen did not look at him or reply.

He snapped the reins, said, "Step off, mule."

Halfway back to Sweet Sorrow, he heard the rumble of the stage coming up the road behind him. He reined the mule over to the side of the road to allow it to pass and when it did, Fuzzy Walls waved at him but did not slow the coach. Toussaint waited for the dust the stage raised and now swirled along the road to settle again.

He had a sudden yen to buy a ticket on that stage and ride it to wherever it eventually would go. He just needed to be someplace other than the place he was in. Even the thought of hunting dreaming rabbits did not appeal to him and he wasn't sure if it ever would again, or if anything would.

Doc's hands trembled as he poured himself a glass of whiskey and drank it, watching the man who'd just saved his life kneel next to the corpse of Bob Olive.

"He's dead," Jake said, then stood and walked past

Doc Willis out onto the wide encircling porch where sunlight and shade mixed.

Doc followed Jake out.

"You saved my life . . ."

"I killed men here today, is what I've done."

"You had no choice."

But Jake was thinking about the oath he took, wondering if now that he'd broken it again did the oath ever truly mean anything to begin with. He wanted to think that it had, that his years as a physician outweighed these last few hours and the acts of murder he'd committed.

"I've never been anyplace quite like this," he said, as much to himself as Doc Willis.

"No, son, nor have I."

"Maybe this isn't the time, but I've been thinking about those folks who seemed to have gone mad—the woman with the child, the man who drowned himself, Mr. Rivers who murdered his wife—the preacher."

"What about them?" Doc said.

"I don't think it was just coincidence."

"What do you suspect it was?"

"I can't be sure. But reason tells me they all suffered from the same thing."

"Meaning?"

"That's what I thought I might ask you. As a physician have you ever come across anything like this before—this sort of random and rampant hysteria?"

Doc felt a chill run down his spine.

"No, I can't say that I have."

"It seems to me their condition could possibly have

something to do with something they possibly in-gested. I can't find any other explanation for it—not on the scale I've seen it around here."

"I don't know why you concern yourself with such matters. Aren't you just waiting to buy a horse so you can make the border?"

"I am."

"These things happen out on the frontier," Doc said. "People go mad from the isolation sometimes. They get drunk and their loneliness spills over. Any-thing will set them off. Sometimes one crazy act prompts another. I just chalk it up to this country, these times, these people."

"I suppose you're right."

"You'll be leaving soon, then?"

"Still waiting on a horse, but maybe Roy Bean will see fit to legally confiscate those of the dead men and let me buy one."

Doc Willis smiled nervously.

"There is no future here for a bright and brave young man such as yourself," Doc said. "You'd be foolish to stay any longer than was necessary."

Yes, Jake thought, I would, wouldn't I?

It was then, as he was descending the porch steps of Doc's house that he saw Roy Bean trotting down the street toward him waving his arms.

"We got troubles."

"They're dead," Jake said. "Olive and Smith. Seems to me your troubles are over."

"That ain't the trouble I'm talking about."

"What now?"

"That wild kid you and Toussaint brought in has busted jail. Smashed in the brains of Gus Boone and is on the loose."

"What is it with you people?" Jake said.

"Whatever do you mean?"

"I mean how the hell did I get put in the middle of all this?"

"It was you who brought him in. If you hadn't brought him in, he wouldn't have smashed in Gus's brains and busted jail and be on the loose—and armed to the teeth, I might add."

Birdy Pride felt forlorn when news arrived that Old James had been shot dead. Her heart sank like a rock tossed down a well.

"He vas a good cook," Zimmerman said. "I could count on him—regular as a coo-coo. I got no one to cook the early breakfasts now . . ."

Birdy said she was going to her crib; that she did not want to think anymore about sad things.

"The world is so filled with the saddest things," she said. "Poor James."

Zimmerman understood completely. He was big and fat as a sausage and generally a man of good spirits, but what had transpired in the last few days had him wondering if he should clear out and sail back to his homeland. He missed the snowy mountains of Austria, its cool green summers, the sound of cow bells, yodeling, the taste of good ale.

"I understand, Fräulein," he said.

*   *   *

Birdy tossed herself upon her small cot, weary from sorrow and the heat and tried not to think of men in general and Roy Bean or Preacher Poke or Old James in particular. Men were just nothing but the bearers of sorrow and heartbreak—even if you did not love them, they had a way of making you sad. Men were just plain sad creatures and their sadness spilled over onto their women. She told herself she'd have nothing more to do with any of them. I need me a man about like Custer needed one more Indian, she told herself bitterly.

She closed her eyes against the heat and when she opened them again, a beautiful young boy with wild long hair stood above her. She felt her heart race with expectation that God in his wisdom had delivered her love's salvation and all former thoughts and rages against men dissipated like smoke in a stiff wind.

"You got any money?" the boy said.

Birdy blinked. It wasn't exactly the words she hoped she might hear from such a pretty boy whose only imperfection seemed to be a stain on the side of his head.

It was hard to tell in that light, but it looked as though he had blue eyes. She favored a man with blue eyes—they were rare as buffaloes. Most men she encountered had brown eyes, or gray, sometimes green, but rarely blue. Her first love back in Darke County had one blue eye—but his other was a combination of colors so he didn't count in her book as a blue-eyed man.

"I've got no money," she said. "I'm a working girl."

"Seems to me if you work you ought to get paid,

which means you ought to have money. Where you keep it? In a can somewheres? Under your pillow? Maybe sewed up in your mattress? I know some to even hide their money in their petticoats."

"I'm Birdy," she said trying to ignore his rough manner. "Birdy Pride. Glad to meet you" and held out her hand for him to take it and do with it whatever he would (she hoped he might kiss it tenderly and prove himself a knight of the order she'd read about in school books back in Darke County) but all he did was stare at it. For such a pretty boy he had poor ways about him.

"Waddy Worth's my name and I'm a bona fide killer, so don't mess with me, Miss. Give me your money—I need it to make my escape out of this burg."

"Take me with you," Birdy said of a sudden, feeling as though she was about to be liberated from a long and hard life of sexual servitude that would end up with her being old and unwanted. "Take me with you!"

"Hell, the last gal I tried to take with me almost got me hanged! Now hand over your money or I'll be forced to do something terrible to you."

"Oh, I don't care, then. Do what you will to me—shoot me, if you must. You'll be doing me a mighty big favor . . ." She set to crying. Some of it was heartfelt and some of it was an act in hopes of making the pretty blue-eyed boy feel sorry enough to take her with him. The thought of letting one more lice-infested, liquored-up, fat-bellied, foul-smelling man crawl atop of her and rut was more than she could bear.

"Shit," Waddy declared. "Just my luck to find a penniless whore. Why, I wouldn't take you to a dog fight if you was a champeen dog. You got any damn thing to drink in this pig flop?"

While he might be about the prettiest blue-eyed boy she'd ever laid eyes on, Birdy told herself he was as foul-mouthed and mean-spirited as an ugly man and it was plain to see that he wasn't about to take her with him.

"I got a little something in this bottle," she said, reaching under her pillow for the small bottle.

"Give it here," Waddy said, grabbing it from her. And before she could consider if she'd done an evil thing or not, he drained it with one gulp.

In less than five minutes Waddy Worth was dead, dead, dead.

Birdy had watched the effects of the mercury take hold, watched as the pretty blue-eyed boy grabbed at his throat and staggered about like a drunk. His pretty blue eyes got big as biscuits and little choking sounds came out of him as he tried to speak.

Quick enough his blue eyes weren't the only part of him to turn blue—his face and neck and lips turned blue, too. He fell down—might say he flopped down—and crawled along the floor and clutched at the bedspread on Birdy's bed. Then his whole body began to shake. He turned to writhing like a snake that had gotten run over by a wagon wheel.

"You oughtn't to have said such mean things to

me," Birdy said. "Now look what's gone and happened."

She didn't think the pretty blue-eyed boy heard her. His whole head seemed to swell and his tongue flopped out of his mouth and looked like a piece of liver. Worst thing was he almost bit his own tongue off but died just before he did.

Birdy wept at the horrible display.

She didn't mean to kill him, just teach him a lesson about civility and not hurting the feelings of others with such harsh talk. But the only lesson learned was she knew now that she would never drink mercury to take her own life. It was just too awful to consider.

She ran quick to find Roy Bean who was coming down the street with that fellow called Jake Horn.

A real nice-looking man, she thought as she ran toward them.

22

THE ORIGINAL Jake Horn—Uncle Jake—crossed the Red River at St. Boniface, and once he got south of the Turtle Mountains, he knew he was in Dakota Territory. Ahead of him lay the high plains—nothing but grass as far as the eye could see, treeless—a sea of grass. He was an old man—nearly fifty—and told himself maybe this was his last good ride, his final adventure, and if it was, so be it.

He knew he was still wanted for various crimes and misdeeds south of the Canadian border. Hell, he'd robbed enough trains to have ballads written about him. But he hadn't robbed a train in years, and hadn't committed a crime of any sort since having gone north of the Turtle Mountains.

He'd gone to Manitoba to hide out from the United States marshals and ended up falling in love with a woman nearly a third his age: Alberta Fair, part of a traveling medicine show. She was a spiritual healer under the guidance of one Colonel Tom Tophat who, besides Alberta, kept several other women in his confidence and employment.

Jake had been suffering headaches and some eye problems and had gone to the medicine show in hopes of buying a bottle of the advertised elixir: *Colonel Tom's Cure All.*

Instead his sore eyes locked with those of the winsome Alberta and he returned that very evening with a bouquet of flowers, asking if she'd go for a moonlight walk with him. She obliged.

"You and the Colonel maintain a private relationship?" Jake asked out of curiosity.

"We all of us enjoy each other's company," Alberta replied as they walked.

"How do you mean, exactly?"

"We're advocates of free love," she said.

"Free love, eh?"

"Yes."

"That mean what I think it means?"

"What do you think it means, Mr. Horn?"

"Everybody in the same bed at the same time?"

"Sometimes, yes, sometimes we pair off, and sometimes we sleep alone."

He thought about it as they continued their walk; she was as darling as a dove—a wisp of a girl who seemed more angel than human to him. He knew it was foolish of him to think along the lines he was thinking along, but he could not help himself.

"Seems as though you're an advanced thinker for someone so young."

"I always had a mind of my own," she laughed.

"My mother called me willful. I left home when I was sixteen and joined the Colonel's medicine show."

"You in love with the Colonel?"

"I love him, but I'm not *in* love with him."

And so it went, the two of them talking and walking in the moonlight and Jake asking Alberta about her ideas on different subjects even as he knew he was already in love with her and by dawn he'd asked her to marry him and she'd agreed with the understanding that it would not be a traditional affair, that she would write her own vows and that such professions as ". . . till death do us part," and so forth, would not be included. She further insisted the Colonel would perform the ceremony and her "sisters" would stand as witnesses.

"I'm not one to turn my back on something at the first sign of trouble that comes along," he said.

"Neither am I, Mr. Horn," Alberta replied. "I'll love you as long as I may, and I expect the same, with no promises of forevers, and no demands on such antiquated notions of fidelity. Is that agreeable?"

"I'll go along with it if you promise me that if you ever get the itch for another man, or a gal, you'll let me know first."

"Fair enough."

And so they were married standing on the banks of the Red River with the gentlest breeze playing through their hair as Colonel Tom read the vows Alberta and Jake wrote. Then Franny, Olive, Jane, and Alice sang a wedding song of their own composition before all of them departed for unknown parts to sell their medicines and practice their personal beliefs.

"You sorry to see them go?" Jake asked as they watched the Medicine Wagon ramble away.

"They were all darlings to me," Alberta said. "And I will miss them. But you are my lover now, dearest, and if all goes well between us, I shan't miss them for too very long."

It was a good marriage for the nearly three years it lasted.

Then one bright morning Jake awoke to find a letter from Alberta in which she wrote that it was time she went in search of new adventures, that while her love for Jake had been of a faithful nature, she felt now the need to explore new frontiers.

*You can interpret this how you may . . . I
warned you of course that such a time would
most likely come, and now that it has I am
compelled to go. I will miss you, Jake, but for not
too very long, as I hope you will miss me also, for
a little while at least. Your Alberta.*

He read it with a heavy sadness. His first instinct was to follow her and talk her out of leaving. But he knew it would do no good—that he could not hold her to him no matter what argument he presented, that if he tried, she'd be like the sad sparrow that died of sorrow in a cage; a story she'd repeated often. The very thing about her he'd fallen in love with was now the very same that caused her to leave him. She was a liberated woman with liberated ways.

He mourned her loss by getting drunk and staying that way for a week until his heart began to heal. That was in the spring and now it was midsummer and he'd mostly got beyond the worst of his longing for her. The letter from his nephew Tristan Shade seemed fortuitous in a way. Tristan hadn't asked for his help, but by god he was sure up to giving it. He even took pride in the fact Tristan had borrowed his name even if he was ass-deep in trouble; *just like the original,* he thought half smiling. If having two Jakes on 'em didn't confuse their enemies, he didn't know what would.

Hell, no matter what happened from here on out, he told himself, he'd lived some life and a man couldn't ask for more than that.

He saw the town a mile away wavering in the heat like a mirage.

Lord, it was hot as he ever remembered it being.

Birdy Pride led Jake and Roy Bean to the body of the boy, Waddy Worth.

"What happened to him?" Roy Bean said.

Birdy told him.

"Mercury?"

Jake was aware of its deadly effects: death by suffocation, caused by inflammation of the glands and infiltration of the tissues of the neck, producing closing of the trachea by pressure thereon. He'd come across it twice before in his practice—both times as a result of a mercury-amalgam-filled tooth the victim had swallowed.

Roy Bean questioned Birdy about how it was the boy came to her, did she know him previously, was he a customer, and why would he take his own life? Was it out of love for her? Had she enticed him, then rejected him just as she had him? Jake knew that it was common for prostitutes to take their lives by drinking the substance.

"Let it be," Jake said. "It doesn't matter, to him, her, or us. What's done is done."

Birdy continued to weep and Roy Bean saw it as an opportunity to get back in her good graces by offering to comfort her. Jake said he'd go and tell Tall John there was yet more business waiting for him. And when he finished telling the undertaker there was yet another body, he encountered Roy Bean again on the street, Roy looking as forlorn as ever over the rebuff of Birdy, who told him she thought that if Preacher Poke came to get right in the head again, she was going to see if he'd marry her.

Jake thought it a good time to negotiate the price of Teacup Smith's horse with Roy Bean.

"He ain't mine to sell, why don't you just take him? Teacup won't mind, I'm sure," Roy Bean said. "Besides, to the victor go the spoils. I'd say that horse of his is rightfully yours."

"I wouldn't feel right about just taking it," Jake said.

"I admire a man of character and principle. Yes sir, I certainly do. You'd make this town a fine officer of the law. And before you say no again, I've gotten the good folks who own businesses to chip in for steady monthly wages—comes out pretty good, too. Although, two of them folks is toes up and will have to be replaced, but I'm sure that won't be a problem."

In fact, Jake had been doing some thinking about the job. In a way, it made sense to stay on as the local town marshal. If he did, who would suspect him of being a wanted man? And if dodgers arrived in town on him, he could simply destroy them. In time, whoever would be looking for him would give up. Then, too, by that time, Doc Willis might be ready to retire—there were worse places to start a medical practice, Jake thought. The work of keeping the law was honest work—or at least it could be—and he liked the folks he'd met so far and they seemed to like him. In fact he liked this country, what he'd seen of it; it felt like home to him. Roy Bean already knew who he was and could be trusted to keep the secret. And those who would come looking for him, would be looking for a man named Tristan Shade, a physician, not a lawman named Jake Horn. And as long as he didn't practice medicine for a number of years . . . And the other thing he'd considered was how long could he keep running? He didn't like what he'd done of it so far. In fact, it had given him a good feeling to stand and fight.

"Let me ask you something, Mr. Bean. Before I arrived here, how much crime and madness abounded in this place?"

Roy shrugged, scratched his itchy head.

"Not much. The most troubles around here was a lot to do with Bob Olive and Teacup Smith—and you already took care of them. Oh, we get an occasional drunk shooting off his pistol in town, sometimes a fight between two cowboys over a whore or something. Little stuff. But mostly it's as peaceful as drinking lemonade in the shade."

"One more question."

"Sure."

"You know from that wanted poster you're carrying around on me that I'm a wanted man—innocent, but wanted nonetheless. How would these folks here take it if they knew as much about me as you did?"

"I know these folks round here, Mr. Horn. And as long as you treat them with respect and uphold the law fair and square, they'd be on your side. Half these folks have left their own troubles behind them—have come to this far-flung station to get a fresh start and don't much care about a man's past as they do what sort of man he is now. They'd back you if you was fair with them. Oh, and something else you should know: I already burned that dodger. You did a righteous thing here today, Mr. Horn. That counts for something."

Heat stood in the streets and most who were out and about stuck to the shady side of things. Dogs laid in under porches where they could. Horses tied up out front of businesses stood with their heads drooping. Flies buzzed over horse apples scattered in the street. Sun baked everything it touched.

"You want Teacup's horse or not?" Roy Bean asked him.

"Let me buy you a beer and we'll discuss it more," Jake said.

Roy Bean was glad he had a human to drink with instead of that sorrowful dog.

Fuzzy Walls brought the four-horse team to a halt in front of the hotel. The horses were lathered, Fuzzy and his shotgun man, Sam Toe, were caked with dust.

"Welcome to Sweet Sorrow, everyone!" Fuzzy called to those inside the coach as he climbed down.

The door to the coach swung open and Prince Puckett stepped down ignoring the common courtesy of allowing women and children to exit first.

"Where's the local law office?" Prince asked.

Fuzzy jerked a thumb back over his shoulder.

"Down yonder sits the jail, all the law office there is is in the jail."

Prince Puckett waited for Sam Toe to toss down his bag. The woman ascended from the coach followed by her two children, who were as whiny as ever. The woman looked the worse for wear. Prince Puckett thought he knew why when he saw the Chinaman follow the last child out of the coach.

Well, he hadn't come all this way to pass judgment on folks' fornicating ways—not even Chinamen.

"Toss me down my bag there, mister!" he called to Sam Toe. Sam cut him a hard look then dropped the leather valise without saying a word.

In the valise were two more pistols, several boxes of shells, two sets of manacles, a dirk, and a pair of socks. A man in Prince Puckett's line of work never knew when he might need extra weapons or a pair of socks.

He went straightaway to the jail where he found only a scraggly headed man sitting on a cot in a jail cell with a blanket wrapped around him and the door flung open.

"You the local law?" Prince asked.

Elias Poke looked up. He'd been thinking about demons and Birdy Pride. The demons had chased him, had made him strip naked and slash himself with a razor and made him attack poor old Otis Dollar who wasn't doing anything but fishing and minding his own business, but at the time it seemed that Otis was a seven-headed monster with fiery tongues intent on eating him alive. But Elias could see now that it had only been something that had come over him after drinking Doc's potion, a potion Doc said would cure his female problems. Instead, all it did was make him see demons and run naked onto the grasslands. He'd been wondering if Birdy Pride knew of his terrible acts and what she would think of such? Now here was a stranger asking him if he was the law.

"No, I ain't the law," he said.

"Who is?"

Elias shrugged. He wasn't sure. He heard rumors that Bob Olive and Teacup Smith had been murdered. He was afraid to go outside and look at the world and what was in it—for there had been plenty of shooting that day, screams, the sounds of horses and wagons running up and down the streets, rumors flying everywhere—some of which made no sense to him. He trembled inside his own skin as though he were freezing.

"I don't know who is," he said.

Prince Puckett looked at the man, saw a pair of wild eyes under brushy brows, a man trembling, with fear or whiskey tremors.

"Why, you old drunk," Prince said. "Why am I wasting breath on you?" and walked back out in the heat where at least it didn't stink as bad as it did inside that little jailhouse.

He looked around. Saw a saloon up a ways.

"Skinny Dick's Pleasure Palace," he read aloud the words painted in black lettering on the false-front. "Sounds like just the damn place I need to be right now" and walked on up.

Toussaint Trueblood arrived at his lodge, unhitched his mule, then went and sat in the shade. His gaze scanned the grasslands; they looked as devoid of life as he felt inside at that moment. Tendrils of heat crawled into his clothes, his calico shirt, and up under his hat and he recalled only one other summer that had been as hot as this one—one when he was a boy of six or seven and his Mandan grandfather had taken him on a long journey from the grasslands to a place of deserts and lone rock formations the color of dried blood and taught him the ways of the snake and the coyote. That time it was hot as it was now.

He closed his eyes.

"What are you going to do now that you have lost your way?"

He opened his eyes and looked around to see who was speaking. Nobody was there.

"I don't know," he said.

The voice did not reply until he closed his eyes again.

"Karen rejects you now because you rejected her then, when she was pregnant with your son, Dex."

Again he opened his eyes. Nobody there. Closed his eyes again.

"How do I know whose boy Dex was?" he said.

"For a man who notices things as well as you do, I'm surprised you couldn't figure it out."

Toussaint felt the lump in his throat.

"You can't blame Karen," the voice said. "She only did what she could do."

"Me, too," he said.

"You owe her much."

"What? What do I owe her?"

Then just as suddenly there was only the heat, the sound of flies buzzing, and he opened his eyes again and then he saw it—the dreaming rabbit standing near a clump of bunch grass, its eyes closed, its nose twitching. Biggest jack he'd seen in years. The kind that would cook up good, provide plenty of bones; the kind he liked to eat. Only this time he did not reach for a rock. This time he simply watched the dreaming rabbit until it, too, opened its eyes, looked at him, then bounded off into the grass.

He stood. It was time to take action. He started off for town, the heat notwithstanding.

There was a sign in the window of the saloon that read: CLOSED, but the front doors stood opened. Prince Puckett went inside. Only one other person was there—an old man standing back of the bar drinking a beer.

"I'll have a beer," Prince ordered.

"I don't work here," the man said.

"You're the barkeep?"

"No."

"Nobody is anything in this dung heap," Prince said. "If you're not him, where's he at?"

The old man shrugged.

"Don't know," he said.

"How'd you get that beer then?"

The old man nodded at the pull handles of the taps.

"Drew it myself."

"How about drawing me one?"

The old man looked at him.

"I told you, I'm not the barkeep."

"I've had a long hot ride, mister, and I'm in no mood to be fooled with. You poured yourself a beer, so pour me one since you're already standing there."

The old man continued to enjoy his beer without any effort to draw another beer.

"Goddamn old fool," Prince said, and reached for one of several glasses stacked along the bar's top, then held it under the tap and drew himself a beer. He took a long swallow, half a glass worth, before saying, "You know where I can find the local lawman?"

The old man shook his head.

"No."

Prince Puckett studied the fellow. He looked familiar. He'd seen this old man somewhere before, but where, he couldn't rightly say. Had him on a swallowtail coat, even in this heat. Could be a cardsharp or a shootist—they sometimes dressed the same.

The old man drank his beer.

Prince Puckett watched trying hard to figure where he saw this fellow before.

Doc opened the tin box, took some of the contents, and dropped them into his glass of whiskey.

It was time, he thought.

He drank the whiskey down and waited (how long he couldn't be sure) till the hands of the clock looked as if they were moving backward, until the light falling through the windows of his office took on the colors of the rainbow. It was time he found out which demons were in him and what they'd do once he let them out.

He saw the reverse painting of Iris on the wall. She was smiling at him, cruelly smiling, as though she were mocking him. He fumbled in his desk drawer until he found the pocket pistol.

"You rotting cheating bitch!" he yelled and fired.

Still she laughed. He could hear her now, alive inside the oval glass, mocking him.

He fired again and again.

And when Jake came through the door, Doc turned his gun on him.

"You stole her! You stole her!"

Jake had come on the run at the sound of gunfire, his Schofields at the ready, unsure of what or who was still set on more trouble and killing this day; he and Roy were just entering the Rosebud when they heard the shooting.

"It's me, Doc."

"You came here and stole my Iris and took her off. I want her back!"

Doc was drunk, or . . .

"It's me, Doc," he repeated. "Put your gun down and let's talk about whatever it is."

Doc saw the man who stole his Iris—the headmaster who quoted poetry and wrote her lovely sonnets and . . .

"Oh goddamn your very soul!"

He fired the last shot left in the chambers of the pocket gun, the bullet missing Jake by mere inches and shattering the window glass of the door.

Jake took him down with a running charge, knocked him to the floor and kicked the gun free of his hand. Pinned him there, seeing as he did, the man's dilated pupils. Doc clawed trying to free himself; it seemed he had the strength of two men half his age and he knocked Jake free of him, scrambled to his feet, jerked open a tray of instruments, his hand grabbing a scalpel.

"Come on," he shouted, slicing the air back and forth.

Jake feinted, causing Doc to swipe at him awkwardly and when he did, Jake brought the butt of the

Schofield down just behind Doc's ear, knocking him senseless.

"What the hell . . ." he wondered as Doc lay there.

Jake knew enough to know that a man like Doc didn't go crazy from drinking liquor alone. He searched the countertops and cabinets, then found the open tin on the desk next to the whiskey bottle. He examined its contents—seeds. Then it all made sense, why the others had gone mad—especially if Doc had prescribed them a concoction of these particular seeds. They were of the jimson plant, what some called Devil's Trumpet or Mad Apple. But why would Doc do such a thing, if in fact he had?

He'd have to wait until Doc got right in the head again to question him.

But the sounds of Doc's gunshots had drawn others, the curious, the way death draws vultures, and one of those curious had been Prince Puckett.

23

❖

PRINCE PUCKETT followed the crowd to a big fancy house set down at the end of the street. He learned along the way from hearing others talk that the house belonged to a physician—a fellow named Doc Willis. Gunshots always interested Prince Puckett, it was his natural bent and curiosity to know where gunshots originated from and why—who shot who and why'd they shot them. Gunshots were part of Prince Puckett's profession, though he liked to be the one doing the shooting.

Jake read the names in the ledger he found next to the open tin of seeds. A short descriptive passage followed each name.

Emmaline Figg. Threatened to expose our indiscretion to her husband if I did not take her from this place; stated quite assuredly that the infant recently born was my issue. I explained to her that was quite impossible but she insisted that I was the babe's father. Of course I could not allow her to ruin me, the horrid cow. Why would she think I'd have anything more to do with her beyond that one indiscretion? Must go; gave her the potion to convince others she was mad in case she carried through with her threat.

Bill Blankenship. I know he had relations with Iris before she abandoned me. Found a note among her effects stating as much. He was one, Smiley Rivers another who had their way with Iris. She gave herself to them simply to hurt me, to prove I couldn't control her, then told me about them, daring me to do something about it. Now each shall pay for their transgressions and hers.

Smiley Rivers. Found him to be dying of gangrene in his jail cell; helped him along to his final reward. Hated that he killed his wife and not himself to begin with. May he rest in hell for what he did.

Dex Sunflower. A mush-headed boy whose only purpose was to ruin young women like my Iris. He complained of suffering the pox, caught, he said, from the Swede girl, Gerthe. I found evidence of the pox but suspect that it was he who gave it to her. And so gave him the potion in hopes he'd meet the same fate as the others.

Elias Poke. A miserable man who professes faith in a god that does not exist. The town will be better off without him in it—once he exhibits wild behavior, they will run him off, as it should be. Fornicates with prostitutes.

Birdy Pride. I could not kill her though I very much desired to.

So there it was. He understood now. He looked at Doc Willis who was just now beginning to stir from the blow to the head. What a shame that a man who'd obviously given much of himself in the service of others had resorted to jimsonweed poisoning in an effort to justify his own damaged soul. Like himself, Woodrow Willis had also violated his Hippocratic oath. In spite of everything, Jake felt sorry for the old man—for what he'd done, he'd done out of a misguided sense of love for a woman who'd betrayed him. This was a feeling Jake understood completely.

"You'd be him," a voice said.

Jake looked up, saw a man holding a silver pistol.

"Who are you?"

"Prince Puckett is the name I go by and I came for you, Mr. Shade."

"You've mistaken me for someone else. My name is Jake Horn."

A moment of doubt furrowed the brow of the detective.

"I don't think so," the man said, reaching into his coat pocket with his free hand and retrieving a tintype that he glanced at then tossed on the desk next to where Jake stood.

"Tristan Shade," the man said. "You ain't him,

you're his twin, and far as I know, he ain't got no twins."

Jake glanced at the tintype, the very one he suspected Celine had taken from his house as part of her grand plan to blame him for the murder of her husband.

"Who hired you?"

"You're a smart man, I hear. Educated, doctor and all, you figure it out. Let's just me and you take a walk on out of here. It's a long ways back to Denver."

Jake knew he had a choice to make: go back and stand trial that would surely find him guilty and thus be hanged for a murder he didn't commit, or reach for his own pistol. Prince Puckett was schooled enough in the art of manhunting that he knew what his quarry was thinking.

"Go ahead, if that's the way you'd prefer it. Fact is, it don't make a damn to me if I take you back or not. The man who's hired me only wants me to bring back your hands. Those I can stuff in my valise. It'd be easier on both of us if you were to reach for those irons—Schofields, ain't they? And lest you think it might be painful, or that I might miss altogether, let it be known I'm the best pistol shot in three counties where I come from. Your choice, Mr. Shade."

The crowd parted when Jake walked out ahead of the gunman.

"Where you taking him?" Roy Bean shouted.

"He's under citizen's arrest, stand back."

A buzz of questioning ran through the crowd.

But waiting there in the street was the old man Prince Puckett had seen in the saloon drinking beer.

"Let him go," the old man said.

Jake hadn't seen his uncle in a dozen years or better—he'd aged greatly, but still maintained a ramrod straight posture and still looked dangerous as a viper.

"Don't try and interfere with this, dad. Go on back and have yourself another beer," Prince Puckett growled.

"Let him go!" someone in the crowd shouted.

Another voice joined in, then another.

"I'll shoot the first son of a bitch who interferes," Prince Puckett warned. "And I'll shoot the second and the third!"

The crowd quieted as the old man standing in the street drew back the flap of his swallowtail coat and hitched it behind the gun he wore in a cross-draw holster on his left hip.

"Then that first son of a bitch will have to be me, son," the old man said.

"Don't," Jake said. "This is my trouble, not yours."

His uncle looked at him without ever taking his attention from Prince Puckett.

Toussaint Trueblood had come onto the scene quite by happenstance—he'd been on his way to take back the shotgun he'd borrowed from Otis, then was going to make a stop at the jeweler's. He moved closer cautiously, bringing up the shotgun, both barrels still loaded.

"Somebody's going to die here today if you don't let him go," Toussaint said.

Prince Puckett glanced at this latest challenge to his authority. He felt sweat trickling down his neck, ribs, and back. This was a bad situation and getting worse.

Then Roy Bean moved away from the crowd, also carrying a shotgun, and the trio of them—the old man, Toussaint, and Roy Bean formed an arc in front of Jake and Prince Puckett.

"There's been enough blood shed here today," Jake said. "I appreciate what you all are doing, but I'm willing to go with this man."

The old man said, "No. That's not going to happen."

Prince Puckett pressed the muzzle against the back of Jake's skull and thumbed back the hammer.

"Easy boys, I keep my piece with a hair trigger. Slightest bump and she goes off."

"Let it go," Jake said to the trio. "Nobody is going to win this fight."

"He's right," the old man said. "He'll kill Jake, we'll kill him. Nobody wins."

Roy Bean lowered his weapon, so, too, Toussaint. They both knew the truth of what the old man said.

"Stand aside and let us pass," Prince Puckett ordered.

The crowd followed but at a distance. The old man and Toussaint and Roy Bean felt helpless to stop anything without getting Jake killed. Prince nudged him to where the stage stood in front of the hotel. He ordered Fuzzy Walls to get up in the driver's seat.

"I'm waiting for Sam to bring the mail," Fuzzy protested.

"Not my problem, get this damn honey wagon rolling. Inside, felon," he ordered Jake.

"You're not really planning on taking me back to stand trial, are you?"

Prince Puckett smirked.

"They said you was smart, now get in that god-damn coach!"

"No."

"What the hell you mean, no? You want me to splatter your brains right here and now?"

"What difference does it make if you kill me now or somewhere along the trail? Go ahead and pull the trigger. I'm not afraid of dying. It all comes to that sooner or later, anyhow."

Prince Puckett pushed the muzzle more forcefully against the back of Jake's head but he refused to get into the coach.

"We're both going to die today, mister. That old man," Jake said. "He's my kin and he'll make damn sure you die with me."

Then it came to Prince Puckett where he'd seen the old man before: his name was Jake Horn and he had a reputation as a bank robber extraordinaire and was rumored to have killed his share of men—mostly those who'd pursued him.

"I'll be son of a bitch," he said, half turning to look at the old man. "Looks like I might just bag me two birds this day." Prince figured there was still reward money on the old man's head. And with a lightning quickness, he crashed the barrel of his pistol down hard across Jake's head knocking him to his knees and with one swift movement wheeled and fired, his bullet taking the old man dead center, and just as quick drew bead on Toussaint and Roy Bean.

"You two want to join him, be my guest," Prince Puckett said.

It had all happened fast as a snake strike. Even Toussaint had never seen a man who was so deadly accurate or so quick.

"You two drag him over here and shove him in the coach. That's money on the hoof."

Toussaint said defiantly, "Drag him over yourself."

Suddenly someone shoved his way through the crowd, ranting and raving as he came. Doc Willis, still drugged from the jimson seeds, wild-eyed and waving a pistol he didn't know was empty. He burst forth from the others, saw Prince Puckett, the brocade vest he was wearing—didn't that goddamn schoolteacher who stole his Iris wear a brocade vest?

"You cuckolding bastard! You stole my Iris!" Doc yelled aiming the revolver at Prince as he staggered toward him, pulling the trigger. The hammer snapped on empty chambers and Prince shot him through the forehead.

Jake pushed up hard from the ground into the back of Prince's legs knocking off his balance. Still dazed, he fought from survival instinct, grappling for the gun in Prince Puckett's hand.

Toussaint and the others raced to join the fight.

Jake got the gun twisted between himself and Prince Puckett.

Hands reached down to separate them.

Two fingers squeezed the same trigger.

The pistol barked once.

The hands of others were too late to save one of them.

Prince Puckett let out a gasp, then fell away, face into the dust, his own bullet having entered his right lung, traversing at an erratic upward angle after having nicked a rib, then severed his spinal cord. He was not dead, but dying. He gulped air like a fish out of water. There was nothing Jake or anyone could do to save him.

A pair of strong dark hands lifted Jake to his feet—the hands of Toussaint Trueblood.

Still somewhat dazed, Jake went over to where his uncle lay, blood trickling from the sides of his mouth. *Lung shot.* Jake asked that the men help carry him over to Doc's office, which they quickly did.

Jake set to work trying to stop the bleeding. The old man lay quiet while his nephew worked over him.

"Why'd you come?" Jake asked him. "You didn't need to come. I never asked you to. I was going to come your way. Why'd you come, goddamn it, and get yourself shot like this?"

The old man half smiled.

"We're kin," is all he said, then died.

24

❧❧

TALL JOHN TOLD his assistant, "Here's how we'll work it. We'll bury the good ones today and the rest tomorrow."

Boblink Jones said, "I'm through after this with burying anymore folks. I'm leaving for Missouri, just wanted you to know."

"I'll give you a raise to stay on."

"There ain't enough money in America to get me to stay on," the youth said. "It's gotten so bad I've taken to dreaming about dead people. Dreamt last night that woman had her throat cut wanted to marry me. I woke up with the shakes."

"Well, let's pray it's come to the end of all that and we get back to regular dying instead of the violent type."

"What makes you think it will?" asked Boblink as he combed oil through Doc Willis's silver hair to make it stay in place. Tall John had plugged the hole in Doc's forehead with putty but it still didn't look normal.

"You hear that?" Tall John said.

"Hear what?"

"That rumbling outside."

Boblink listened. He could hear the rumbling.

"What is it?" he said.

"Thunder, I think."

"Thunder?"

"It's going to rain, I believe. I can always tell when it is."

"How can you tell?"

"I can feel it in my back. Starts to ache like the dickens."

"Rain! I'll believe it when I see it."

"I could be wrong, don't get your hopes up too high."

"I'd go out and dance naked in it if it was to."

"I don't think you ought to, might get arrested for indecency."

"You mean by our new town marshal?"

"Well, now that the killing's about over, he'll probably need something to do lest he get bored and quit."

"He seems like a nice enough fellow."

"He might be, but I doubt he'd want to see young bucks dancing naked in the streets of his town."

Boblink grinned.

"I sure would like to see it rain, wouldn't you?"

"Indeed I would. Rain seems proper weather for a funeral."

"Then it best rain a lot for all the folks we got yet to bury."

The rain came that night. It fell by the bucketful. The sky flashed with lightning and the ground shook with thunder and the rain came pouring out of the sky as though it, too, had missed not having fallen in ever so long.

The streets of Sweet Sorrow turned into small rivers, and roofs leaked and those under the leaky roofs didn't mind, but rather gathered things to catch the rain in. Folks went out in it and let themselves get soaked to the skin and some took off their hats to catch the rain in so they could pour the water over their heads.

Elias Poke thanked God for the rain, not for himself, but for the poor folks in Sweet Sorrow who'd waited so long for it to come. And he thanked God for making him right in his thinking again, and forgiving him for his wild and wicked ways.

Birdy appeared in the church doorway, her hair wet and plastered to her head and her dress soaked and clinging to her.

"It's raining, Preacher," she said.

"I know it is, little dove," he said.

"Can I come in?"

"Yes, I was just on my way to come and find you."

"What for?" she said.

"I want to ask you something, Birdy."

She was afraid of what he was about to say. Her heart beat like that of a wild rabbit.

He asked her to sit down and when she did, he sat beside her.

"It was dreadful wrong what we did here the other night together," he began. "And it led me into a madness that I'm lucky to have survived. I've prayed and prayed ever since for God's answer and finally He has given it to me."

"You're going to leave, ain't you, Preacher? You're going to leave like all the others . . ."

"No, child, I'm staying, for as long as folks will have me be their preacher."

"Then what?" she said, her eyes filling with tears.

"I want to ask if you'll marry me, Birdy Pride. Be my wife. Oh, I know I'm somewhat older than you. And I ain't the most handsomest of men—I'm sure there are others you could—"

She kissed him hard before he could get any more words out. Sometimes a preacher can just talk too much.

Toussaint sat under the overhang of his lodge drinking coffee and listening to the sky talk while the rain fell en masse so hard it sounded as if it were boiling. It dripped off the overhang and the cooling relief it brought gave him an abiding pleasure. He studied the small silver ring he'd bought earlier at the jeweler's—the thing he'd gone after when the shooting had begun again and he found himself in the middle of it.

He looked at the ring with thoughtful consideration.

He didn't know what size ring Karen wore because

he'd never bought her a ring even when they were married. He decided after long consideration that if it fit her—if she'd at least try it on and it fit, then it would be the beginning of something between them. And if it didn't fit, well, he'd wear it on a leather string around his neck because it was important to him that they be married again, if not in reality, then in spirit, and to honor the spirit of their son.

The wind blew some of the rain in under the eave and it fell on his face and he closed his eyes and told himself from this day on, he would hunt no more dreaming rabbits. That all creatures had a right to dream without fear of death. There had already been too much death on these grasslands to last him a lifetime.

Karen Sunflower saw in a flash of lightning Otis Dollar sitting in his wagon in the rain outside her cabin.

She went out onto the porch and called to him through the hiss.

"What are you doing, Otis? You're going to drown."

"I came to . . ." A crash of lightning obliterated his words.

"You came to what?" she yelled.

"I came to tell you something," he yelled.

"What is it?"

"I came to tell you . . . that I love you, Karen. And that I'm sorry what happened to Dex . . ."

She could see in the intermittent flashes Otis's sorrowful face, could not tell if it were tears or rain running down his cheeks.

"Go on home, Otis," she said. "Go home to your wife. She'll be worried about you."

"I want to come back sometime and talk to you," he yelled.

"No, Otis, we've nothing to talk about."

She saw him looking out toward the spot where Dex was buried, then back toward her.

"It's okay, Otis. Everything is okay. Go on home, please."

He looked pitiful. She waited until he rode off into the rain, but did not go back into the house right away. The rain had a quality to it she missed, a feel about it that gave her some small comfort in a world that lately held none. She reached forth a hand and let it fill with rain then brought it to her face and neck and let its coolness relieve her fevered skin.

Dex, she knew, was in a place where it never rained too much, or the sun never got too hot, where the grass was always green, the air always just right, the rivers always pure and full of fish and angels guided him each hour of his journey. He was not out there where Otis had looked. He was in a better place.

She wished only the same for herself when the time came. In time she'd come to peace with Toussaint as well. This much she knew to be exact.

"Those folks backed you up the other day," Roy Bean said. "That tell you anything about them?"

"It does," Jake said.

"I'm glad you decided to take the job."

"If only temporarily, until you can find a professional lawman."

"Hell, son. This ain't exactly New York or Chicago—it ain't even Dallas. Might be a spell before another proper man comes along to apply for the job."

"Still, I'm not sure I'm exactly cut out for such work."

"You couldn't prove it by anyone around here that you're not, me included."

"What about you?" Jake said. "Are you still going to try and get elected judge?"

"I'm not plum sure. I've been missing my wife and kids a great deal. I might wander back down to Texas and check on them before I make any final decisions."

"Sweet Sorrow won't be the same without you."

"Birdy's going to marry the preacher."

"So I heard."

"It was a fine funeral they held for Doc and your uncle today, in spite of the rain, or maybe because of it."

"It was. Preacher preached a fine sermon and Tall John and his boy did a nice job. Jake would have been proud of such a burying."

"Jake? Was that his name? I thought it was T. Shade."

"Yes, it was . . . Some of us called him by his nickname."

"Well, here's to old dogs and kinfolks," Roy Bean said, lifting his glass of beer—the two of them sitting alone in the Rosebud. "And here's to Peg Leg Watts, and old Doc Willis, and all the others gone before us."

Jake matched Roy Bean's salute by clinking glasses.

"And to the future of us all."

"And to rain."

"And to rain," Jake said.

And the rain fell for three days straight much to the joy of everyone.

BLAZING WESTERN FICTION FROM MASTER STORYTELLER

BILL DUGAN

BRADY'S LAW
0-06-100628-9/$5.99 US/$7.99 Can

Dan Brady is a man who believes in truth—and in a justice
he won't get from the law.

TEXAS DRIVE
0-06-100032-9/$5.99 US/$7.99 Can

Ted Cotton can no longer avoid the kind of bloody violence
that sickened him during the War Between the States.

GUN PLAY AT CROSS CREEK
0-06-100079-5/$5.99 US/$7.99 Can

Morgan Atwater's got one final score to settle.

DUEL ON THE MESA
0-06-100033-7/$5.99 US/$7.99 Can

Together Dalton Chance and Lone Wolf blaze a trail
of deadly vengeance.

MADIGAN'S LUCK
0-06-100677-7/$5.99 US/$7.99 Can

One successful drive across the open range can change
Dave Madigan's luck from bad to good.

AuthorTracker
www.AuthorTracker.com

Available wherever books are sold
or please call 1-800-331-3761 to order.

DUG 0604

ACTION-PACKED *LAW FOR HIRE* ADVENTURES BY

BILL BROOKS

PROTECTING HICKOK

0-06-054176-8/$5.99 US/$7.99 CAN

Determined to hunt down his brother's killer, city-bred
Teddy Blue joins the Pinkerton Detective Agency. But Teddy
gets more than he bargained for in the wide open West, when he's
assigned as a bodyguard to the famous "Wild Bill" Hickok.

DEFENDING CODY

0-06-054177-6/$5.99 US/$7.99 CAN

When he's hired as professional protection for "Buffalo Bill" Cody
out in the wild, Teddy's caught in a deadly tangle that may
prove too much for one hired guardian to handle.

SAVING MASTERSON

0-06-054178-4/$5.99 US/$7.99 CAN

It's just Teddy Blue and lawman Bat Masterson against
pretty much the whole damn town of Dodge City . . .
with the killers lining up to take their shots.

(((T))) AuthorTracker

Don't miss the next book by your favorite author.
Sign up now for AuthorTracker by visiting
www.AuthorTracker.com

Available wherever books are sold
or please call 1-800-331-3761 to order.

LFH 0304